GREEN VALLEY

GREEN VALLEY

LOUIS GREENBERG

TITAN BOOKS

Green Valley
Mass-market edition ISBN: 9781789093520
E-book edition ISBN: 9781789090246

Published by Titan Books
A division of Titan Publishing Group Ltd.
144 Southwark Street, London, SE1 0UP
www.titanbooks.com

First mass-market edition: May 2020
10 9 8 7 6 5 4 3 2 1

A CIP catalogue record for this title is available
from the British Library.

Printed and bound by CPI Group Ltd, Croydon CR0 4YY.

1 'Yes, of course she's here.' David's voice was a muffled echo, his impatience degraded to a hazy simulation.

I twisted the tight spiral of the telephone cord around my finger, listening for forgotten inflections to prove to myself that it really was my brother-in-law and not a Zeroth fabrication. I hadn't spoken to David in eight years, and for many of those years I'd hardly thought about him. 'When did you last see her?' I asked. 'I mean, in reality?'

'I don't know. What difference does it make if I saw her physically or not, Lucie? What's this all about?'

Fabian stepped into the study doorway and gave me a concerned look. I raised my hand and mouthed, *It's okay*, then rolled my chair across the floor and toed the door shut on him, the receiver's spiral cord stretching, the phone dragging with a jangling clatter across the desk behind me.

'We have information that something's happening on your side of the wall. In Green Valley,' I said into the phone. 'That children are in serious danger.' If you could call two dead boys 'information'. I scanned Jordan's message again. The second, a child of about nine, had been found that very morning in the memorial yard at Hershey Field, bristling with nanotech and Zeroth implants – like the other child, he could only have come from Green Valley. I could have just come right out and told David that children were dying, but it had been a long time, and I wasn't sure yet how much I could trust him.

'*We?*' he batted back at me. 'So you're still with the police. Is this an official call?'

'It's not an official call – yet,' I said, mustering a threat I had no authority to make. 'I just want to know that Kira's fine. When did you last see her, in the flesh?' I repeated.

David clicked his tongue, as if checking on his daughter's safety was an annoying bind. 'All right, all right. Maybe in the morning, yesterday. I'm sure I saw her eating something, and then she went on Mathcamp. I can check the logs.'

Whatever David said next faded through flurries of static. I pressed the receiver closer to my ear. You'd have thought Zeroth Corporation, whatever remained of it, could at least still come up with a decent phone connection. Then the static ebbed again and David's voice sighed through the line: 'Oh, that's weird.'

'What is?'

A pause and a scuffle. 'Nothing. Don't worry about it.'

'David, what's weird?'

'It's just that I can't… currently –' a wash of blurring static swirling his words – 'just a glitch, I'm sure.'

I noticed Fabian's shadow shifting protectively in the strip of light under the door. 'I want to see her. I want to come in. Now,' I murmured, my voice low into the mouthpiece.

'Into Green Valley? You can't,' he said slowly and carefully, as if explaining to a child, as if I was the one who'd lost my mind. 'Green Valley is a quarantined enclave. You can't just drop in for a visit. Those are the terms of the agreement you people forced on us.'

'Bullshit,' I hissed. 'There are supplies, there've been contractors in and out since you closed. I know you can get me a visitor's pass.' Fabian had retreated to the kitchen; I heard him ratcheting the coffee maker – but still I kept my voice down.

'Yeah, and why would I?' David said.

'Because I want to see Kira – today. That's why. Or would you prefer to wait for a warrant?'

'You and I both know that won't happen.'

'Are you sure?' I said. 'Any judge would rule that child endangerment counts as "exceptional circumstances".' The threat sounded unconvincing, even to me: the vague 'exceptional circumstances' clause stipulated in the Green Valley Partition Treaty of 2020 had never once been invoked in the eight years of its existence. Stanton and US law enforcement had turned a blind eye to Green Valley since the partition.

'Child endangerment? Really, Lucie? An online math course?' He sighed again. He clearly didn't accept that Kira was in any danger. He was either unaware of the children missing from Green Valley, utterly deluded, or lying very well. Or maybe he just thought it had nothing to do with him or Kira. 'All right. If only to get you off my back. I can do that. I'm important here,' he added, to my surprise – David having to convince himself of his powers? That was something new. 'Come to the liaison office. I'll tell them to expect you.'

I hung up, then dialled the office to call in sick.

Barbra Reeve sniffed me out immediately. 'You don't sound sick to me.'

'I've got a family situation,' I said.

'With whom?'

I bristled. It was the imperious way she asked, and the fact that as director of Sentinel she knew all my secrets anyway. It didn't take a spy to figure out that I didn't have much family to speak of – my only sister dead, my mother gone soon after, a father who never even made the picture. There was no point in lying. 'My brother-in-law.'

'The one who lives in Green Valley?'

My only brother-in-law, as you are well aware. 'That's right. He invited me in.' I wasn't going to let her put me off.

But that wasn't her intent. 'That's bloody marvellous, Lucie. Come and see me first.'

• • •

9

'Don't go to Green Valley.' Fabian advanced on me the instant I came out of the study, unashamed of listening in. 'You know what it is.'

'I don't. Not really,' I said.

'You know what it isn't,' he insisted. 'It's not real.'

'Those are lazy Omega catchphrases, Fabe. Of course it's real. Flesh and blood people living inside a great big warehouse because of a vote.' *A stupid, misguided vote*, I wanted to say, but that would have started an argument I couldn't finish right now. Fabian, after all, was one of the people who had brought the vote about, campaigned against the abuses and invasions of the 'digital tyranny'. Twelve years ago, his beloved Omega group had stuck a stake through the heart of the global surveillance economy right here in 'Silicon Stanton', one of the first in a series of mini-revolutions across the world.

'They're the ones who chose to wall themselves in and live in that fake place,' Fabian said. 'They could have set aside their tech like the rest of us and lived an ethical, socially responsible life.'

'Not everybody had a choice, Fabe.' Before he could stop to think about that, I added, 'Anyway, I have to go. Somebody needs my help.'

'It's David Coady who needs your help, isn't it?' Fabian trailed me into our bedroom and looked out at the wind and the glowering sky outside.

When I didn't respond, Fabian prodded for a reaction. 'Yes, *David*. I heard you talking to him. I can't believe you want anything to do with him. Chief evangelist for that… that mass-surveillance cult.'

His patrician profile silhouetted against the stylish elegance of his flat, framed by his neat white shelves of dust-coiffed revolutionary texts, the righteous certitude painting his face, made me feel as safe as it had when we'd first met.

It was hard to believe he still knew so little about me.

'Trust me, Fabe. You don't have to worry about David. Zeroth doesn't have the power they did, and they're not getting it back.'

'I'm not worried about him. I'm worried for you. You don't know what it's like in there.'

'And you do?'

'No, of course not, but—'

'Well, then. Aren't you interested? You've spent all these years fighting the *idea* of Green Valley, of Zeroth, but you don't even want to know what they've become.'

'I don't believe they can *become* anything other than what they always were: a malicious virus in society.' He scraped the hair away from his brow, agitated, his heavy wristwatch jangling. 'During the Turn, we saw them for what they were, Zeroth and the rest of them. I don't even know why we conceded so much in the treaty. They should have all been prosecuted.'

Fabian hated Green Valley, where it came from and what it stood for: digital surveillance and control, abuse of privacy rights, organised repression of dissent, complicity and conspiracy. Before we'd met, Fabian had been a key funder and abettor of Omega's work, a central mind in its think-tank. The remnants of Green Valley's dangerous vision were what he, the party backed by Omega's might, and the whole post-Turn political establishment spent their days fighting. They were adamant that they would never allow that abusive cabal to rise again under their watch. But my methods, working for Sentinel... If he knew how I really spent my days, that I spied on Zeroth and Green Valley through illicit electronic screens, he'd see me as the enemy, no better than Zeroth, even though we shared the same target.

What I told Fabian about my work wasn't *all* a lie, I comforted myself. Fabian knew half the truth. Make it two-thirds. He knew I worked for the police as a consultant analyst. But he thought what I consulted on was cold-case management and analogue data-handling structures, which is what I'd originally been employed to do. In the past two years, though, my work had diversified into the Sentinel project, and that was the part Fabian couldn't know about. The secret was poisoning the air between us.

'You conceded so much because you were desperate to make them disappear,' I said at length. 'So that's how it stands: they own the land and they're not doing anything wrong.'

'That we know of.'

'Well, this is my opportunity to have a look and report back. Don't you want to check your assumptions?'

'Of course, but I don't see why you have to go there. It could be dangerous.'

'Jesus, Fabe, we can talk around and around this, but I need to go.'

As I grabbed a jacket from the closet and zipped it up, he spoke to my back. 'Who's Kira?'

'Kira's my niece. Odille had a daughter.'

I closed the door on his questions.

2

I hurried to the station to see Barbra Reeve and came down the steps twenty minutes later, my mind whirling through everything I'd learned about Green Valley over the past couple of years. Intelligence blind spots, the enclave's hardwiring, delivery and waste management systems, the logistics of their communications systems, what someone could bring in with them, and what, if anything, they could possibly smuggle out. After years of painstaking effort, Sentinel was one tranche of hardwired code away from activating a total tap on their information systems. Reeve had been planning a risky incursion into Green Valley to find the right component, but now I'd been issued with an invitation through the front door. Barbra Reeve could barely conceal her excitement as she delivered her instructions and the extraction kit.

But on the ride out to Green Valley, my mind went to Kira. Why had I never told Fabian about her? I guess she felt like an echo from another life, when Odille was still alive, living with her perfect husband and her perfect baby in her perfect house in Green Valley. But then she died – cancer crashing the perfection party and leaving David alone with a ten-month-old baby girl just as the Partition Treaty was signed and Green Valley was sealed off. At first, I was torn at being so suddenly separated from Kira, my last living connection to my sister – but I had no choice, just like the other families who'd been split by the terms of that urgently expedited treaty.

As time went by, I reconciled myself to the loss, convinced that Kira was fine in there. Despite the Turn, so many people secretly wished they could be inside – this was Green Valley, after all, so much safer and healthier than the real world: Reality 2.0, with its cutting-edge circadian lighting systems, far safer and more nourishing than our carcinogenic sunlight; taintless hydroponic food and natural vitamin blends for optimal nutrition, which was so much more efficient and environment-friendly than common farming; all underpinned by their humanely intelligent integral VR system, which many people still privately envied.

I had allowed thoughts of Kira to fade away with my grief for Odille, confident that she was growing up pampered, happy and safe. Until a couple of hours ago, at least.

'You sure you don't want me to wait?' the taxi driver asked as I stepped out. 'For if you don't make your meeting.'

'Thanks, no,' I said, handing him a large tip. His was the fourth cab I'd stopped outside the precinct, and the first prepared to come out here. The driver nodded and pulled off, and I watched his yellow car down the deserted road back to Stanton, dwarfed beside the concrete wall. It wasn't the first time I'd been close to the wall, but I was shocked again by its massiveness, rising starkly to where the concrete roof met it in a seamless curve thirty-two metres up.

Breeze-blown litter scurried on the tarmac; the taxi had disappeared and I'd been staring at empty space. Debilitating panic would not help Kira, I knew: I had to snap out of it and *do* something.

To my left lay the boarded-up shops, the abandoned houses and the derelict park in what we'd come to think of as the exclusion zone. It had once been the peri-rural edge of a middle-class commuter suburb overlooking Zeroth Corporation's lush campus, but the concrete wall – fast-tracked extraordinary planning permission paid for from Zeroth's still-substantial war chest – meant that life in Stanton started a few streets further away now, cringing away from Green Valley.

The air in the wall's shadow was frigid and stagnant. There was nothing alive here, no evidence even of birds or rats. I could see only two or three rushed graffiti tags on the concrete expanse that should have been an ideal palette for blazers across the city. Those skittish scrawls spoke less of the kids who'd sprayed them than of the unseen ghosts that had chased them away. From what we knew, not even homeless squatters had risked taking up residence in those free houses. The shadow of the wall was a curse.

Shivering myself deeper into my thin jacket, I hitched my backpack higher on my shoulder and crossed to the door set insignificantly into the concrete.

It was a small door, a reinforced glass door like any street-front office, labelled in Zeroth's distinctive lettering that you used to see everywhere: *Green Valley External Liaison Reception*. As if it wasn't a gigantic tomb I was checking myself into, as if it was a simple, everyday business transaction. I had to remind myself that Zeroth was still a legitimate business, as far as it went. No matter how they had metastasised in Stantonites' imaginations, Zeroth remained a software and communications company, with people living in a swathe of land they legitimately occupied in a legally formed independent enclave, no matter how idiosyncratically built on. Stanton and the rest of the country had their fair share of huge, covered shopping malls, hotels and office parks, so why should Green Valley feel any different? Choosing to live inside a concrete dome didn't automatically make you a criminal or a zombie or a vampire.

Stop thinking, I told myself, pressing the button for the bell.

After a few seconds, the magnetic lock buzzed and the door clicked open. I pushed through into the office's reception area and a fug of incense-saturated air. There was the curved plywood desk I'd been expecting, a fading fitted carpet patterned in Zeroth's eye icon in corporate lime green against a calming sky blue, but rather than an office, it felt like I'd just entered someone's living room. A mismatched cluster of framed photographs lined the countertop, and the board-mounted Zeroth posters – *Zeroth: better than first* – on the walls had been draped with bright fabric hangings that looked like they were from Colombia or Bolivia. A loop of plastic Christmas lights in the shape of flamingos had been strung from one corner of a vacant television screen across the wall to the edge of a filing cabinet, which was topped with a fire-coloured batik cloth and a Japanese vase of plastic orchids.

I glanced behind me, towards the door, checking I was in the right place, but the sign was still clear enough. It was only now that I noticed a woman in blue jeans and bare feet and a tailored pink sweat top sitting on one of the couches, which was also upholstered in faded corporate blue and green, but layered over with throws and crocheted blankets. She was sipping from a pink plastic cup and looked at me with an open face.

Nodding at her, I went to the desk, looking for a bell on the countertop. Behind me, the woman on the couch siphoned the dregs of her drink noisily and after a moment said, 'With you now.' I turned to see her stretching as if she'd just been sleeping, and then she padded around to the end of the counter. She walked with confidence, elegantly languid. She had very pretty feet, brightly painted toenails. Her hair was smartly tinted and her skin smooth and healthy; she may have been around forty-five, I guessed, from the lines at her eyes, but looked younger. 'Let's see,' she said, turning on the bulky computer at the desk, something that reminded me of my childhood.

As the computer started up, she looked me in the eyes and I immediately recognised a professional assessment in her glance; her eyes skittered over the ID points on my face, noting the angles and the ratios, ready to compare me to my photograph that she'd have on file.

'We were expecting someone today. Wasn't sure what time. You must be the someone.'

'Yes, I'm Lucie Sterling,' I said, and held out my hand.

She shook my hand firmly, holding my gaze with green eyes. 'Gina Orban, external liaison.' She glanced down at the screen and tapped a few buttons. She raised her eyebrows as she read the information in front of her. 'Family, huh? Are you David Coady's sister? None of my business, I suppose.'

'Sister-in-law,' I said.

Gina Orban frowned. 'Oh, so you're Eloise Parsons' sister. She's an interesting person.'

Eloise? Did that mean David was remarried? I did my best to swallow the surprise – did people even do things like marriage in here? 'Oh, no. My sister was…' I hesitated.

'None of my business. It's not often we get visitors, so I'm asking too many questions.'

'How often do you process people out?' I asked as casually as possible, just an interested tourist.

'You mean Valley people going outside?'

'Yeah.'

'Never. None of them leave.'

'Oh.' Even though I knew it in theory, the extent of their confinement was a disconcerting thought, especially here, up close. Sentinel had watched the liaison office ever since the partition and the footage backed Gina up: there were very few visitors from outside, and it was only ever them who came out. The children hadn't come through this office, we were certain, and the only other exit that we knew of was the supply bay.

She took a long-sighted squint back at the screen and raised her brow. 'Personal authorisation from a subwizard, no less. Makes sense, I suppose.'

'What's a subwizard?'

'Oh, you know. It's tech speak. They were all little boys when they invented this. I guess they thought calling themselves wizards was more rad than calling themselves kings or gods or whatever. Mr Coady's what normal people might call a community leader. Or was. I'm not sure. I don't keep up.'

Her tone – irreverent, disobedient, disloyal? An attitude I wasn't expecting in the front office of what we on the outside essentially viewed as a doctrinaire cult – put me off guard. I held my tongue.

'Anyway,' Gina Orban said, padding out from behind the desk again, 'are you aware of the procedure? Have you been in before?'

'No.' She knew I hadn't. Not even before the partition. Odille and David would always come and visit Mom and me in the city. Mom was already housebound by then.

'We need to fit you with The I. I'm not sure how much you know about it, but it's a complicated system and quite a rigmarole to install, so it's particularly unusual to grant a short-term entry clearance like this. People don't just drop in to Green Valley for tea. I'm guessing the visit is important.'

'Yes,' I said. 'It is.'

'It's none of my business. I'm just curious. Not much comes through this office.' I couldn't tell whether she meant information, goods or people, or what.

I was eager to get into Green Valley, but didn't want to be curt. Any information this casual and evidently lonely officer might let slip could be useful. 'I don't mind,' I said. 'What do I need to do?'

She led me to one of three doors at the far end of the reception room. 'I'll need you to take off everything you're wearing and put it in one of the lockers, along with any devices, currency, contact lenses, jewellery, baggage, electronics, everything but your natural self you were born with. Cover yourself with the towel in the locker and let me know when you're ready and we'll begin.'

She said it so neutrally, it was almost like I was being asked to check into a spa, or an abattoir. I objected, 'From what I knew of it before you… before Zeroth sealed, The I was a device you wore in one eye and it acted like a sort of personal computer screen. I'm not sure why you're asking me to…'

She smiled at this, a waxen smile that only affected her lips and left the rest of her face frigid. '"Personal computer screen,"' she mocked. 'Wizard Whitebeard wouldn't be pleased to hear his visionary work reduced to a "sort of personal computer screen". Anyhow, it's evolved. It's how Green Valley functions, in its entirety. It *is* Green Valley, really. To be in Green Valley, you need The I. And The I's evolved since the Turn.'

I tried to look politely surprised. I knew the technology was still being developed behind these walls; at Sentinel, I'd been analysing intelligence that suggested it, but I didn't see all the information, and there was no one analyst who understood it fully. Anyway, I didn't have to understand how it worked to use it, I told myself, repeating that complacent phrase that was almost blasphemous after the Turn. It had been such a comforting line to take back then, absolving ourselves of all responsibility, dropping our fates into the hands of seductive strangers, corporate entities in whose benignity we could feasibly believe.

Gina noticed my hesitation. 'Nobody's forcing you. You don't have to come in. You could get a message to your brother – your brother-in-law – some other way.'

I took a deep breath. I had work to do. 'No, of course I want to. David and I have something to discuss, and besides, I'm really interested to see what it's like.' Trying to convince myself, too, because my heart had started clawing at my ribcage.

She directed me to the changing room and handed me a small brass bell by its tongue – Tibetan or Persian, I guessed, when I saw the intricate etchings on it. 'Ring this when you're ready.'

Like the reception, the changing room's institutional edges had been softened by domestic touches. The stand of four metal lockers had been painted in pastel tones – mint, lilac, peach and sky blue – and detailed with hippie flowers. The slatted wooden bench was covered with Arabian cushions, while the row of basins was ornamented by candles, one of them alight, bottles of scented hand creams and liquid soaps. A hand-scripted card was pasted to the broad mirror above the basins with a platitude that sounded somehow menacing: *What You See Behind You Is Not What Lies Ahead.*

I chose the peach-coloured locker. The rusty hinges scraped as I pulled it open and I wondered just how few people came through here, and just how bored Gina Orban was, and what sort of thing extended boredom might do to a person's mind. Hand-painted daisies beamed at me as I pulled myself free of my turtleneck, but when I started on the button of my trousers darkness flashed in my peripheral vision. I whirled around and saw myself in the mirror, only me, but still that shadow was settling somewhere in this room. The candle's flame danced and tugged as if something had hurried past it.

It's just me, I said to myself. *There's nobody else here.* But still, I went to the mirror, looking into it, my face pressed close, cupping my hand between my brow and the glass to check that someone wasn't watching me from the other side. When I was pretty sure there were only the white tiles and the wall behind the mirror, I quickly stripped down to my underwear and reached for the large towel, which let off a small plume of stagnant white cotton dust as I unfolded it. The towel had probably never been used, but it had sat here for a long time. After shaking the towel out and wrapping it around me, I put my things into the locker, then rang the bell.

'You'll have to take that off, too,' Gina said when she came in, barely glancing at me, but noticing my bra straps. 'I've really seen it all,' she said.

Reluctantly, I unhooked my bra and dropped my underwear. This was the price I had to pay to get into Green Valley, I reminded myself, but it was already rising higher than I was comfortable with.

Gina hooked a hanger with a green-trimmed blue tracksuit on the locker and placed an unused pair of trainers below them. 'As soon as you're fitted, you can wear this when you go in. Hardly the height of fashion, but it doesn't matter in there. They won't be seeing you; they'll be seeing your avatar. Same goes for everything you see in there. You'll be walking around a real place, of course, and talking to real people, mostly, but you'll be seeing, feeling, *tasting* it in its enhanced state, as The I sees it. Sunshine, singing birds, unicorns, the works. In Green Valley, the virtual *is* reality. Or so I'm told.' She took a tablet screen out of a small cabinet beside the lockers and slid her finger over it, then turned the screen to me where a photograph of a woman appeared. She was of medium build and medium height, wore blue slacks and a white blouse, low-heeled shoes and had unadorned shoulder-length blonde hair. She had a symmetrical face with full lips and a small nose, and slightly larger than normal eyes.

'Who's she?' I asked.

'That's you.'

'Me?' I said, knowing what she meant, but demanding that she explain it as if I didn't. It was the principle: you shouldn't nonchalantly get away with giving someone a new body without comment.

'That's your avatar. It's how people will see you in Green Valley. You'd be very welcome to customise her, but we're running low on time.'

'It's really fine,' I said. 'It doesn't matter to me at all.' It did, though. Still, I was titillated by the idea of being this fantasy blonde for a day. I wondered if people would treat me differently.

'I call her Plain Jane,' Gina said. 'But to be honest, I wouldn't mind having her bone structure and her model face and her defiant boobs. The wizards designed her, of course.'

Again, it was hard to ignore the sarcasm dripping from her words, the undisguised resentment; referring to Jamie Egus as 'Wizard Whitebeard'. She was inviting me to probe. 'Tell me, Gina,' I said. 'Why are you here? You don't seem to... fully buy into the Zeroth ethos.'

She laughed: a hoarse, empty rattle like an echo in an abandoned house. 'Lie flat on your stomach and let me start.'

I did as she said. She knelt down next to me and zipped open a soft briefcase. 'You could call me uniquely cynical, I suppose,' she started. 'About Green Valley, and about Stanton. I don't belong to either of them.' As she spoke, she folded the towel up and rubbed a cold liquid over the small of my back. 'I used to be an occupational therapist on Zeroth's staff in the heyday, before the Turn. When they were developing The I, I was offered an alpha trial. I suffered some of the worst recorded cases of motion sickness and aversion, so impressive that they made me the development team's guinea pig. Voluntary, of course. They would never have forced me, but they paid me extremely well. At that time, they were launching simple virtual reality interfaces to the public – enhanced social networking, collaborative gaming, mindfucking porno experiences, you know. But half the potential clients got nauseous, puking on their POV sexbots and their dragon joust opponents rather than having fun.' She rubbed the ointment up my spine, making it tingle, scratching or drawing something on my neck and then pinning patches of hair back on my head. 'They suffered from what they call the uncanny valley effect,' she continued, 'suffering fight-or-flight panic attacks in the middle of virtual tropical holidays. Everything looked too real, but their cerebral cortices knew that it was all an illusion. On a primitive, instinctive, cellular level, the parts of their brains that hadn't been fooled were screaming out that they were being tricked, that they were in mortal danger. This was obviously not good for business, not good for uptake of the new devices. Development figured if they could beat the symptoms in me, they'd beat it in ninety-nine per cent of cases and that would be good enough. It worked out well. I'm one of the guinea pigs who led to Zeroth's VR dominance. It left me with certain… side effects… but they've been good to me, and I have a peaceful existence here.'

Then Gina rammed a spike into my lower back. I wanted to scream with pain, but then I realised there was no pain. A cold ripple rushed out from the spot and zapped through my spine in an electric rush. I bucked and arched with the pulse, and then it was gone. I groaned. 'What the fuck was that?'

'Sorry. A little discomfort, but that's the lumbar transponder.'

Before I could ask any more, she'd stuck something into the base of my neck that paralysed me. That same seismic cold ripple, but this time either I couldn't move my body to accommodate it or I couldn't feel my body arching. I was vaguely aware of cushions scattering off the bench, Gina's hands replacing them, a sense of better comfort, the mortification of seeing my bundled underpants crumpled under the bench. *If I die here…* I thought distantly. Claws pushed between my follicles, hooking my head, without physical pain but with the instinctive substrate of pain. My body screamed for me to move, to run, but I was paralysed and, to be honest, feeling all right, not bad at all, and I didn't know what I was panicking about. I should *just relax*. And all the while, I was looking at the bundled pants and thinking of how I'd lie on my bed as a girl, rubbish strewn all around me, protected by the tinny clatter of my headphones, safe and soft and warm.

And then a gasp and a crash and a spike through all my veins and I realised I was lying naked on the bench and Gina's warm hand was flat and calming on my back. 'Okay,' she was saying. 'Ten seconds to calibrate. Hang in there.' Rubbing my back with her warm, soft hand like a mother should when her child cries. 'Got you. How's that?'

At length, I was able to turn my head and see Gina looking at the tablet screen. I turned my head the other way, tested my limbs. Apart from a small added weight on my lower back and in my neck, a tug of trapped hair when I moved, it was okay. I reached down for the towel, which was half covering me again, and pulled it up my back. 'Is that it? Can I get dressed?'

'Sure. Give it a minute, then try to stand. If your balance is out, we'll fine-tune.'

I pushed up to sitting, tightening the towel around me. I should have felt violated and angry, although this woman had only done what I'd asked her, and she had such soft, sympathetic hands and I couldn't be angry even when I tried. And then I did try. I thought of those things that always made me angry – catcallers, bullies, cold-callers, power cuts – but the emotion shot by me like an express train through a station, and then it was gone. I tried to feel angry about the fact that some device was controlling my mind, but I couldn't, so I tried fear. I thought of a group of drunken men on a quiet road, the sound of a wolf-whistle in the middle of the night.

Briefly my adrenaline surged, but before I could catch the feeling it dissolved. Outrage, shame – gone. I tried to find it funny. I tried to laugh, but the sound died on my lips.

'We put guests into full SSRI mode. Especially short-term. There's no time for you to adapt to the environment, so we essentially balance your emotions by controlling your serotonin and dopamine levels with nanorobots. It may seem a little strange, I guess. But I've heard it's pretty calming, too. It's an electronic opiate. Do you like it?'

'I don't want to,' I said, managing to stand. I hadn't intended to be so honest with her, but I'd been somehow compelled.

'Good. Your balance is great.' Gina looked away, discreetly arranging her kit in her case as I changed into the tracksuit. I remembered to fold my underwear and placed it on the shelf in the locker, checking at the same time that the tight package I'd brought remained tightly tucked where I'd left it, in the inner pocket of my coat. 'Now comes a part some have found pretty nasty, I'm afraid. I'm sorry for it, but it's essential: we need to check your aversion levels. Come, sit comfortably.'

'Aversion levels?'

Gina came to sit beside me, the tablet screen in her hand displaying a series of dials. 'At first, when people came to visit Green Valley, they'd want to quit out manually. Maybe they had motion sickness, maybe the experience was overwhelming – who knows, maybe it was boring them. But some of them, despite all the advice to port out correctly, here and only here, saw fit to try to unplug The I and rip the interface off themselves. Let's just say the results were not good. "Suboptimal" in Development's terms. They needed to find a way to prevent this. Using the physiology behind the cortical aversion that users like me experienced when faced with the virtual world, they developed an aversion signal that would fire any time the system was tampered with. It would render a visitor physiologically unable to remove the rig, anywhere except here.'

'Like an electronic dog collar?' I said, acutely aware that my body had been attached to a dangerous electronic circuit. 'The one that zaps the dog when it strays over the boundary?'

'Yes.' Gina raised her lips in that cold version of a smile. 'Something like that.' And without warning, she tried to kill me.

It started as a quiver somewhere deep in the lower part of my head, deeper than my head should go. Something – *lots* of somethings – were running through tunnels dug into my brain. They were running in mortal dread. And the closer they got to me, to the sensing part of me, over their vague blurring terror-coloured shoulders I could feel what they were running from and it was all I had ever feared and all that these thousands of fleeing shadows had ever feared bundled up into a mass like a fist that was coming so fast it was going to shatter me as it hit and before I could scream it was in me and I was flying in a thousand shards and each of them burning with an acid of fear and I needed to scour—

But then it sucked back into itself like the vacuum of space eating an explosion.

I was aware of faint light seeping through my eyelids and past my fists where I was pressing them into my face. Gradually, I sensed my locked muscles as I curled foetal on the floor; I relaxed them and heard the echo of my scream still ringing off the wall. I slowly relaxed my arms and moved my neck to see a puddle of my own piss spreading over the blue linoleum floor.

'Aversion levels are calibrated well,' Gina said.

I pushed myself back onto the bench, not able to speak, not able to yell at this woman who was torturing me. If I could, I would have put my hands around her neck and wrung the life out of her, but as I thought it, the mood dissipated, and, knowing that it was wrong somewhere in a deep, muffled part of my mind, I felt grateful to her.

Then I could open my mouth and make a word with it, and all I could say was, 'Why?'

'The I *is* Green Valley,' she repeated. 'It's how it works. So just a reminder that that's an indication of what you'll start to feel if you tamper with The I in Green Valley. If you're in any trouble at all and want to detach, you just come back here. Call me if you're lost.'

'You'll need to give me your number. Do the payphones take regular money?'

Gina stopped and looked at me and I realised how foolish I sounded. Of course there were no payphones in Green Valley, no telephone numbers. 'Use The I. Ask a helper when you're inside. I could explain it all to you, but we'd better get moving. You're booked in until 5 p.m. You don't want to spend the whole day talking to me, do you?'

I shook my head.

'Good, then,' Gina said. 'Just the lenses left and you're ready to go.' She glanced at the puddle on the floor and the front of my trousers. 'I'll get you some clean clothes. Should have foreseen that,' she muttered as she left me sitting there, trying to steady my breathing.

The lenses were the oldest and most familiar part of The I's rig, and that's why Barbra Reeve and Bill Schindler, head of Sentinel tech, wanted one.

At the height of Zeroth's commercial success, over eighty per cent of Stantonians wore The I – you needed it to bank, to receive a salary, to find work, to access your driving points, to catch public transport, to buy tickets, to make cashless payments. Sure, there were billions of people on Earth who didn't use The I, but they were the poor, invisible to the marketers, marginal. Very few people who had a choice would deliberately marginalise themselves.

The I had started off as a single lens that fitted in one eye and provided a simple overlay rather than the alternate reality it became. You could look at a concrete factory wall, and see it overlaid with a virtual firework display; the fingers of a winter tree might be hung with sungold mangoes and flocked by scarlet macaws. It had started off fun and uplifting, an illustration of The I's creative capabilities, but by the time the Turn came around, this playful augmentation had become an uneconomical legacy feature, hijacked by hard-sell advertising.

When I got my first job out of university, I bought my own I, and for several years I kept just one release behind the latest version. The I developed rapidly – by the Turn, it could signal the user's optical, auditory, olfactory and gustatory nerves to create sophisticated VR magic. And those of us working at Sentinel knew that The I was still being developed after the partition, despite Zeroth no longer having a market. Just what these developments involved was less clear. Barbra and Bill Schindler suspected that, given Zeroth's lack of resources, any developments to the lens would be overlaid on successful old technology – and this offered the greatest chance of redundancies that would make it vulnerable to hacking. A current-model lens was their best chance of finding some of the new code hardwired behind outdated encryption. Also, it was small enough to hide somewhere and smuggle out, which is why they'd requisitioned me with a dummy lens and the signal-proof baggie, now hidden among my clothes in the locker. Barbra hadn't warned me about the spinal transponder Gina had fitted to me, but I guessed it would have fine control over tactile senses and motion. The discomfort of the installation, and even the mortified terror of the aversion test, had receded to dark memories, and I was excited now, looking forward to trying Green Valley out, but especially to seeing my niece again, for the first time in years.

Compared to the rest of The I's rig, the contact lenses were painless. Just like the device I'd been familiar with, they slipped with minimal discomfort over my irises. I could sense them calibrating to my eyes, the tiniest wave of motion when they first went in. They settled so comfortably I could easily forget I was wearing them.

Gina led me to the exit door, *Green Valley Town Square* printed on its opaque face. 'I'll guide you out at five,' she said. 'Enjoy your visit.'

3 I tiptoed as if I were picking a way through marshland, even though I knew I was on solid floor. I could imagine – or was I really sensing? – the whir of my mind and the creak of the bones in my ears jostling to comprehend and to calibrate. In front of me, just as the sign had said, was Green Valley's town square, and to my surprise, it looked precisely as it had when Green Valley closed. The iconic image used to serve as the centrefold in tourist brochures: *Visit the beautiful campus of Stanton's world-famous Zeroth Corporation, developer of Me Music, Z-Play and The I. See the eco-friendly office parks and residential village of Green Valley: soft technology with a diamond edge.*

That was before it had been entombed in concrete, and I had to remind myself that the clean blue sky and the puffy clouds and the sunlight were an illusion piped into my sensory nodes by the hardware embedded in my body. But the sunlight *felt* warm, like real sunlight. I took a few tentative steps beneath the spring-green alders – yes, warm in the dappled light, slightly cooler in the patches of shade. It was impossible, but I was being made to feel it. A bird pipped and took flight as a kid rattled by on a skateboard, gone before I could stop her.

Under my feet were the cobblestones the brochures had called *small-town hygge in a brand-new world*, but at the same time, I knew I was walking on flat, hard ground. Geographically just inside the wall, I couldn't be anywhere near the old town square – where it used to be. Then it struck me with a gut-floating lurch that the town square might be everywhere, anywhere a user wanted it to appear.

I rapped my knuckles on one of the trees – it was solid wood. I reached up and picked one of the leaves, twisting and shearing it between my fingers. It broke apart and left green juice on my palm. This was a real tree, and a real leaf, I would have sworn. Squatting down, I ran my fingertips over the ground, and where part of me knew there was bare concrete, I felt the texture and the ridges of cool cobbles; I scratched up sand between them, seeing it under my fingernails and on the tips of my fingers. All the while, I imagined there was the slightest delay, a nanosecond of rendering happening in the circuits along my spine. Surely that was just paranoia. Standing again, I flaked a piece of bark off the tree and put it in my pocket, a talisman to anchor me to reality.

Not your *pocket, Lucie*, some part of me spoke. *The pocket in the outfit Zeroth has lent you.*

Nausea gurgled deep in my stomach; running shadows encroached from my peripheral vision, but as soon as the panic started, it was damped again and I could look up and take a deep breath, barely remembering the fear. Biocontrolling nanorobots were shooting signals between my synapses and along my spine.

Now I could walk on, past young mothers with strollers and middle-aged people walking their dogs. A couple jogged by, wearing tight gym clothes and listening to music on players strapped to their upper arms. They smiled at me as I passed. I made my way to the whitewashed bandstand in the middle of a quadrant of lawn and looked out over the railing. In front of me was the row of Main Street shops the brochures used to proclaim, and lining the other three sides of the square were the smart townhouses we'd all envied. The wall had disappeared, replaced by a row of houses on the tree-lined street and blue sky behind them. No cars. People walking, jogging, cycling.

Three soothing notes sounded in my ears and a middle-aged man materialised in front of me. 'Lucie?' he said. He was wearing textured guanashina slacks, a sharp indigo suit jacket and hand-stitched lace-ups, his elegantly patterned tie adorned with a silver pin, and his gracefully silvering hair gelled into a perfect wave. He seemed to have matured from the expensive hoodies and designer jeans I recalled, but his face was the shape I remembered, the charming, idiosyncratic curves that had snagged Odille, and who could blame her?

I stepped forward as if to shake his hand or give him a hug – I wasn't sure – but before I could, David floated backwards and I realised two things: that this picture of my sister's husband was an avatar, and that he – whatever physical substance of him lay under the image – was not here; this was a phone call.

'Hi, David? Can you hear me? Can you see me?' I said, as a smaller image of Plain Jane appeared floating to the top-right of my eyeline. A green halo shaded around her, indicating, I guessed, that the connection had been established.

'You're here,' David said. 'In Green Valley.'

Self-consciously, looking at the casual blonde that was meant to represent me, I blurted, 'It's not really me, but I guess you know it's me.'

'Don't worry, I understand,' David said, but vacantly, without smiling. 'Listen, um, Lucie. It says here that I invited you. Thanks for coming, but I'm not sure if it was… I can't remember why you're here.' An affectless vacancy reflected on the avatar's face.

'For God's sake, David.' I stepped forward again, but the image glided back in response, locked into its ratio. 'I came to check on Kira.'

'Oh. Yes,' he said. 'It's hard to remember.'

'It's been ages,' I blurted, trying to squeeze eight years into this tenuous connection. 'How have things been in—'

But he wasn't listening. He whirled around to look at something behind him, something I couldn't see, and I caught fear in those generated eyes. 'No, I'm not—' The connection cut out and David disappeared. The halo around Plain Jane went red, and her thumbnail image dissolved away.

David's absence ghosted in the air in front of me. A woman walking by, hand in hand with a toddler, didn't seem to notice or care that I was standing in the middle of the sidewalk, staring at nothing, a bewildered expression on my face.

Gina Orban said something about a helper. I should try to find one, I realised, and ask how to return the call, or how to find him.

'Excuse me,' I called after the mother. She turned and smiled, the toddler staring up at me, chewing on his finger. This child, at least, didn't seem distressed or in danger; the kids in here seemed all right – but at the same time, I knew I was seeing only what The I wanted me to see. 'Can you tell me how I can—'

But I was interrupted by three chimes in my head and a soothing voice. It was familiar, but it took me a moment to place her. Then I had it – this was the voice of Clara, Zeroth's digital assistant, one of the three voice options on The I. Millions of people had woken every morning and spoken intimately with Clara before the Turn. As if nothing had changed in the world, she said, 'Calendar entry received for Lucie Sterling,' followed by a recorded clip of David's voice, neutral again: 'I'll see you at the Asbury Café in five minutes.' Then the computer followed up with, 'Do you want to travel to the Asbury Café now?'

'Yes?' I tried, aware that the mother on the sidewalk was waiting for me patiently, the toddler tugging at her sleeve.

I shook my head and made a don't-worry-thanks face, not wanting to speak in case it confused the computer. The woman nodded and walked off.

'How do you want to travel to the Asbury Café?'

I had no idea how I'd get there in five minutes if it was far away. I still hadn't seen a Green Valley shuttle or even a cycle hub. 'How far is it?' It was odd, after all this time, how natural it felt to slip back into conversation with The I as if it were human.

'The Asbury Café is two hundred and thirty-seven metres from your current location. Estimated travel time in current traffic conditions is one minute and twenty seconds.'

'I guess I'll walk, then.'

'Displaying directions to. Walk. To the Asbury Café,' Clara said, as a map overlay appeared in front of me, with a pulsing arrow and a route charted across the town square.

The café was in the row of shops fronting Main Street, a wall of glass displaying young professionals scattered along wooden counters against bare-brick walls and being productive at communal tables. It was exactly like a scene from Zeroth advertisements dating back ten or fifteen years, and I'm sure I recognised a hipster with a red folding computer with his green-haired partner, and a bald wrestler-strong man in a white T-shirt drinking a protein shake further down the communal table. I pushed through the smooth-hinged door and scanned the customers. Some looked up at me and some didn't. I tried fruitlessly to gauge which were real and which were part of the scenery. They all looked as real as people in cafés did on the other side of the wall; except, of course, in Stanton people wrote with pens on paper, had facial blemishes, baggy eyes and thin hair, and usually were speaking to each other or reading books rather than staring into electronic devices.

I sat at the counter in the window so that David would

see me. An incredibly toned man in a tight shirt came over to ask me if I needed anything.

'Just waiting for someone.'

'Sure.' He smiled, with perfect teeth. 'Just shout when you're ready. We have muffins fresh out of the oven.' As he spoke, I sensed a whiff, right up my nose – emitting from *inside* my nose – of the rich, warm scent of chocolate and raspberry muffins, something I was sure I hadn't smelled before he'd spoken. I was hungry and thirsty, a cosy feeling, because I knew I could be satisfied here. I found myself scratching the wood of the countertop, to prove to myself that I could make a mark in it. Scoring a rough L in the surface, I picked up some wood grit under my nails – my avatar's nails – which by now were becoming quite dirty. I didn't know if this meant the counter was real or just exceptional software design, but I repressed the question, or it was repressed for me.

Then David was there, pushing through the door and indicating that I should follow him to a booth at the back of the café. 'Not that it matters, really. It can see us everywhere,' he said as we slid into the booth. Up close, off the call, he sounded like David, and the years tumbled away. For a second I fully expected to see Odille follow him through the door. But Odille was dead. Before I could even try to understand what he was saying, I was compelled to reach over and grab his arm. When he didn't float away from me like his phone avatar had, I took his shoulders in both my hands and pulled him to me. He was solid and warm and real – the man who had once loved my sister.

'It's good to see you, David,' I said.

'You too,' he said. 'But it hurts. I loved Odille so much. You know that, right?'

'Of course I do. I'm sorry for what I said on the phone.'

He let me hold him for a while longer, but then extricated himself, touching his jawline, which was airbrush-smooth.

'What did you mean, *It can see us everywhere*? What is *it*?'

'The watcher,' he said.

'What is that? What does it watch for? Has it got anything to do with the—' I cut myself off just in time. I hadn't told David about the dead boys from Green Valley, and though I'd warned him of a danger to the children, he hadn't asked what kind. He still thought I was being just another hysterical anti-tech outsider.

'It watches for any unusual activity that might threaten the integrity of Green Valley. It's here to protect us.'

This sounded like a PR line, so I pressed him. 'Protect you from what, David?'

'Do you want a muffin?'

I don't want a fucking muffin, David. 'I came here to see Kira. It's time you took me to her.' But then, unaccountably, I did want a muffin, and a large cup of coffee. That would feel very good. David had already beckoned the waiter over.

'He's not real, is he?' I said, when he'd left with my order.

David shrugged. 'It's hard to tell. Someone may have made him. He may have made himself.'

The bathroom was like something I'd seen in a magazine. The same varnished brick with beaten copper basins in a unisex washroom. As I pulled down my trousers to pee, the cubicle door hinged open. I jolted up and pulled at my trousers, but I realised there was nobody there – the catch wasn't holding the deadbolt. I caught a glimpse of myself in the washroom mirror, a blonde woman's hands pushing down the belted waistband of her jeans, while for a second I held the soft material of the Zeroth sweatpants. Then, with a subliminal shift, I was feeling denim and stiff faux-leather and metal studs between my fingers. I bolted the door again, and this time it caught.

When I was washing my hands, warm water and subtly fragranced soap foaming from automatic, touchless dispensers, I stared into the face of Plain Jane in the bank of mirrors, her face moving seamlessly at my prompts: smiling, frowning, licking her reddened lips and baring her teeth, a silent scream. Over her shoulder, for a moment, something else was looking back. Someone shifting behind her. For a burning second, I saw a tall, dark form that shimmered with moving images. I couldn't bring it into focus – the place where a mouth and the bottom of its nose should have been was smudged like coal-black pastel, and a jaundiced glow seeped out from its eyes. All this in a second, because I spun around to find nobody was behind me, and when I turned back to the mirror, only a scared-looking Jane peered back at me. As I watched, her face settled to contented neutrality as my own heart slowed and my mind calmed. I hadn't forgotten the faceless creature, but I was unable to generate a strong emotion about it.

The fingerprint of fear reminded me that I had come here for a purpose. Something I had to keep reminding David of, too.

My order had arrived while I was away. I picked up the muffin and bit into it, and in my mouth for a split second wasn't the fresh crumb of baked dough but a fungal sludge. Instinctively, I made to spit my mouthful out, but before I did, The I stepped in and made the flavour bready, delicious, chocolate-and-raspberryish. I frowned, swallowed, took another appreciative bite and swilled it back with some of the strong and fragrant brew. It was really good.

'Where is Kira?' I asked David. He gave me a questioning look. 'Kira, David.' I leaned in and whispered urgently, 'You asked me here so that I could see her. Is there something you need to tell me?'

'You wanted to see her,' he said. 'Here goes.'

An image flipped across my field of vision and I couldn't stifle a gasp. The girl, smiling and tanned, hair raked nonchalantly away from her brow, had Odille's face: her cat-like cheekbones curving in and then plumping out again at the jaw. A genetic copy of the sister I'd lost.

'She's beautiful. She must be nine now.'

He looked at his hands. Zeroth's fast-track success story, hottest director in the industry back in the day – counting on his fingers. 'Nine. Yes… nine. That's right.'

A caption under the picture of the smiling girl asked if I wanted to save it. I blinked yes, even though I knew there wasn't any point – I couldn't keep the image once I'd left Green Valley. 'Has she been… happy?'

'Of course. Very.'

'I didn't even know you'd married again. Who is she?'

'Eloise. We've… we knew each other before Green Valley closed.'

'While you were still with Odille?'

'No. Well, yes… We were friends. Colleagues.' There was no emotion on David's face.

'Oh.' It was all The I would allow me to say. The shock and rage were being ground up and expelled in the pit of my stomach. It allowed me to focus on the reason I was here, though. 'Where did you last see Kira?'

'At home, I'm pretty sure. But the record is corrupted.' David's attention was drifting. He glanced over his shoulder.

'Jesus, David! Do you need an electronic record to remember everything?'

'You don't know what it's like. I've been here a long time. Life is different. It's hard to explain.'

'And where is she now?'

'At home.'

'I want to see her.'

'I don't think it's a good idea to take you to the house.'

'Why not? That's why I came here. The only reason.'

'Eloise is there. She won't be… happy that I invited you.' He frowned at me again. 'If you're sure I did.'

'Why? Has she got something to hide? I've told you that we have information that Kira could be in serious danger. Wouldn't Eloise want to keep her safe?' My voice had risen, spitting out a gout of anger that The I couldn't process quickly enough, but I didn't care. The computer people could stare. Nothing was truly private here, in any case. That's how the technology worked, that's how Zeroth worked, that's how Green Valley worked. It's exactly why the world turned away from it – so we could have a private goddamn conversation.

David raised his hands, his avatar visibly agitated by the conflict. 'Relax. I'll take you to the house.'

I tried to cling on to the anger, which was already being made to dissipate through the waste channels of my limbic system.

Natural anger and fear were rare commodities in Green Valley. They could be valuable, motivating weapons.

4

David's house wasn't far from Main Street. It lay towards the middle of the settlement, away from where the liaison office had been when I'd left it. I tried to keep the position of that doorway to reality lodged in my mind, like a beacon, as we walked, but the gentle curve of the suburban streets soon disoriented me.

I'd seen these streets before, in pre-Turn brochures, when Zeroth's brand of utopia was a marketable vision – the wide, tidy sidewalks lined with trim lawns and lush subtropical plants that took advantage of the unique microclimate in the valley. Boles of ancient trees dripped with Spanish moss and fruit trees sparkled with blossom and flittering birds. This is how it had looked in the hagiographic videos people used to make about Green Valley years ago, and somehow they had made it look exactly the same now. There was no way it could really have survived eight years in a concrete bunker, even with the most advanced hydroponics; it was an incredible illusion.

Another thing nagged at me. If these birds and these trees and the smart whitewashed siding of the colonial-style houses were just a digital veneer, couldn't the citizens design anything? Why wouldn't they remodel their houses and customise their avatars? Someone could make themselves into a seven-winged fairy and live in a floating bubble of water with dolphins if they wanted to; someone could choose to live in an igloo in a moonscape. Why stick to human forms and the reality-bound design of Green Valley, circa a decade ago?

'Jamie thought, and the collective agreed, that it would help with continuity,' David told me, when I asked. 'We knew that people might struggle to adapt to the fact that we had chosen to stay here and not leave. It would make it more familiar if we adhered to certain design rules.' When he talked about Zeroth's business, he sounded confident and professional, and I was starting to understand: The I was part of David's consciousness, he'd become so used to its assistance that it had channelled and shaped his abilities. Talking about Zeroth's vision was his job, so The I facilitated it. Trying to engage with an anomalous risk to his daughter was an extracurricular misdirection of his capacity, and The I wouldn't abet it.

'And you're part of this collective,' I asked, 'with Jamie Egus and other senior Zeroth staff?'

'Yes,' he said, but his shoulders started to hunch and his stride began to shorten as we turned into the driveway of another pristine colonial-style house. He led me up the five steps and onto the porch, then tapped timidly on the front door – on his own front door. 'Eloise? Elle, are you there?'

There was no answer, so David turned the knob and opened the front door.

'You leave it unlocked,' I said. 'That's impressive.' But the moment I said it, I knew I was being stupid, and the uncomprehending glance he shot me as he led me into the house confirmed that.

The open-plan living room was stylishly but coldly decorated in tones of dove-grey and white: soft furnishings and *objets* artfully arrayed, a whitewashed stone wall framing a fireplace that didn't look like it had ever been needed. The only blight on the neatness looked self-consciously styled too, a page from a catalogue suggesting joyful family life: a half-eaten cheese sandwich and a decorative sprig of tomato leaf on a green ceramic plate perched at the edge of the coffee table, three perfect half-moon bites cut out. A tumble of piously ethical wooden blocks on the floor next to a red-and-blue wooden truck. A single tiger-striped sock lying in the middle of the pristine dove-grey carpet.

'She's probably in her workshop,' David said. He glanced at a closed door to the left of the living room, from where a deep hum emanated, and his face and shoulders seemed to relax.

'Why are you afraid of her?' I asked.

He turned and smiled. 'Afraid? No, I'm not afraid of Eloise. Honestly, I guess I'm embarrassed. I didn't want to introduce you to her. She's become so… strange. But she's busy now, and won't notice us, so I can show you around.'

David led me through the living room, down a short passageway, to a door decorated with a photo of a girl in a resin frame with seashells and sailing boats trapped in it. *K I R A* was spelled out in bright and chunky lopsided letters glued to the lower edge, as if I needed telling. The girl in the picture had Odille's smile, her flyaway curls, the shape of her brow, all merged with David's handsome features – she was breathtaking, and I felt like I was looking at an image of a ghost.

David pushed the door open, and as we stepped into the bedroom, three identical little girls, about five years old, looked up from where they were sitting in bright, child-sized wicker chairs along a low whitewashed table, colouring pictures. There was nothing familiar in their faces, not like in Kira's, but they were pretty and their hair was in cute, wild ringlets; they wore identical blue-striped T-shirts and knitted orange scarves with fox-head hoods. In triplicate, they turned their faces up and said, 'Hello, Daddy.' David nodded distractedly, twitching his mouth but not saying anything as he passed them, going to the bedside. Like mirror images, they followed their father with their big eyes.

I couldn't let David get away with ignoring the girls, so I squatted down in front of the table and said, with overcompensating cheer, 'Hi! I'm Lucie. Your dad's... friend. What're you drawing?' I looked at the paper in front of them, but it was blank. They swivelled their heads towards me and stared at me with three sets of the same eyes.

'Oh, ignore them, Lucie. Please. They're not real. Eloise made them years ago, when she still had time for romantic gestures. They're badly coded, but it'd hurt her feelings if I erased them. They're going to go one of these days.'

'Where are we going, Daddy?' the girls said. 'Are we going on holiday?'

'Yeah, something like that,' David muttered as he prowled to the nightstand, tidying the objects on it – a plastic water clock, a frog-shaped tape dispenser, collectors' cards from a range of toys I didn't recognise – picking each one up and turning it over. The girls turned their faces back to their blank drawings. My gut churned. When I stood up, the blood ran into my legs and I was swamped with grey numbness and then was hit with an underlaid vision of this room, the bedclothes all over the floor, an acrid wet patch in the middle of the sheets, the bedside lamp knocked over and those toys tipped and scattered. I stumbled back against the wall, hearing a hollow clunk that shouldn't have come from solid brick. I felt the tug and struggle of The I calibrating my system, and within a minute, I was back to normal again.

'Are you all right?' David said.

'Yes. I stood up too quickly.' I turned my face away from the triplets as I joined David where he was leaning over the bedside cabinet. When he straightened, a low purple glow emitted from his right hand.

'This is weird,' he said. He showed me a small rectangle glowing in his palm. A picture of a proud yellow rooster was painted on the chit, a Spanish or Portuguese design, floral and bright against the rich purple background. 'This isn't hers. It's not even… from here.'

'What is it? A credit card?' Like many people in Stanton, I still carried a couple of those defunct plastic cards with me, well after the Turn. I'm not sure why – a talisman against the past, or maybe just because the slots in my purse had stretched to accommodate them and if I threw them out, my library tickets and banking punchcards would slip out every time I opened it. But the rooster started moving in a cartoonish way, strutting to the right and puffing out its chest before belting out a soundless crow. 'Oh,' I corrected my guess, 'it's a screen. A super-thin cell phone, right?'

David responded by holding the chit up, and opening and withdrawing his fingers. The glowing rectangle remained suspended in the air between us, the rooster settling back into its side-on portrait position. When I tried to take hold of it, my finger went straight through the projection.

'It's a custom-built v-card. Not one of Zeroth's.'

'Like those stupid things we used to shoot each other before the Turn? Virtual animoji?'

'Exactly. From that era.'

David glanced at me, as if remembering the woman we had in common in a long-distant life.

On the purple rectangle, the yellow rooster had roused himself and was starting his strutting routine again. I prodded at the v-card, surprised, despite experience, that my finger didn't send it whirling or sliding, just glided right through. 'Where did it come from?'

'The only way someone could have left this in here is if they hacked their way into Green Valley, cloaking their presence very well, but not perfectly. This old card's got outdated encryption. That's why I detected it.'

I stared at the cartoon prancing through its routine again, understanding that it was just a column of unprotected code

The I had snagged from an ancient, forgotten corner of the intruder's dossier. 'Where's Kira, David? Do you even know? In the café, you said she was at home.'

'That's what the… It's just a glitch. She's perfectly fine. Just as she's always been. I can show you the bloody records if you want me to.' Defensive, the slick mask slipping.

A glitch. His words reminded me of what I'd seen a minute ago – the fallen bedsheets, the knocked-over lamp. 'You say someone hacked in,' I said, working to keep my tone level in front of the triplets. 'But I think it's more than that. What if someone's been here – physically? What if a stranger's been in your daughter's bedroom? Why can't you find her? Why are you so oblivious? You're just plugged into your own personal reality, like everyone else here.'

'We made a drawing of him, Daddy,' the triplets piped up.

I wheeled around to face them. 'Show me,' I said, and they all turned and raised their blank pieces of paper.

'Oh, go away,' David said.

'Is it possible that they know something?' I asked. 'That they saw something?'

'No. They're primitive programmed objects. They have a small selection of preset responses that trigger when you do or say something specific.' He yawned and said, 'I'm tired.'

'Good night, Daddy,' the girls said, vanishing.

'You see? Now you start to understand.'

But I didn't. We hadn't said anything that would lead the triplets to say they'd *made a drawing of him*. How could that response have been programmed?

'We should go. Eloise might come out,' he said, leading me out of Kira's bedroom.

'I'd like to see her,' I said. Of course I wanted to see David's wife. Kira's replacement mother. 'She might know where Kira is.'

'No. Really. I'd rather not do this.' He tried to ward

me towards the front door, but I dodged his arm and hurried over to the door he'd glanced at when we came in. The humming was louder from here, accompanied by a rushing sound.

'No, Lucie, stop,' David was saying behind me. 'Please.' But I twisted the door handle and pushed my way inside.

A thin, naked man was sitting on a blue-cushioned office chair in a green meadow at the edge of a blue pool. In the air in front of him floated four screens scrolling data and images. To his left, a rainbow waterfall jetted into the pool, releasing a deep hum as it streamed out of the back end of a gleaming white horse. No, not a horse – a unicorn.

'She shouldn't be rendering like this in Green Valley,' David said. 'It wastes energy we don't have to spare. If the rest of the collective found out, she could get expelled to the Edges.'

At any other moment, I might have laughed. This was the first sign of humour I'd noticed within Zeroth's sterile, corporate vision. 'I don't understand,' I said, my eyes still drawn to the rainbow fountaining out of the unicorn's butt. By his grim expression, it was clear that David didn't share the joke. 'Surely they know everything. This is all online.'

'She builds good encryption. And she relies on my discretion.' David wasn't trying to keep his voice down, talking about Eloise as if she wasn't there. 'She really doesn't give a shit for the rules. And one day she'll get us in trouble.'

For a second, I felt validated by David's evident scorn for the woman who had taken Odille's place in Kira's life. How the fuck could someone like this be trusted with a little girl?

David pursed his lips as Eloise swivelled round on her office chair planted in the middle of the meadow, splaying her skinny, hairy legs, the little pouch of her belly rolling over a scraggly bush of black pubic hair and a sleeping cock and balls. I stifled a prudish gasp. 'How did you get her in?'

Eloise asked David as her avatar shimmered into a casually clothed woman of about forty, the skin of her face naturally lined, her hair simply pushed back with a green band.

'Special request. She's seeing to a… personal problem.'

'Hmm,' Eloise said. 'Must be an important problem. Anything I can do?'

David peered closer at her screens. 'What are you doing here?'

With a gesture, Eloise replaced the scrolling data with a picture of an octopus on a colourful reef. 'I've mined eight coins today. Then I traded up on a spike.' She swiped and plucked her fingers around the empty space in front of her, then turned back to face us. Eloise studied me with deep, intelligent eyes – not the eyes of a madwoman. Her gaze was still, reading something that nobody had told her, something that The I wasn't feeding her. 'So, how do you like our town? I see you're wearing Jane. Short visit, huh?'

'Yeah,' I said. 'Your town's amazingly… real. It looks just like I imagined it.' All I wanted from her was to know where Kira was, but I suspected I wouldn't find that out by asking directly. I needed to coax, to come at the question obliquely. 'I was asking David why the residents weren't allowed to stretch their imaginations a little more. Why there isn't more of this.' I gestured around us.

She shrugged. 'Lack of imagination? Lack of confidence? Lack of resources? Full-on fear? Who knows? I guess the collective is worried that if you let the Lambdas have their way there'd be dragons and Ferengi roaming the streets, everyone would be having gang-bangs with hydras in pink champagne jacuzzis.'

'Jesus,' David muttered.

She shrugged. 'She asked, sweetie. It's your fault anyway,' she added. 'You outsiders. So mistrustful you had to destroy the promise of the internet. How's it going out there? Are you back to riding cows and drawing on walls with burnt sticks?'

'You shouldn't make assumptions,' I said. 'Not everyone's like that. Don't you get the news in here?'

'Never trusted the news.'

After the Turn, everyone thought we had reached some final consensus and that there was no more need for politics. If I were to tell Eloise the honest truth, I'd tell her the world had become stifling out there, ripening for an explosion. But instead I said, 'I see that. Maybe you're not so interested in what's happening out there.' I indicated the door – the world outside, or her own home. I looked into her eyes again, catching some understanding there, or imagining I did. 'So tell me, Eloise? Does everyone in here have to follow the collective's rules?'

'There are still some who do their own thing. But they cluster at the wall, at the conceptual edges. As close as Egus could come to expelling them, I guess.'

'Come on, Eloise,' David huffed. 'You know as well as I do that it's a consensual arrangement. They have as much freedom as we do.'

'More, I'd say.' Eloise shrugged. 'Plus it's consensual only because the collective can't exactly send them out of the enclave, allow them to reveal our dirty secrets to the cavemen outside.'

David tutted in disgust. 'You talk a lot, but you wouldn't go and live there, would you? You like the comfort of the rules a little too much. Try and pull this shit off out there and you'd be branded a fool and exiled from exile land.'

Eloise shrugged and turned away, back to her screens.

'This is why I didn't want you to meet her,' David said. 'She's such a phoney. Enough bullshit, Eloise. Do you know where Kira is?'

She turned to face us again, and now she looked like

nothing other than a worried parent. 'What do you mean *where she is*? I thought you were watching her today.' In Green Valley, watching a child meant something quite different.

'Nuh-uh, not my turn,' David said.

'It is, David. Check the schedule,' she complained. 'Anyway, here she is.' She brought up a map and pointed out a beacon. 'She's in the garden with Cisco. Don't know why you couldn't have checked yourself.'

David frowned. 'I tried. There was a glitch.'

'System update this morning. You need to keep up.' She turned back to the screen. The interview was over.

'Can I see her?' I asked David as he led me away from Eloise's lair and through the sitting room to the front porch.

'I don't think that's a good idea.'

'Why not? That's why I'm here.'

'Yeah, but who should I say you are?'

'I'm her aunt, David. Or—' Did Kira even know I existed? 'You have told her about me, haven't you? She knows Odille had a family – that she's got family outside?'

'Yes, yes, of course,' he said. 'But it's not that easy. I can't just say, "Here's your real mom's sister, stopped by for a visit." We'd need to find the proper time and way to introduce you. She doesn't know you, Lucie, and though she knows intellectually that Odille was her mother, Eloise is her mom. You can't just… appear. It would be confusing, bewildering. And on top of that, you're wearing Jane. What is she supposed to think? Who are you supposed to be?'

'Okay. I get it.' Even though it skewered me, I did understand. As much as I wanted to meet Kira – Odille's blood, my family – I couldn't do that to her. 'But I just want to know that she's fine. Can you just show me to her? I could look at her through the window or something.'

David softened. 'How about I introduce you as someone else? Then you can meet her and she doesn't have to know who you are. You'd just be a random stranger. For now.'

As if there would ever be any chance of me being anything else to her. I never would – the hopeless fact of it dragged a lead weight through the middle of me.

'Sure. Okay. Thanks.'

He led me through the kitchen and out to the back garden, where I saw the girl from the picture, a beautiful mutation of my sister, standing with a boy and poking a stick into a tall cypress tree.

'Hey, sweetie,' David said as we approached.

'Hello, Daddy,' she said. 'You wanna see our spider hotel?'

'Sure.'

I hung back as David peered into the tree and Kira told him about her game. The boy hadn't turned, almost deliberately swivelling to avoid my gaze. The evasive motion reminded me that I was looking at projections. I needed to know the real girl beneath this figure of Kira.

I stepped forward. 'What you got there?'

Kira turned to me with a blank look.

'This is, uh, a colleague of mine,' David said. 'Uh—'

'Jane. My name is Jane,' I said, holding out my hand.

The girl looked at my hand, up to my face and then put her palm in mine. I concentrated in that one second of physical touch on the solidity in her palm, the grip of her fingers, a precious second of connection to tell me that everything was okay.

The boy still didn't turn, moving as I moved, evading me like the eyes on a trick painting, and Kira's hand seemed to jitter for a fraction before it pulled away, the substance of it feeling light and hollow under the avatar, like a deflating balloon. For a second I doubted, but just a second.

It was the smile that did it – that convinced me that Kira was safe and well. It tore away the decades and brought me home, to the warm light of Odille's face.

5

'Thanks for that,' I said as David led me back into the house. While I was buoyed by the fact that Kira was safe after all, and that she appeared nurtured and well, I was also dumped by an immeasurable sadness. I had just come face to face with everything I'd lost.

If Kira was fine, though, the dead boys certainly weren't. What had happened to them, and how could we be sure that the same wouldn't happen to Kira or the other children here? What I'd seen today had led me to trust David enough.

'Listen, David,' I said. 'The reason I called, the reason I came, is that we found two dead children in Stanton – and they came from Green Valley.'

'What?' His shock was genuine – I was certain he wasn't putting on an act, electronic mask or not. 'What do you mean? When?'

I told him the basics – the two dumped bodies, The I architecture, the nanotech in their blood – so that he was in no doubt. 'This is why I came, and I'm glad that Kira's here, but you need to keep an eye on her. Do you know anything about missing children? Do you have any records?'

'God,' he said, wiping his face with his hand. 'It's not really my area.'

'You have to tell your police or security services or whatever passes for them in here. There has to be a record, hasn't there? Everything's tracked in here, isn't it? Everyone's movements.'

'Sure. Of course. Yeah,' he said. 'I'll get onto it. I'll speak to them.'

'Keep me updated, all right? And I'll let you know if I find anything useful out. We've – *you've* got to keep Kira safe, okay?'

'Sure. Don't worry about it,' he said, his confidence already returning after the shock. 'It must be an anomaly. Things are fine here, amazing safety record. That's what we always stood for, you know?'

I ignored his bald appeal for approval. That ship had long since sailed. I left the house, glad when Kira's laughter ringing out from the back yard was the last thing I heard.

'Clara,' I said, recalling the syntax we'd used all those years ago, 'display route to liaison office.'

'No route found,' the soothing voice replied. 'Please select a valid destination.'

'Clara,' I said, recalling the frustration we'd all grown used to, 'take me out of Green Valley, to the exit.'

'Which direction do you want to travel?'

'Clara, dial Gina Orban.'

'Please select a valid contact.'

'Jesus Christ. How do you get the fuck out of here?' I said, aware as I did that the shameless abuse of a faceless AI was a nasty habit of humanity that I didn't want to perpetuate. 'Sorry. It's Gina Orban, right. I thought she was called the liaison officer,' I said awkwardly, knowing the syntax of doubt would not compute.

'Please select a valid destination.'

'Cancel,' I told her, and started walking. Even The I and all the virtual rendering in the world couldn't make Green Valley any larger than it really was. If I placed one foot in front of the other, I would physically move across the space enclosed by the concrete shell. If I continued doing that for an hour, I would walk from one end of the enclave to the other. Before long, I would come up against a wall, even if it didn't look like a wall, and from there I could trace my way around it and find the liaison office.

I strode on with purpose, retracing the route to Main Street, then chose a direction and set out. The skating kid was back, rattling over the cobbles, and the fit thirty-something joggers were doing another loop around the square. Was the kid a simulation? Wouldn't a real kid have school today? But then, I didn't know much about how Green Valley worked. Education would certainly be via The I. Perhaps some pioneering educationalist had come up with a way to skateboard and learn algebra at the same time. Maybe that's what David had meant by *Mathcamp* – after all, Kira hadn't been at school either. There was a whole heap of questions I hadn't asked him about Kira. Was she even seeing the same Green Valley I could see?

As I walked past the coffee shop where I'd met David, I glanced in through the window. There was the buff waiter, offering muffins to the creatives at the communal table. The guy with a red computer was still there, along with the green-haired girl. Sure enough, down the table sat the same bald wrestler guy, in broad-gestured conversation with someone on a screen.

Next door was a deli, advertising organic produce and free-range steaks by the pound. Even Sentinel had no details of what produce was brought in to Green Valley. Zeroth had made lucrative and exclusive contracts with farms outside who kept their activities shrouded in secrecy. It was another thing Stanton police ignored: if there was nothing illegal happening, there was no reason to probe into perfectly reasonable trading practices – trademarks and patents and hard-won contracts with clients who valued their privacy were nothing new, and since the Turn, the population demanded that the police didn't go snooping around in private affairs. We'd won our privacy back.

I walked on as Main Street curved to an end and fed into a residential crescent that looked exactly the same as

David's street. Birds trilled in trees so rich with produce that they drooped demurely towards the model-garden flower installations; a dog was barking somewhere, and closer by I heard children laughing. Across the road, the houses watched me silently from behind their floral fringes. The dog barked: *yap, yap-yap-yap*; *yap, yap-yap-yap*; the noise fell into an unintentional rhythm as one of the children shrieked higher than the others on the downbeat of the third bark. Then it happened again a few barks later, and again. I zipped my top up higher, conscious of temperature for the first time.

Knowing I was curling back towards the centre of town, I tried to reorient myself, but after a few more curves, I didn't know which way I was facing. Instinctively, I resisted bringing up the map. *They* would know where I was if I allowed the map permission to detect my location. *They*, the big covert corporate-state monster that we, in the rational and free world outside, had turned our backs on. *Use your natural instincts*, I told myself pointlessly, looking up at the false sky for signs.

As I was about to give in, a grating sound broke the peace behind me. I turned to see the top half of a man wearing a cycling helmet gliding along the sidewalk on the other side of a hedge. He emerged on a kick scooter from behind the hedge and turned up the driveway I was marooned on. At the porch, he dismounted showily, planting his foot and sliding the little back wheel out like a Tokyo drifter.

'Nice wheels,' I said.

'Hi,' the man said, unclipping his helmet. He squinted as he surveyed me, unable to find a focus or a readout on me. His eyes darted nervously. 'Are you with the birthday party?' He nodded towards the house, guarded. A birthday party. Maybe I should ask this guy if he knew about the missing children – that sort of news should surely spread among the regular sort of parents who take their children to birthday parties. But I decided against it – any regular adult would be justly suspicious of a kidless stranger lurking outside a kid's party, asking questions.

'No. I'm just visiting. I'm looking for somewhere.'

'We don't get many visitors here,' he said. 'Do you know how to use the map?'

'The place I want to go doesn't seem to be listed.'

'Oh.' He screwed up his face. 'That's strange. This place should be entirely mapped.'

His suspicion was deepening; he shifted his stance and turned to face me. I didn't want this man to know where I was going, so I came up with a lie. 'Someone told me about a place where people are free to build what they like, outside the Green Valley borders. He called it the conceptual edge, but I'm guessing that's not a place name.'

His stance relaxed. 'Oh, yes. The Edges. You could call it a place if you want. We used to get a lot of tourists in to look at the architecture. That was before… Not many visitors through now, as I say. There's not as much activity at the Edges any more, but you may still find something. Here are the coordinates to the west-side outpost.'

'Is that anywhere near the wall?' I asked.

'Yes,' he said, 'built all along the north-west boundary.' His tone was relaxed and generous now, a proud citizen telling a visitor of the glories of his hometown. I wondered if he was an early visitor like David, missing the old days of tourism and influence, lamenting the cramping of his vision. As he spoke, a flash appeared in my upper eyeline: *Message received from Tim Keevy*. 'It'll be bookmarked on your map. But use the map – there's no straight line there unless you can fly.' There was no sign on his face that he was making a joke. 'Wandering around, getting lost, can be dangerous.' He smiled thinly and turned to climb the steps to the house's front door. It was only when the children started screaming again that I realised they'd been dead silent while Tim Keevy and I had spoken, as if he'd put them on pause.

The liaison office was in the western wall of Green Valley, so the Edges wouldn't be far from it. If I got to the wall there, I could trace it around to the exit. My time was running out. I called up the map and followed the walking directions to a block of unnamed roads a quadrant away. Soon, I turned into another snail-curled street, which blushed red halfway along. I slowed my pace and glanced around me. If I'd taken closer notice of the type of plants outside that children's party house, the exact droop of the elephant ears and the red-speckled rhododendrons, the curve of the bower in front of the watching windows across the road, I could have confirmed for myself that I was back where I'd started. But the flashing icon on the map, that icon billions of people once trusted to ward them home, showed me I was in a different quarter altogether. It was just a product of the homogeneous architecture, surely.

Yap, yap-yap-yap. Yap, yap-yap(shriek)-yap.

Yap, yap-yap-yap. Yap, yap-yap(shriek)-yap.

A bolt of panic spurted through me and was suppressed, leaving me heavy and forgetful as I stepped towards the red patch in the road. The redness was made of perfectly shaped, identical scarlet polka dots about the diameter of tennis balls painted over every surface: on the tar, on the kerb, over the neat strip of lawn edging the sidewalk, across the paving blocks and even on the shrubberies in front of the house, assembled so that the shapes lined up into yet more perfect dots from precisely where I stood. As I watched, the dots divided and reproduced and pushed on from every side of the blotch, until they were advancing with compelling tidal logic over the house's porch, crawling across its windows, onto the roof.

It was as if I'd stepped into an installation by Naoko Tamura, an artist who had been very popular ten, fifteen years ago. She'd started off several years before as a dynamic and unique creative commenting on madness and perception, but her colourful, photo-friendly work had soon been drained of its meaning and co-opted by the commercial mainstream, even featuring in Zeroth ad campaigns just before the Turn. Could this really be her work, right here, or was it just a flush of Zeroth counterfeit?

The thought was blotted out of my mind by polka dots climbing my legs, swarming their way up, until they were gathering over my chest. They were two-dimensional, and should have been weightless, but they slid and flickered as they moved in a creeping scuttle. The weight of them began to clamp around me, restricting my muscles. My pulse beating in my neck, a cluster of dots finding their way under the hair at the nape of my neck like an insectile lover.

As more dots clustered up my neck and over my lips and against my nostrils, I froze in anticipation, giving in to the swaddling pressure, waiting for them to crush and suffocate me, to snuff me out.

But it didn't happen. The dots suddenly stopped – they were nothing, not even paint – and I was standing in the middle of the road in mortifying suspension, profoundly ashamed by my lack of resistance.

'We give ourselves to the projected light, don't we?' someone said. A withered voice. Gradually, a shape resolved itself out of scarlet rounds and gutter concrete. The figure, grey and spotted itself, was half-pressed into the surface of the road, and she raised her head and looked at me as she extruded herself to standing. 'You wanted the end to come, didn't you? You wanted your fate to be decided for you, not bear it yourself. Didn't you?'

I nodded. Scarlet spots were flaking off the

tar-and-concrete woman as she stood, and fluttering like dead leaves to the ground around her. Around my feet, my empty dots were piling up too.

'Only you can cast yourself into the void,' she said. 'Your ending cannot be simulated.'

'You're talking like you're not from Green Valley. Outside, we don't trust simulations either.'

She didn't seem surprised that I was from outside. As if in thought, she raised one grey hand towards her mouth, her small, dark eyes intensely focussed, but then flicked a fingertip. The dots all around her turned bright yellow, leaving my eyes to struggle with the sudden glaring shift. In perfect synchrony, every dot suffered its own apocalypse, imploding like dead stars at the end of the universe, and the effect was a spectral ripple that was impossible to take in until it was over and the suburban street was just a suburban street with an old woman in a grey woollen kaftan talking to me. 'This world is seductive. It's impossible to leave.'

'Can you tell me more about the Edges? Who else lives here?'

'It's a haven – from control. The people who come here are people who like to play.' Her face moved in what I took for a smile. 'You might encounter a few. Some of us like to be seen, some don't.'

She gestured over her patch of street as if to encourage me on. I didn't have much time, so I thanked her and walked away.

At the end of the road was a T-junction, the straightest stretch of road I'd seen apart from Main Street and the periphery of the town square. According to the map, I was at the physical edge of the enclave – there was nothing beyond the thick line denoting the wall and the boundary of Green Valley. Strung to my left and my right were a series of arches under what may have been designed originally as an aqueduct or a viaduct. Some of them had signs hanging over them and tables or small constructions arrayed outside. It could have been a gentrified artists' market in any wealthy city in the real world and I wondered, given my brief exposure to the imagination of the polka-dot woman, why even rebels against Green Valley's architectural strictures would line themselves up in such a space-bound arrangement. Perhaps it was a remnant of the tourist age, when physical tourists and cyber-tourists would flock here and buy digital art and comics and games and plans and software from the Green Valley creatives. The tourists would have appreciated the familiarity of a recognisable market, and it would be in the interests of the artists to draw them here without losing them.

But now, eight years after Green Valley had closed, there was none of the promised explosion of possibilities. Could it really be that humans are shackled to the earth, that utter freedom terrifies us? We like straight lines; we want the feel of the ground under our feet.

But as I turned left and approached the stalls, the renovated industrial façade of the first enclosure in the strip began to dissolve away subtly and merge with a starker space. I peered into the half-darkness, tripping over a soiled mattress jutting out of a studio's doorway. A soft-fried egg, days old, trickled across the mattress towards a plucked, raw chicken wearing women's underwear. 'I'll show you how it happened,' the chicken said. There was a house made of chopped hardwood and rubble, solidly packed, crawling with living plastic crabs; a chrome-plated Mickey Mouse bent Donald Duck over a sale table; a woman dressed as a bird kept flying into a window. Although these artists had used the technology to enhance and activate their work, most of it felt sterile. This art show might have been made twenty years ago, a time-worn copy. It made sense that Green Valley, cut off from the world, might have become moribund, but it was disappointing. Perhaps some part of me had wanted to believe in their vision, some part of me applauded their bravery: I'd wanted to believe it had worked.

As I let The I tamp down a sense of deflation that might fester into a deeper depression, a message flashed up: *Incoming call.* Unlike on the video call with David earlier, only a small still image of Gina Orban's face appeared in my eyeline. 'Hello, Lucie. You have half an hour left. Can you find the office, or do you want me to get you?'

'I'll get back, thanks. See you soon.' I checked my position on the map and set the liaison office as my destination. Near the T-junction, a bright light glared from the first studio in the row. Glancing through the wide, arched doorway, I saw that the walls and the floors were uniformly covered in high-gloss white tiles, and a handsome black ram with spiral horns stood near the doorway, sniffing the air and nervously tapping its hoof on the porcelain floor with a hollow, fragile knock. Curious, I slowed and stepped closer, catching a glimpse of a shallow white gully leading to a drain in the middle of the floor.

I turned away, but the ram spoke to me in an ancient accent. 'Come inside. You know you want to. I'll let you wield the knife.'

Despite the clean glare of the room, the air was tinged with a thick, foul odour of rot. It was all The I could do to push images of congealed blood away from my mind. I shook my head and tried to hurry off, but something was holding my legs. I looked down to find narrow and sticky rust-buckled leather straps around my ankles. I was being pulled inside the tiled room.

'I didn't ask, Lucie,' the ram said. 'Sacrifice isn't optional. You came here to see what we do.'

Whatever was pulling the straps was too strong. I tried to keep up with the tug so that I could stay on my feet, but it started dragging me faster, and harder, and I twisted and tripped and slammed onto the ground and was dragged the final ten metres into the middle of the room. The entranceway became a fourth tiled wall as I was hauled upwards by my ankles and looped over a hook suspended in the ceiling. I think I was screaming, or I should have been, but I felt tired and docile hanging by my ankles amid a steel-hooked row of skinned sheep carcasses all disgorging blood from their necks. It was quite pretty, I thought, looking down from above, to see four neat streams of blood converging from each corner of the red-spattered white room into the drain in the middle. *This is all we are*, I thought, or I was made to think, or I heard said in my head in my own voice. Whichever way, it made sense.

The I was struggling to balance the mixture of terror and mind-saving evasion and the fact that I was hanging upside down and all the blood was pooling in my head, a massive pressure building, begging for release, crying to be let out.

The ram sauntered close enough to tickle my forehead with its woolly fringe.

'This is what we do,' it said, the foul stench of a million deaths smothering me as it spoke. 'Sacrifice.'

'It can get quite interesting, can't it?' Gina said.

I wanted to sit up and hit her, and that was good. It meant the retraction was happening as it should. I was gradually starting to become myself again. When the transponders were detached, I could feel their absence by the way my body wouldn't level itself. The whole day, I'd been experiencing everything harder and deeper than normal, in an unconscious effort to assert myself over The I's control, so I knew I'd need to recalibrate myself – in an analogue, human way. I'd have to let it pass, give myself time to recover.

I was glad that Gina had come to collect me at the Edges. I got disoriented after I left David's house and I couldn't remember my way out. It was almost as if I'd blacked out for a while and surfaced again, with only a nagging sense of dread, like a half-remembered nightmare. Gradually the fog lifted and I started to remember all I had experienced, but when it came to that pungent ram, my mind still battled to find the seam between reality and hallucination.

Gina left me to shower and get dressed into my own clothes. My feet were sore from walking, my muscles stiff with spent adrenaline from all the new impressions. I was developing a thick headache but I remembered Barbra's mission before I left. I checked my jacket pockets – they were untouched. The signal-proof pouch was still there. I slipped the right lens of The I into the pouch and replaced it in Gina's lens case with my old I lens, which had been safely disabled and wouldn't be broadcasting any lies.

6

It was near six when I got to the precinct. Though it had felt like a week, I'd only been in Green Valley for five hours, and I guessed Barbra would still be in the office.

I took a stabilising breath before hurrying and greeting the desk officer. 'Hi. I know I shouldn't be here after hours, but I've left my keys behind. I got all the way home and scratched around in my damn bag… they have to be on my desk. Well, I goddamn hope so. You mind if I go take a look?'

'Sure,' he said. 'You gotta sign in, though.'

'Of course,' I said, hoping he wouldn't look too closely at the dirt under my nails. Most of Green Valley had come off in the shower, but not all. After signing in, I patted my jacket's inner pocket – the signal-proof pouch was still there. Even though I trusted the Sentinel tech's capacity to block its signals, and the fact that I'd been able to smuggle it out of Zeroth's liaison office undetected proved that it was working, I couldn't help imagining radio-wave tendrils punching a microscopic hole through the pouch's defences and speeding their way back to Zeroth to expose me. The sooner I handed this thing off, the better. And if Barbra wasn't in the office? I'd have to hold onto it till the morning, feel Zeroth's tentacles clawing out to it all night. Fuck, I hoped she was there.

Not for the first time, I found myself nostalgic for life before the Turn, when you could call someone on their cell phone and they'd speak to you immediately, or you might expect people in non-critical jobs to read their text messages in the middle of the night on the weekend. To follow this train of thought was cultural blasphemy, but I did it anyway. Were we really better off after the Turn? Or had our privacy been a fair price for the comforts we'd enjoyed?

On the far side of the fourth floor, Bert Halstrom, the Sentinel doorman, stood by a blank desk, guarding the grey door. 'Ma'am,' he greeted me as I approached. 'You're expected.' I put my messenger bag on the table and allowed Bert to flip through the contents, shining his bright little torch, which was also a metal-detecting wand, into the darkest recesses. When he was done, I allowed him to frisk me.

If The I was emitting any signals, Bert's wand didn't seem to detect them. The pouch was evidently doing its job.

Shielding the keypad with my body, I pressed a code into the mechanical combination lock and flipped the lever. The grey door unlatched with a click. At a second door, I entered a different code into what was disguised as another manual press-button lock for the eager eyes outside, but which also read fingerprint biometrics and compared them with a database before clicking open. In the second anteroom, low-lit and featureless, a palm and retinal scan allowed a blast-proof, air-sealed resin door to slide aside for me, revealing the Sentinel common room. It was empty of analysts at this hour but Barbra Reeve and Bill Schindler emerged from a conference room.

'Did you get it?' Schindler asked.

'Evening, Lucie,' Barbra said, stopping me as I reached into my jacket pocket. 'Come.'

She led us up the stairs to her office on the overlooking mezzanine, closed the door, and rendered the glass wall opaque with the touch of a button. I'd seen the effect before, but it still charmed me, the glass – or, more accurately, the thermal layer between two panes – shading so subtly, and the lighting in the room coming up so organically, that you didn't notice when you could no longer see the common room outside.

I imagined what a regular voting, tax-paying citizen might

think of this window. Simply because the glass was controlled by electronics, and especially because it was installed in a police office, the citizens outside would be suspicious of it. It wouldn't make a difference to their knee-jerk paranoia if they stopped to consider that the window had nothing to do with surveillance, that it was simply an elegant and convenient variation on blinds. No, it would strike them as black magic, and they'd bring pitchforks and flames to it. As much as I understood their reaction to the abuses before the Turn, it meant we were missing out on aesthetic advances. It was because I harboured heretical thoughts like this that I was standing in Barbra Reeve's office right now.

'As Bill was saying' – Barbra leaned against her desk, her pretended patience vanished – 'did you get it?'

At last, I could take the pouch out of my pocket. I placed it on the desk, relieved to have it away from me. I couldn't quite shake the thought that it was still communicating with Green Valley, distributing my biometric and positional information, and the wizards behind their green curtain were compiling and monitoring that information, biding their time. The thought betrayed my own superstition; I was just like everyone else, at heart. 'I managed to bring out a lens, as we hoped. I have no idea whether you'll be able to get anything from it. The tech's changed a lot since The I we knew. Much more than I imagined.'

'Don't worry about that,' Schindler said, reaching over and sliding the lens out of the pouch and into a transparent container. 'We've been on top of it.' He held the device up to the light, turning it this way and that, scrutinising the hardware with an unconscious smile widening on his face. He turned to Barbra. 'Do you mind?'

'Go ahead,' she said.

Schindler pocketed the case and walked to the door. 'Good work, Sterling.'

When he'd closed the door behind him, Barbra said, 'His team's on standby, ready to dissect it. If there's any way in, they'll find it. It's what they've been preparing for.'

Fabian was angled on the couch in the bay window with a glass of wine in one hand and a novel in the other. His mouth twitched in tacit acknowledgement that he'd noticed me coming in but he carried on reading. We usually let each other finish our chapter, but not that evening. I dropped my things on the dining-room table and went right over to him, shoving his legs aside and wedging my way onto the couch. Then I took the glass from his hand, put it on the coffee table, and stuck my tongue into his mouth, grabbing him and pulling him over onto me. My core shuddered at the weight of his body; I wanted to be crushed by it, absorbed into him. I glanced at his face as he squirmed away. His smile had broadened, but he was still cheekily gripping the book above us and was side-eyeing it, trying doggedly to finish his page.

I worked my fingers at the cloth of his trousers, buried my face in his neck, breathing his scent in until it filled me, nipping at his skin, wanting to bite hard, wanting to eat him, to have him inside me, the flesh of him. I wanted to churn with him, every mass-bearing pound of us. I wanted him smeared all over me and me inside him and him smothering me. I needed something hefty and physical and hard and sore, something that would make me scream, something that would make me real again.

When I was convinced, at last, I stayed lying over him, looking out of the window at the alders gently sprinkling their leaves in the amber glow of the apartment's lights onto the sidewalk three floors below. My clothes were half off, twisted around my legs and neck and arm, but I revelled in the discomfort as Fabian pulled a throw over me and ran his fingers along my spine.

'What was that about?' he asked.

'You were right. Green Valley's totally fucked up.'

'Hm,' he said, nuzzling his chin into my hair.

'I'm sorry about earlier.'

'Nothing to be sorry about.'

'I should have let you have your say, at least.'

'You would have done what you needed to anyway.'

'Yeah.' I laughed.

I reached for one of his hands and guided it to where Gina Orban had fitted the lumbar and cervical transponders. When I'd checked my reflection after being retracted at the liaison office, there was barely any evidence they had ever been there: three tiny pinpricks at each site that you'd only notice if you were looking for them, and a red suction indentation that had already faded and smoothed away. I pressed Fabian's fingertips to my lower spine, wishing that if I pressed in just the right way, he would be able to see what I'd seen.

'Listen. About Kira...'

'Your mystery niece. I didn't even know you had one.'

'I'm sorry. I tried to figure out why I never told you. I wasn't trying to hide anything from you, honest. It's just... it was long ago.'

'Tell me about her.'

I reached for my wine. 'Another time, okay? I promise. It's been a bit of an overwhelming day.'

'Is she all right, at least? Did you find that out? You sounded so worried about her on the phone this morning.'

'Yes, it was a false alarm after all.' I didn't want to go into the reasons I had feared for Kira.

'Well, I'm glad you're back in one piece,' he said, kissing the top of my head. Glancing at our reflection in the window, I saw a pietà: saintly Fabian cradling me, enveloping me, protecting me.

I pushed myself tighter into his warm nooks, comparing this with the odd sensation of hugging David. 'After just a few hours there, I feel... dissolved, half real. I can't imagine what it's like for the people inside.'

Fabian's body grew taut and he pushed up to a slump. 'They get used to it, I suppose. We can normalise anything.' His voice was brittle. 'They chose it.'

I sat up and tugged my shirt straight, moved to the far end of the couch, my arms folded. 'They chose this years ago. What if things have changed? What if they regret their decision? Do they have to be stuck with it for life?' This was really something I should have asked David.

'Those are the terms they agreed to. Anyhow, from what we know,' Fabian said – the royal *we*, the Omega *we* – 'they become so enmeshed, so dependent on the system that they wouldn't be able to face life on the outside.'

I couldn't tell him that I knew as much about life inside Green Valley as his Luddite research group. Kira, that little version of Odille with her whole life ahead of her, was surely trapped in a system she hadn't chosen, addicted to a machine. Tears welled up in my eyes and I bent down to blink them away and pull up my underpants, untwisting them up my legs, then made a show of looking out the window, at the night-life cars and the people passing below.

Fabian rubbed at my thigh with his foot, regretful. 'Tell me more, then, Luce. What was it like in there? What did you do?' I knew he was asking only to rekindle the dead air between us, not because he was interested in Green Valley, but still, I loved him for trying.

I shook my head and said, my tone as conciliatory as possible, even though I was hammered by a weight of portent, 'I need to get my head around it, then I'll fill you in.'

He stood up and headed to the kitchen to get something on for supper, relieved, perhaps, not to have to chat equably to me about Green Valley scum.

Fabian was sleeping with his back to me, allowing me to press into him for warmth and contact, but not turning and reconnecting to me when I flipped myself over. And I was flipping over a lot that night. Every time I closed my eyes, I descended through a curtain of grey mist and back into Green Valley, my mind churning with all the faces and the parade of simulacra I'd seen. Every time I drifted off, I was shunted awake by some bad image, the afterburn of flickering lights in blackness that I knew would harm me.

At two o'clock, after listening to the alarm clock ticking until its officious little shuffle grew unbearable, I gave up, grabbed my clothes from the bedroom chair and went to the study.

I'd lived with Fabian for six years, but still occupied his apartment like a guest. Or, even more, like one of the art installations he curated: *Untamed Woman Trapped in Civilised Jar*. The apartment was pearl-toned – all high ceilings with resounding space and artfully bevelled edges. Tall double-glazed sash windows looked over the healthy treetops and nonchalantly draped light over the shine-polished hardwood parquet; the living rooms were lined with custom-built bookshelves creaking with treatises on the functions of art and the philosophy of politics. The kitchen was buffed marble and steel; the beds and couches mohair and cashmere. The home of my nurturance, the home my mind still inhabited, had been a dingy space with a constrained, barred view of rusty iron and gum-spattered, weed-cracked sidewalk. I sometimes felt as if I'd been shaken out into this elegant, urbane place and left to scurry around, observed from outside and above by polite society.

But that was my neurosis, none of Fabian's doing. He accepted and tolerated and loved me, with a gracious equanimity that I suspected only someone from his privileged background, someone who hadn't had to scrabble for care or sustenance, could muster.

When Fabian worked at home, he generally sprawled his material across the dining table, and he'd invited me to call the study my own. Fabian's luxurious books and cabinets of artistic treasures owned the room, but my little desk fitted snugly between the wall and the window, a calm, clear surface dotted only with a small pile of notebooks, a wooden tray of letters and documents – and the telephone, whose soft purr now rippled the silence. I snatched up the receiver.

David spoke before I could say anything. 'She *is* missing, Lucie. Someone's taken her.'

'What? Since this afternoon?' The transgalactic static washed between his words, trying to keep them from me.

'No. It wasn't her in the garden.'

'What the hell do you mean? I saw her. I touched her.'

'The avatar was falsified, days ago. I've looked all over and I can't find her. And… her bedroom. It's been invaded.' His voice was low, a desperate whisper. 'Someone's been in there. Someone's taken her. I need your help, Lucie.'

My heart gripped at my chest. 'Oh, God. Is there anything I can do from here?' And then anger pushed through – he had all the tech; how could *Zeroth* need *my* help tracking someone? 'Surely there are records, footage?'

'Yes, but there's something wrong with the system. The playback's corrupted in all the crucial places.'

'It must be someone inside, then, who knows how to do that.'

'I don't think so. That rooster, the old code, you remember? There's more like it. And that stuff doesn't come from in here. It's not compatible with Zeroth code. They might be getting help from inside, but whoever took her came from outside. I managed to filter and rebuild her location records and traced her all the way into Stanton, a location near Claymarket, before the signal disappeared – six days ago, Lucie. That's why I think you can help. Someone in Stanton has taken her and is deliberately hiding her—'

'How could you trace her outside Green Valley?' There shouldn't be any cell or Wi-Fi signals outside the wall... except for Sentinel's covert systems. Had David just admitted that they were aware of Sentinel's work, piggybacking on our devices?

But, no. 'GPS,' he said. 'You haven't shot the satellites out of the sky yet.'

'Oh, right. And when you say her location data disappeared, could it mean that it's already... too late?'

'Oh.' He didn't speak for a moment. 'No. Whatever her condition, we'd still be able to locate the tracers. It doesn't mean that, Lucie. You have to help me.'

'All right. I'll do what I can.' I said it with false bravado. 'I'll call you if I find anything out.'

'No, don't call me. I'll call you. I'll set up a secure line.'

'Why? Do you think someone inside is listening?'

'They're always listening, Lucie. Always. And this is something they won't want to hear.'

I tried Jordan Martinez's desk on the off-chance that he'd be at the precinct, but it just rang. I followed up with a call to the charge office front desk and left a message for Jordan, dictating it to the constable at the answering service. 'There's a girl missing, nine years old. If you come across anyone, please let me know. I'm at home.' That vague message wouldn't express my urgency to Jordan, but I couldn't leave any more details. I certainly couldn't mention Green Valley or Zeroth to the front-desk constable who had no idea about Sentinel's work. Maybe Jordan would read between the lines; we were often on the same wavelength. I considered him a friend in the precinct. His unadorned, unprivileged background, matched with a no-nonsense blend of honesty and practicality, resonated with me: maybe he was the sort of human I imagined I'd become if I ever got over myself.

'He should call office hours or any time?' the constable asked.

'Any time, please. I'll be here. It's pretty important.'

I could hear the constable's shrug. 'You don't want to ask the detectives on duty? It's Brydon and, let's see… Rahman.'

No, it had to be Jordan. A senior detective in the CID, Jordan was my go-to contact on the detective force, and he'd been the one saddled with the Green Valley kids' dossier. 'Don't worry. I'll check in with Martinez in the morning.'

After taking a deep breath, I dialled the next number on my list, the one I had avoided earlier. I wasn't expecting an answer, but if I didn't try I'd spend the rest of the night roving about the house restlessly. The dial purred like a cat as it cycled through the numbers.

'Stanton path lab, yeah?'

'Hi, Maya? It's Lucie Sterling. I'm surprised you're there.'

'Hey, Lucie. Yeah, late shift. I'm babysitting tonight.'

'Who? What do you mean?' For a moment I thought she was making a tasteless joke. Maya Kanté, the sharp-minded medical intern who kept shifts at the morgue for pocket money, had already developed the blunt sense of humour of a pathologist, but in her case it didn't usually extend to laughing about the death of children. She was still young and retained some of the sensitivity a career in the field would eventually erode.

'Jordan's here too,' she explained.

'Oh, okay. Why's he up?'

'Tallying up patrol's notes on the new little girl.'

I sat up straight. 'Which little girl?'

'Found a few hours ago.' Then, to someone else in the room: 'Come again?'

Something rustled, and clearly, behind the muffled tone of Maya's voice, I heard her heart beating – a steady, untroubled double thump. A few more lines of unintelligible conversation, then Maya lifted the receiver from where she'd been muting it against her chest. 'He says he sent you a pneum.'

'Hang on.' I leaned over, opened the hatch and found nothing inside. No capsules, and no noise of a sucking vacuum either. There'd been pump breakdowns at the Malvern junction down the road for weeks now, but I wouldn't have got a pneum this soon anyhow. I jabbed at the send button pointlessly before going back to the phone. *Why didn't he just phone me?* 'Nothing yet. What did it say?'

'He says if you're looking for a little girl, to come down. We've got one… looks six or seven, but we're thinking maybe she's older.'

I was already standing up, but I had to ask. 'Any ID?'

'Uh-uh. Not many seven-year-olds carrying passports or drivers' licences.'

Facial recognition used to help; computerised dental, retinal and fingerprint files, for your personal safety and security. All I had to compare against, thanks to the Turn, was the digital photo of Kira's face in my memory. 'I'll be right there.'

'Jordan says you'd better hurry. External's likely to want her first thing in the morning.'

'Why?'

'She's a little underdeveloped, this girl. And there's weird nanotech in her blood, just like the others. There's only one place she could have come from.'

7

Every time I walked through downtown Stanton from our flat to my office at the central police precinct, I was reminded of who I was. The route took me past the tenement where I had grown up, the Claymarket Hole nightclub in its basement, the laundromat and the Eet Mor twenty-four-hour convenience store, where one of Raj Khan's sons still manned the counter on every dead shift. Tonight it was Bobby Khan, slumped on a stool behind the desk, his feet on the counter, an amazing balancing trick, flipping through a surfing magazine. When a customer carrying a cat and a large carton of milk and a bag of crisps approached the counter, Bobby looked up and caught sight of me peering in as I passed, and offered me a smile and a half-lifted wave. After the vacant perfection of the patrons of the Asbury Café in Green Valley, Bobby's lopsided yellow teeth, the evacuated blast of spiced fry fat and the flickering, patently unsafe neon sign flashing *NON ST P GOOD ESS* under the steady drip of condensation from the air-con unit never looked better to me.

My upbringing was common enough. My mother had raised Odille and me on her own, the three of us abandoned to quiet poverty by my addicted father. That's all: a story of lack, like so many others.

In the top drawer of my desk in the study, two photos were tucked into a notebook. Photos taken at school, both of them: me standing next to seventeen-year-old Odille when she won the district tech fair, and Odille standing next to fourteen-year-old me when I placed second in the regional debating contest. Both photos from not long before she left home. We had a sense, even then, I think, that we had an unusual relationship. No other kids photobombed their siblings' school prizegiving pictures, but we were desperately, needfully proud of each other, and behind each photo, only the two of us would recognise the ghost of our mother standing proud and failing behind the lens. She worked herself to a sliver, as if she could never work hard enough. She died exhausted by sacrifices. That was motherhood to me; I'd promised myself then that I would never be like her.

I'd made it out of here, hadn't I? Although Claymarket and the miserable hole my mother left remained a smouldering wound in the centre of my being, there were stretches when I no longer believed that this grimy space defined me. Claymarket at root, my office and my work, and yes, the apartment on the leafy street by the museum, the cashmere activist who made me at home there – I was made up of all of them. I hadn't changed; I'd expanded.

Hauling my keys out of my messenger bag and sorting through the colour-coded tabs, I was painfully aware of the jangle and clatter shearing the pre-dawn streets. I glanced behind me to check that nobody was following. Total surveillance would have been a comfort, right about then. Eventually, I found the right three to unlock the security gate and vestibule door. After the Turn, several electronics companies had offered to remodel their systems to simple closed-circuit devices that wouldn't record or report, but would simply unlock doors if you had the key-card that matched the lock, but they didn't take off. Citizens didn't trust them not to be secretly storing or distributing their information, and after the abuses and the blatant lies the digital industries had been complicit in before, who could blame us? Keys, cut from metal, and locks, made of rollers and pins, were once again our trusted, not-so-silent gatekeepers. After the Turn, like in the old days, you'd need to physically follow and steal someone's keys to get through their door; you couldn't hack into people's private spaces en masse by remote control. Or so Stantonians believed.

On the cusp of the Turn, an old schoolfriend of mine had been raped and robbed in a back alley. It hadn't been fitted with the surveillance cameras that had sprouted over most streets in the city. I'd been as certain then as I was now that if there had been cameras in the alleyway, the police and the courts would have had evidence to confirm her account; they would have identified the men who'd arrived in place of the boy she'd gone there to meet, and someone would have been held to account. It was that sort of heretical thinking that kept one of my feet there in Claymarket and prevented me from fully inhabiting Fabian's lush and idealistic world.

Locking the gate and the vestibule door behind me, I turned to the inner door and tried the latch. To my surprise, it was locked too; it shouldn't have been, when a pathologist was in. I let myself in and found the corridor in near darkness, lit only by dim emergency strips.

'Hello?' I said. 'Maya? Jordan? You here?'

The lino flooring of the long corridor bloomed in little white-feathered mint-green patches as my eyes adjusted to the gloom. Four wide exam-room doors to my left, eight narrower office and supply-room doors to my right. At the far end, the corridor split towards the staff area, the library and the intern studies to the right, and towards receiving and storage to the left.

Maya usually worked in the third path exam room, under Dr Rossetti, but if Jordan was with her, maybe she was in the library. I hurried along the corridor, avoiding looking through the porthole windows into the darkened labs, and turned right.

Here, at last, yellow light was pouring from the door, and I heard voices.

'Jesus, Maya,' I said, rounding into the library. 'Why don't you answer when I call? You should keep the lights—'

The stench of sheep fat and congealing blood was so thick I could hardly breathe. The room tilted upside down and I was being suspended through a hook by a rope around my ankles, waiting for the curved blade.

The slit pupils of the black ram.

The blood dripped like rain around me.

'Look closely, Lucie,' the ram said, and I opened my eyes.

It stood up, lithely changing form from a skinny-legged ovine to a man and then going beyond a man, a giant haloed by shadow, which turned into light – a thousand lights of a thousand screens playing a thousand nightmares. I tried to look away. The ram was all I could see and when I tried to anchor my gaze on its face, there was nothing, just a constant, shifting smudge, like mud at the bottom of a river. He made me look with my eyes jammed open; he made me select my worst vision from the nightmares collected there.

A screen flickering grey footage of a woman in a white coat, a man in a padded jacket, doing something to the body of a little girl. The yellow lights too bright, the spatter of the blood coating and recoating the tiles, clumps of it sliding as it thickened. A giant with yellow eyes burning from a smudged face. The straps at my ankles failing, the shudder as the buckle popped. I was falling, my head smashing into the crimson tiles.

A soft landing.

Thick hands under my arms, propping me up against the armchair's edge.

A glass of water in my face.

'I'm okay,' I said. 'I'm okay.' I rubbed my eyes.

'Come,' Jordan said. 'Sit properly.' He lifted me up and into the chair with barely a heave, stuffing a cushion behind my back, another behind my head.

I took the water Maya was offering me. 'Are you sure you're okay? We heard you stumbling about.'

'I'm fine. Sorry,' I said. Looking around, I saw the corridor was fully lit. Talk radio was playing from one of the labs. The chill had gone. 'Have the lights always been on?'

Maya gave a sideways twist of her face, the metal and ink there contorting to a smirk. 'Uh, yeah. Like, tonight, I mean. Not for the whole of history, I guess.'

'But they were off when I came in. I called for you and nobody answered. You were definitely not in lab three.'

Maya shot a glance across at Jordan, who said, 'We saw you come in. You looked a bit spaced out. We spoke to you but you just walked past us. Like you were sleepwalking. You sure you don't need to get some rest?'

But I just shook my head. 'No. No.'

Had Gina left some part of The I in my system? That could explain the double vision, the overlaid playback. The thought sent panic scurrying through my nerves, and this time it wasn't tamped down by any mind-control drugs. 'Shit,' I said.

'What is it?' Jordan said, leaning forward.

I knew I'd have to tell him something, but not yet. 'Nothing,' I said. I rubbed my hand over my face, then pushed tentatively up off my chair. My head was clearing and I was fine to stand. 'Can I see the body, Maya?' I asked, careful not to admit that the child in there might be more to me than a case, an administrative detail. The truth was, I couldn't admit it to myself.

'Sure.' She led me out of the common room. Jordan picked up a dossier from the table and made a show of leafing through it, though his attention stayed on me till we'd left the room.

In storage, Maya slid a drawer open. I concentrated on the green-tiled wall, the chrome fittings, the muted stainless steel, tracing my fingers over it, knocking my knuckles against the cold surfaces. *This is real*, I told myself; *the ram's slaughterhouse is a computer graphic. This is my actual life, these sensations are being made by physical external objects; those were virtual, falsified stimuli.* Although it had felt like I was in hell, I'd only been in a real studio made of bricks and wood and iron on the outskirts of Green Valley, an actual room in a concrete shell on the Earth's surface.

Maya folded the sheet halfway down the girl's body and placed a file on the steel table above her head. Though I'd tried to keep the memory of Kira's photograph clear in my mind, the sight of the girl's face still made me gasp. It took me a deliberate moment, comparing that memory with the blotched face of the dead girl, to understand that it was not my niece lying there, straight brown hair parted off the green-tinged brow to either side, at peace.

My knees quaked with the force of my relief and I shot my hands out to steady myself, grabbing for Maya's file to disguise my lurch and flipping to a photo of the body where it had been found. The child's hair tied back in a ponytail, ill-fitting clothes: new green corduroys cinched by a thick piece of string around the waist, a slightly grubby pink T-shirt. Then the next pictures, the belly sunken between the sharp ridges of her hipbones jutting as she lay on the cold metal. It was unnatural to see a child like that.

Looking from the corpse to the photo and back again, I fought a numbness in my mind, its refusal to accept. I made myself note the autopsy's Y-shaped slashes into her torso, puckered beneath their broad stitching, no longer any blood to bridge the gashes. Her little oval face seemed restful, but not in angelic repose: there was exhaustion there, desperation brought to a sudden halt.

She is real, I thought to myself. I wanted to touch her shoulder, wake her up. 'Were you in on the autopsy?' I asked Maya.

'Yeah. With the prof.'

'Did you find the cause of death? Was it... was she killed?'

Maya shook her head, and the metal in her nose and ears tinkled. 'Not that we could tell. Apart from the lower-range musculoskeletal development she shares with the two boys, there's no obvious cause of death. Although we did find severe serotonin and adrenaline imbalances.'

'What could have caused that?'

Another tinkle from her face, far too airy for this oppressive room. 'We don't know. Professor Rossetti can only imagine – because of where she came from – that it might have been panic associated with some form of withdrawal. But the initial tox screen was clear.'

'So no drugs?'

'No.' I scanned the girl's body, her sleeping face, the gnawed fingernails and the picked toenails coated with a layer of coloured lacquer. At least no drugs had been forced on someone so young, and all the other horrors that would imply. 'But she's teeming with biotech,' Maya went on. 'She has to be from Green Valley.'

'And there's still no ID, I'm guessing.'

'Nope.' Across the shelf, Maya watched me from beneath the straight edge of her dark fringe, her black-rimmed eyes behind her black-rimmed glasses observing me as I fought myself. I traced my gaze around the girl's hairline, over her temple, past the vale of her eye and over her cheekbone, in and then out again over the jaw. Again, I fought the urge to reach out to her – I didn't need to touch her to prove to myself that she was real.

'Do you have her clothes? Her possessions? I'd like to look at them.'

'Jordan's got them,' she said, and I left her to shut the girl away as I made my way back to him.

In the common room, he was bent over the file, writing a note in his hooked left-handed scrawl. He looked up when I came in. 'The one you're looking for?'

'No.' I sat down across the table from him as he raised his eyebrows. Stanton wasn't the most peaceful city on Earth, but three dead children in a week… that was enough to raise the eyebrows of a seasoned detective like Jordan Martinez.

Jordan looked into my face and read me. He put down his pen. 'What's the deal?'

I decided then to tell Jordan the truth. I knew I could trust him, and this situation was a serious one; I would need his help. 'My niece is missing,' I sighed. It was a relief to tell someone who might care.

He straightened and stared at me. 'Oh. Shit.'

'She's nine years old. She was my sister's daughter. She lives in Green Valley.'

'What? You let your sister take her *there*?'

'I didn't *let* her do anything. I had no say in the matter. Besides, my sister died just before the partition, so neither did she.' I watched Jordan's face change and carried on talking before he felt the need to come up with a sympathetic response. 'I went to Green Valley yesterday.'

'You *what*?' Jordan pushed back in his chair and his face flared in alarming blotches of purple. 'What the—'

I faced up to him. 'Hang on, hang on. Before you say any more, listen.'

'Green Valley? Jesus. Seriously, what—'

'Will you listen to me, Jordan?'

Jordan wound down with a few more mutters, but shut up and waited.

'Thank you,' I said. 'I know your thoughts on Green Valley.' I imagined Jordan as a guest at one of Fabian's dinner parties, the two of them bonding over their attitude towards people from Green Valley. I flinched at the thought: shabby and smoke-smelling, Jordan was the sort of office friend you drink with sometimes and generally look forward to seeing on Mondays, but never invite to your home. He would be made to feel like an ash stain in Fabian's apartment. 'Her father invited me,' I said. 'When the two boys turned up, I wanted to see her in case she was in trouble too.' I shook my head, not telling him that I'd been fooled into believing she was safe. 'I guess she was.'

'So tell me, then,' Jordan said, his ringed eyes drilling into me. 'Did you find what you were looking for?'

I glanced at him. Was there any possible way he could know what Barbra had sent me to do? No, surely not. He knew nothing about Sentinel, or about the component I'd smuggled.

He went on. 'Did that lying place offer you any answers?' I had to remember: he'd just found a child's body, clearly from Green Valley and entirely justifying his prejudice. 'Did you speak to any parents? To anyone whose child had gone missing? Find any suspects?'

'I hardly spoke to anyone – real. It's… strange in there. All mirrors and masks. All I found was more questions than answers,' I said. 'But David did show me something he found by her bedside. Something that could be material evidence. A kind of calling card.'

'Where is it?'

'It wasn't the sort of thing I could take out with me. Besides, I'm not sure if it… really existed.'

Jordan shook his head and sneered. 'That place is a fucked-up waste of time. Nothing's real. They all play make-believe in their little bubble. You should see the runaround we're getting from their goddamn "liaison office" just to talk to someone in their security services.'

'Have you got through to anyone yet?'

'Uh-uh. A circle of we'll-get-back-to-you and on hold. And we can't just go there and talk to a real person. They're going to make it disappear. They'll just outwait us. We should just fucking let them rot.'

'We have to keep trying, Jordan,' I said, implicating Jordan in the case, trying to make it stick with him, 'because my niece is missing, and three little children are dead. We need to find out their names and where they belonged. Who did this to them.' My face was starting to betray me, beginning to melt and seize and for some mortifying reason I was about to cry in front of Jordan. 'I don't expect the PD to give a special fuck, and I know it's just you doing all this work on your own, but my niece might be like that little girl in your fridge. Not just because…' I stopped talking, wondering when we'd find Kira's body, imagining the skinny little girl in the morgue wearing Odille's sweet face. I got up quickly and turned away towards the door.

'I'm sorry,' Jordan said. 'I wasn't thinking. I get sick and tired sometimes. We've been up all night here, cleaning up their mess, and they've never asked for our help.'

'I know,' I said, brushing my eyes and turning back to him. It was big of him to apologise. 'I understand. The official line on Green Valley jurisdiction is the most logical: just leave the Green Valley freaks to their own fate – the fate they deliberately chose. But that has to change when we're dealing with dead kids – right here in Stanton. I'm asking you for help, not just because of Kira, but for this little girl who ended up here. She's not a freak; she's not a simulation. These children *are* our business.'

Jordan nodded, pursing his lips in an earnest way.

'Maya said you've got her things.'

'Yeah,' he said, pointing towards a specimen table at the back of the room. 'I'm just checking them against patrol's report. The captain wants a summary first thing. This is why I'm not getting my beauty sleep.'

'Can I look through them?'

'Look, but don't touch.'

I went over to the table and looked at the girl's paltry life arrayed there. A paper gum packet with two pieces left in it: strawberry mint. An almost-empty sample-sized tub of strawberry lip gloss. A balled-up tissue. A piece of grubby plain string in a small, fraying loop that she'd probably worn as a bracelet. Three cheap plastic hairclips and two sparkled elastics that looked pretty new, the type you get on cards of a dozen at the chemist. Someone had done a limited job of caring for this child. Was someone doing the same for Kira right now, or was she dead already?

I shook the thought off and moved across to her clothing: the rope, something like a bell pull or the tassel of an ornate, heavy curtain, that had held her trousers up. The oversized green corduroys, worn blue canvas shoes, white cotton underpants with blue spots. And the plain pink T-shirt, the type you get in three-packs at the thrift store.

'What's this on the shirt?' I asked Jordan, who was hovering a couple of paces behind me to make sure I didn't touch anything. There was a thick dusting of powder on the T-shirt, and looking again, I noticed it blushing out from the seat of the trousers too, on the heels of the shoes.

'Flour. Bread flour, we think. Forensics are still busy.'

'Flour?'

'The body was found outside a bakery in Claymarket. She didn't die there, though.'

8 The alleyway was guarded by two officers. I shrugged into my hood and quickly walked by, catching a glimpse of a police-tape cordon near the bakery's back entrance and a cluster of white-suited techs working the area along with a couple of plainclothes detectives.

I darted into the back lot of the building across the alley and spotted a dumpster in deep shadows at the far end of the lot. I could just about poke my head over the wall from there.

Slow water dripped off the rusted ladders and balconies, the oblong of sky above brick-grey, weatherless neutrality, the condensation being sucked out of the fog in the cold night air and gathering into russet drops around me. Dirty yellow streaks of light from nearby windows shivered on the surface of the puddles, as cold wind petulantly ripped through the alley.

I could have asked Jordan to escort me to the scene rather than sneaking around alone, but I hoisted myself onto the dumpster anyway. The movement and the noise sent several things scurrying away behind it as I peered down at the crusted slit windows into the back room of the bakery. Normally at five in the morning, the windows would be steamed up and glowing with a warm light, figures in white rushing to complete orders; but no bread was baking here this morning. Cubby Rosenior would be losing money for every hour he remained shut, and he'd be telling everyone he knew about his pain.

Intending to move across the wobbly lids to the next

dumpster, I turned and shifted my foot, finding a warp in the thin sheet metal that boomed like a massive gong as it snapped from convex to concave. More scurrying, but something bigger this time. A definite sigh; a heavy, putrid exhalation.

It's a person, I told myself; *just someone sleeping here who I've disturbed.*

I heard footsteps on the asphalt coming from behind me, from the mouth of the alleyway: solid, confident, well-shod. The clicking step of new shoes, not a worn-out shamble, *click-click-clack*, coming calmly into the alley. New shoes, not hooves; *not* hooves.

Taking a deep breath, squeezing my eyes shut and then opening them, I turned.

A neatly uniformed officer, his hand on his holstered weapon. 'Help you, ma'am?'

'Yes, thank you,' I said. 'Give me a hand down, will you?'

He came over and offered me his arm. I used his shoulder to vault off the top of the dumpster. As I righted myself, I took him in. He was from the precinct patrol. The guy's face was as tightly pressed as his uniform; his hair shone as slickly as his polished shoes and fell over his brow in a precise blonde flip. 'This is a crime scene, ma'am,' he said half-heartedly. 'What's your business?'

'I'm Lucie Sterling, special consultant with Stanton CID.' I reached for my ID card slowly. The officer watched my hands closely but didn't judge me a big enough threat to unholster his gun.

He scrutinised the card and checked my face against the picture, then handed it back. 'Special consultant' was a deliberately vague title that could involve any work, and was designed to be bland enough not to provoke questions. 'Okay, but you still need a detective with you if you're going to enter a scene.'

'I know. I was just having a look.'

He glared at me. 'You can visit the site with an authorised detective.'

Knowing that there was nothing more I could do, I was dumped by a wave of exhaustion. I'd been running on adrenaline for hours and now it washed away, leaving bitter scum in its wake. The Sentinel office wouldn't be open until nine, and there was no point in standing here for another couple of hours, making small talk with Officer Flip. The idea of nursing a couple of coffees and reading my book in a back booth at Verla's was tempting, but I knew Fabian would be worried. 'Officer,' I called – he was already clopping his way back to the street, and he turned fussily.

'Yes, ma'am.'

'Do you have a junction handset I can borrow?'

'No, ma'am. There's a callbox on the corner of Onyx and Nymph.' Another half-hearted remark, because he knew as well as I did that any public callbox in Claymarket was purely symbolic. The creep had a junction set, but I couldn't force him to lend it to me. I'd call from Verla's.

Walking out of the backlot, I was aware of the skittering ghosts I was leaving behind me. I tried not to look back. For the moment, at least, that gore-matted ram was not trailing me. I hoped that whatever had got into my blood in Green Valley was working its way out.

'Where have you been, Luce?'

I cupped my hand around the receiver and glanced from the small, doorless booth at the early-morning diners in Verla's coffee shop: the dead-tired workers at the end of a shift, the early-risers fuelling up for the day, and the bone-thin ghosts trying to refill with lost life as they hustled from their first job to their second and back again. All of them sitting alone, seats apart, tightly wound in the shrouds of their own lives. They wouldn't be interested in some stranger's domestic minutiae, but I spoke quietly anyway.

'I couldn't sleep. I went for a walk.' Keeping my voice down on the phone made me sound like the liar I was.

'Are you all right?' Fabian said. 'Can I do anything?'

'No. No. It's just… I think Green Valley really messed with my head, with my body. I needed to come down.'

'Have you?'

'Yes.'

'Why don't you come home, then?'

'Hardly worth it. By the time I get there, I'll have to leave for work.'

The untruth weighed heavily on the line between us. Did he suspect the real nature of that work? It would almost be a relief if he brought my lie out into the open. But all he said was, 'You're going to be exhausted.'

I sighed. 'I know.'

'Any news about Kira?'

'Not yet.'

'Let me know, right? And come back early tonight.'

'I will.'

Fabian wouldn't ask me to promise. We were more grown up than that.

9 At five to nine in the morning, greasy toast and coffee from Verla's churning in my stomach, I joined the cluster of administrative workers waiting outside the precinct's front doors, eager to get inside. I greeted a couple of archivists I knew, then flipped my hood over my head and hunkered into the leeward corner of the entranceway to wait for security to open for us. Stanton's bylaws discouraged non-essential work outside office hours, a progressive stance taken after the Turn. Hyperproductivity and twenty-four-hour industriousness had been recognised as another repressive part of the digital economy we had rejected; only critical staff could work non-office hours, and analysts at my grade still needed special clearance for overtime.

A man rounded the corner with his big black umbrella pointed into the wind and I started, heart hammering in my throat, that nightmare ram invading my senses again, when I'd just about managed to tamp the memory down and convince myself it was only the remnant of some electronic dream. Every car passing on the road was a menacing shadow. By the time the door finally opened for us, my jaw was clenched so tight it hurt, and cold acid flowed through my muscles.

Up on the fourth floor, Jordan was typing at his desk, making whiffling sounds over the soft-touch typewriter he'd recently requisitioned when his carpal tunnel syndrome flared up. When he noticed me coming in, he paused and looked up, rubbing at the black support bands around his wrists. 'Get any sleep?'

'No.'

'Uncomfortable to sleep in an alley, I guess.' I pursed my lips. That officer from the crime scene had been quick to report to his masters. 'I told you I'd take you there if you wanted to see it.'

'Yeah, thanks. I'll take you up on that. But I wanted to get a feel for myself.'

'It's pretty dangerous out there.'

'You don't have to tell me that, Jordan.'

'Anyway, black ops have been asking for you.'

I checked my watch. 'Are they here already?' It didn't worry me that Jordan called the Sentinel directors 'black ops'. Sentinel hid in plain sight. That was the point. It was like in the old days when everyone knew where the CIA and MI5 had their offices, but they weren't just going to saunter in and get to read top-secret files. Everyone on the CID level knew that there was something secret going on behind the big grey door, but they didn't know what – I'd heard speculation that the unit was political liaison, or internal investigations, even non-digital surveillance – old-fashioned spookery, as Jordan plainly guessed – but if any of the detectives could even vaguely imagine what really happened behind that door, they were discreet enough to keep their thoughts to themselves.

'They seem particularly eager to see you,' he said, mockingly adopting Barbra Reeve's upper-class tone by rolling an invisible pea in his mouth as he spoke.

I left Jordan to his report, passing the CID desk to the dark side of the floor, running the gauntlet of Bert and the scanners and locks before coming into the Sentinel workroom. Looking over us, Barbra stood, hands on her hips, surveying her workers in their hive. A dozen or so analysts were settling around four table clusters working multiple screens. While a couple spent a moment charging their coffee and muttering preparatory greetings, most of them had got straight to work, the analysts leaning intensely into the screens. The unalloyed dialogue between their trained eyes and the minds behind them and the images and data reeling out in front of them made me think of Eloise – apart from the fact that they had clothes on, and the brutalist office space emitted a different tone to her rainbow unicorn waterfall.

I made eye contact with Barbra and she beckoned me up.

'Any luck yet?' I said.

She cocked an eyebrow, sensing my increased urgency. 'They've been working all night.'

'How long do you think it will take?' If Schindler's team managed to hack into The I, I'd be able to find Kira in ten minutes. The longer we waited, though, the colder the trail would get.

She shifted back and folded her arms. I was still standing in the middle of the office, not invited to sit. 'You know this is bigger than dead children, don't you?' Barbra said. I bit my tongue – I hadn't told her what the family situation with David was, but I imagined she already knew I had a nine-year-old niece in Green Valley. Was she deliberately goading me, trying to draw me out? 'We have what we need now. We got lucky with the pretext to enter Green Valley, and we need to process the component properly. After all this time, there's no need to rush.'

I entered Green Valley, I wanted to remind her; *I* brought back the device. And my niece is not a *pretext*, I wanted to say. But I knew that would get me nowhere with Barbra Reeve. If I gave her any reason to believe my relationship with Kira would affect my professional judgement, I'd be back on filing duty before I'd closed my mouth. Instead, I took a breath, and said, 'We should try to clear up loose ends. I could ask Detective Martinez to take me to the scene, but it might be more helpful if I can use some of Sentinel's footage. The city doesn't want unsolved deaths on their hands.' A jumble of excuses and pleas, like a child begging for a treat, and still Barbra stood unmoved. 'If a journalist stumbled over the story,' I tried, 'it might cause a panic.'

She tilted her head and stared into my face. 'How do you think that might happen?'

'You know how things are. People talk a lot. People like to share their news and they don't have the outlet they once had.'

She scrutinised me for a moment longer and I thought I'd pushed it too far. Barbra Reeve was the last person I should try to threaten. But then her face eased into a smile and she nodded. 'All right. I can see that you care for these kids, and that's admirable, even though they're not our responsibility.' I was blindsided, bit my tongue. 'I'll let you use Sentinel resources, but only while we're waiting for Bill's team to crack into the component. We can use it as an exercise. After that, I'll need your full attention on what he brings us. Then these kids are purely a CID matter to the extent that they're in Stanton's jurisdiction. Agreed?'

'Thank you. Do you—?'

'No, I have no idea how long it will take, Sterling.' Barbra shrugged. 'The physical interface and the encryption are bound to be hard to break, but Bill's team is good. Several hours. Do what you can, but you must come back when I call you.'

'Thank you,' I said again, and hurried out of the office and down the stairs to my workstation in the common-room pool. Barbra's windows cleared themselves as I fired up my terminal.

Sentinel had originally been set up as a public unit that used analogue methods to prevent the recurrence of digital terror, but over the years they'd expanded well beyond that original brief, funded and supported by politicians and lobbyists who knew that Omega wouldn't be the favoured lobbyists for ever, and that once they'd fallen, there'd be a renewed demand for fulsome – electronic – security and policing services. If Omega knew the extent of this operation, they'd find a way to disband the entire law-enforcement system in their indignation.

First, I pulled up video footage from the lamp-post cameras on Nile Street where it led into the alley, and the end camera on the alley itself, which Sentinel had fitted into a street lamp that never worked and had just become part of the general clutter and decay. Nobody would ever come across it, any more than they would wash the piss from behind the dumpster and build a garden conservatory for the homeless people who slept there. The alley behind Cubbington's bakery, like much of Claymarket, remained what Barbra would call a low-priority vantage, but the two surveillance points were decent enough, and remained operational.

I set the two feeds back to the previous afternoon and scanned through them side by side, pausing whenever I saw a figure coming through the alleyway. I watched Cubby Rosenior and another man locking up, then later someone unlocked the back of the shop next to the bakery. I paused and checked the map – Gandalf's bookstore. The owner of S-Town Bodega closed up and emerged from the alleyway, stopped at the corner of Nile and Mildura, then got on the number 85 bus towards – pause and check – his home in Horizon Park. Half an hour later, a cat fight erupted and was broken up by something being thrown from an unseen window of an apartment above. A brief downpour started, and someone who was dressed like a homeless man scuffled into the alleyway and took shelter against the wall, lighting a cigarette and waiting out the squall. At 6:33 p.m. on the feed, it happened.

A figure in padded jacket and balaclava, rainproof trousers

and thick workboots came into the alleyway carrying a large bundle. It was hard to tell the build of the person under the bulky clothes. I could only imagine hesitation or deliberation in the grainy image on the screen. They half-turned and placed the bundle carefully, gently, across the bakery's back entrance, the child's ragged little sneakers poking out of the end of the grey roll of blanket. And then the person did something odd, kneeling over the body. The suspect's back was towards the camera and hid what they were doing to the child, but they stayed bent over the child's body for fourteen seconds before standing again and hurrying back, covered head down, a light stride, almost a skip-run. Back to the car on Nile Street, parked right outside the alley mouth. The car was an unremarkable model, a grey Toyota Camry with a trunk big enough for a child's body, not the sort of car you'd drive dressed head-to-toe in camouflage dark. The streetside camera had picked up a clear registration number.

Although people had become complacent since the Turn, it was still unlikely that someone would dump a body with legitimate licence plates, so I was surprised when the registration number brought up an active record for a car that hadn't been reported as stolen. It belonged to someone called Vidal Barrett, a lawyer based at the edge of Claymarket. I noted his office address and his home address, telephone numbers and pneum coordinates, logged out of my terminal, scanned out of the Sentinel office and hurried over to Jordan, who was leafing through a thick wad of notes, slumped over his desk, propping his head up with his hand.

'Have you got a moment, Jordan? Did you get the report in?'

He rolled his eyes towards me so that he didn't have to raise his head from his hand. 'Yeah. I've got to go over this evidence for the Shing trial. The minutiae of creative accounting. Save me.'

'I've got a lead. The person who left the girl's body at the bakery was driving a car that's still registered to a name and address in town. It could be a fake, but it doesn't look like it.'

He straightened. 'How did you...? Never mind.' Glancing at the grey door. 'What happens in Oz stays in Oz, right?'

'I've got an address matched to the vehicle he came in, and I have authorisation for an extraordinary visit.'

Jordan narrowed his eyes at me. By 'visit', Jordan knew that I meant a search of the apartment, and by 'extraordinary', I meant fast-tracked past the usual bureaucratic processes.

'I'm low on time,' I pressed. 'I only have a couple of hours. Will you come with me?'

'Thank God,' he said, leaning over and taking a pre-signed warrant dummy out of his desk drawer. 'I was about to fall asleep here.'

10 The apartment registered to Vidal Barrett was in an unpretentious neighbourhood just north of the Museum District. Jordan parked half a block away and we ran across the road between gaps in the traffic, me clutching my messenger bag to my stomach. From what I'd read in his dossier, Barrett kept office hours at a small general-practice firm on the gentrified fringes of Claymarket. He was divorced, and had a sixteen-year-old daughter but the mother, Dierdra Smith, had sole custody. So there was a fair chance there'd be nobody home right now; unless, of course, there was a cleaner or a lover or a tenant. Barrett had no arrests, no convictions; took his degree at a community college an hour down the highway in Racino. There was only his driver's licence mugshot on file, a grainy thing taken years ago, and apart from decent bone structure, a nice smile and a terrible haircut, there was little I could glean from it. Despite my training, I started building a picture of him in my mind: shabby suit, balding, cramped office, drinking habit, struggling to keep up with the alimony but doing his best. Why would a man like that be dumping dead children in the middle of the night?

Stop it, Lucie, I chided myself. I knew nothing about this man and I was being unprofessional. We were here to find out what this Vidal Barrett might have to do with the dead children; whether he'd taken Kira too. I had to be calm and clear, not work up a fantasy of unsubstantiated conclusions.

The building had a smart brass-framed door and a small

but bright marble lobby. Although it was a small block, the landlord had hired a security guard – a measure that had become common since the Turn – but the desk was vacant. There was a visitors' book and a mug, a novel and a small radio. Without thinking about it, I scanned the ceiling and the top of the walls for any tell-tale signs of pinhole cameras – a newly painted spot, an unusual crack or a divot in the beading. So often, techs had tried to worm in invisibly with a microbit and came away with a chunk of plaster. I didn't notice anything, and although it was highly unlikely that this average building had been fitted for another case, anything was possible.

'Let's go,' Jordan said, mistaking my hesitation for worry about the security guard. 'We can sign in later, and you'll earn your good citizen's badge.'

I hid my grimace as we headed up the stairs to the third floor. Jordan and I got along so well because we both accepted that sometimes we had to bypass abstract regulations to do our work, but what I planned to do once we were inside would test our relationship. I clutched my bag closer to me, not looking forward to the confrontation. The hallway was carpeted with quality thick plush that was starting to wear a little down the main thoroughfares. Dim, energy-efficient bulbs shone coldly from sconces that had been made for much warmer light, and illuminated the thinness of the most recent paint job, smudges and chips showing through the single coat that had been applied perhaps a year or two ago.

We knocked three times, waiting for a good while for an answer. I listened, but there was no movement inside, and no sign of life in any of the four other apartments on that floor. Single- or two-bed flats in a commuter limbo, hard-working people feeling the suck of economic pressure under their feet, it made sense that they'd all be out – at the office, or at the bar; no family. We should have waited for the guard and shown our warrant, but Jordan put on his gloves and took out his lockpicks, another part of our extraordinary-visit service.

He closed the door quietly behind us. The first thing that hit me was a fresh and floral perfume, something you'd expect a young woman to wear. The flat was neater than I'd expected – we'd entered straight into an open-plan reception area, which led all the way to the south-facing bay windows overlooking the building's scruffy rear garden. The plastic chairs of a green garden set were neatly leant over a table with a sun umbrella folded in the middle of it; a barbecue and a slime-filled water feature in the corner. I moved away from the window and turned a circle in the living room. A couch with a handmade patchwork quilt on it, three crammed bookcases with a clutter of empty vases on top of them, a stack of LPs towards which Jordan gravitated. A nice thick blue rug lying over the stripped wood floors, a coffee table laden with one meal's worth of plates... breakfast from this morning, milk hardened into a yellowish sheen on the bowl. And beside that a notepad with a girl's handwriting on it – scrawls, scratchings, doodles, names and dates; the evidence of distracted studying.

The washed-up, two-bit attorney in my mind started to dissolve away and to reform as I went into the kitchenette and looked at what was stuck on the fridge: a set of magnetic poetry jumbled up except for a line – *PLEASE I LOVE SOME MILK TODAY*; a souvenir magnet from Flamingo World; and a photograph of a man and a teenaged girl. The man clean-shaven and buff in a tight-fitting T-shirt, the smile familiar from his licence photo, but his short black hair in a far better style. Vidal Barrett had aged from his awkward youth to forty very handsomely. The girl was almost as tall as him as she leaned her head on the side of his, her straight dark middle-parted hair half-obscuring the design on Barrett's T-shirt.

Behind the kitchenette, a short passageway led to a bathroom; a woman's make-up and shampoo jumbled on the tub's side, along with unisex skin products and a can of shaving foam. In the cabinet under the basin: toilet paper, soap, bleach, tampons. In the mirrored cabinet above only over-the-counter medication: paracetamol tablets, a bottle of antacid, a tube of haemorrhoid ointment, facial waxing strips. The first bedroom was the smaller one, the bed made, the slatted blind closed, a pile of books on the bedside table; in the closet, three suits, some casual trousers, T-shirts and sweat tops. At the end of the passage, the second bedroom was the larger one, with a corner view over the hills through grand curved windows. A desk and a bookcase were positioned against one window and a child's double bunk bed took up the far end of the room. The bottom bunk was piled with clothes and books and bright accessories that spilled out onto the carpet, while the top level was where the girl slept, the bundled comforter and pyjamas exuding a floral-masked funk that hauled me straight back two decades to Claymarket and my redolent little bedroom. This overflowing patch was the girl's corner of the otherwise orderly house. With so many belongings here, it looked like she spent more time in this house than just an occasional visit, and I wondered if Mr Barrett was transgressing his custody rights.

I was about to open the closet in the bedroom when there was an urgent rap at the front door. For a moment my mind was blanked by an image of yellow eyes and matted black wool, but the shade passed through me without stopping. When I got out into the living room, Jordan had opened the door and was talking to a uniformed officer.

'Urgent message for Ms Sterling,' she said. 'The director needs you back.'

'Did you tell her we're here?' Jordan said, scowling between me and the officer.

'Yes,' I lied. It was a half-lie, because I knew that doing anything on Sentinel terminals was effectively telling Barbra Reeve, if she wanted to know. 'I'm on my way. Thanks, officer.'

When the officer had left, I stretched my rubber gloves over my fingers, opened out my satchel on the kitchen counter, pulled a stool from under the kitchen counter, and climbed up on it.

'What're you doing?'

'Look away, Jordan,' I said as I began to drill the little hole in the ceiling behind the kitchen's light fitting.

'Lucie, what the fuck? This is not part of the deal.'

'I told you, look away. Go and stand outside. You're not seeing this. You don't know it's happening. It won't trouble your conscience.'

He opened his mouth and scowled at me as I installed the microphone and the fibre cameras, attaching them to the control module and inserting it into the base of the light fitting. Then he shook his head and walked out into the hallway, leaving me to set bugs in the bedrooms. I could have installed cameras in the bathroom too, but something stopped me. Call it a sense of decency, if you like. Or call it haste.

After circling the place one more time, making sure that everything looked the way we'd found it, I joined him. He closed the door behind us, checking that the lock was undamaged, then stalked off down the steps ahead of me. The guard, back at his desk, barely raised his eyes to us. Jordan had started the car by the time I'd hurried after him and got in.

For a couple of minutes he didn't say anything, but his nature got the better of him. 'What the fuck?' he said again. 'You can't go around doing that, Lucie. You know I've committed three officers to this case. I've stuck my neck out for you, and you have to trust me. If she's in the city, they'll find her. We know how to do police work. I don't care what you people do in your magic room behind the door, but this is the real world out here. We're not some… fucken… tyranny. Citizens have rights.'

His hypocrisy made my jaw clench. I looked straight ahead and concentrated on keeping my voice level. 'I thank you for that, Jordan. But if that man has my niece, I'm going to do everything in my power to find her.'

'*If*, Lucie. *If*. For Christ's sake. I don't believe you have any proof, otherwise you wouldn't be sneaking around his apartment while he's out. We'd get a legitimate warrant, we'd go to his office and arrest him.'

'If he's not involved,' I snapped back, 'it doesn't make a difference. *If* he didn't do anything, nobody will see those feeds.'

'You will,' he muttered.

I'd expected an argument, but I hadn't expected him to be so disgusted. I hadn't expected to feel so ashamed.

When I got back to the station, Barbra took me into her office with the biggest smile I'd ever seen on her face, which worked out to be a kind of weird snarl. 'We got in. Just as expected, there was a legacy vulnerability our coders managed to exploit. We're currently channelling a live dump of some of Green Valley's key data streams, including Egus's accounts, live utility metering, systems control data and so on.'

'Just metering and accounts? You're not getting live access to The I? You can't see inside?'

Barbra smiled. 'It's a great breach, Lucie, but it's not the God particle. Wouldn't we love to be able to monitor everything and everyone at all times. Even Egus and his friends didn't manage that in their heyday. Got pretty close, though.'

'Won't he know?' I asked. 'Egus, I mean.'

'Bill is certain the transfer is cloaked properly and Zeroth won't see us piggybacking on the stream. They've disguised our tap as one of Zeroth's own redundancy loops.' She stopped and looked at my face. 'Don't be disappointed. It's an excellent ingress. We can consolidate these data streams with the old user data we already have on file. We can trace any suspect who ever owned an I, just like Zeroth.'

'You mean the Zeroth records weren't deleted? Wasn't that the whole point of the Turn?'

'Safekeeping, Lucie, is different from usage.' She offered a beneficent smile again, as if to a favoured pupil. 'It's slow, it's frustrating, I know – we've been fighting this battle for a long time. But you've done great work. I'll need you on analytics immediately – we have a hell of a lot of data to process.' She put her hand on my arm, a gesture as strangely unsettling as her long-toothed smile. 'Of course, I can't officially commend you. But you should be proud of yourself.'

I wasn't feeling very proud of myself. I was bristling. At that moment, when only one suspect was of any interest to me, snooping on an entire city full of people seemed arbitrary and pointless. Barbra was already settling into the chair behind her desk, staring at something on the screen in front of her.

'Can you tell me: why are we even watching them?' I said.

She looked up, her eyes taking a moment to adjust to me and away from the screen, then frowned as various options scrolled down the menu in her mind. Finally, she settled on magnanimity towards the staffer who'd just delivered the project this major coup and was obviously tired. She took a deep breath and reinstalled the wolfish smile on her face. 'To keep them safe. Everything we do in this office is to keep citizens safe.'

11

I tried to hide behind a Day-Glo orange upsized plaster cast of a Minoan death mask, but the woman had spotted me. I'd seen her and spoken to her several times at these events of Fabian's but I still couldn't remember her name or anything about her.

'Isn't it just so… unique?' she asked me.

I nodded.

Just remember one or two small details about people, Fabian had often counselled me, *and lead off a conversation with them, then you'll soon be into an illuminating discussion. You find these things awkward because you forget to unlock people's trust.*

It should have been easy for me. My profession, after all, was analysing and collating significant details about people. It wasn't that I could manage data and not real people; I often had warm discussions with people on the bus and at the precinct and with Bobby Khan and the regulars at Verla's – I remembered their names. But there was something about Fabian's colleagues, or friends, or apparatchiks, that blocked me. It betrayed my limited imagination, I knew, but they all looked and sounded the same to me. Academics, politicians, commercially successful artists, other curators like Fabian – they made me feel stupid and small.

Even though I'd gone home and dressed smartly, compared to them I felt sweaty, tired and underdressed. This opening had been on the calendar for months, a big night for Fabian. I had to be with him tonight, but my attention was anywhere but here. I'd spent the afternoon staring at a split screen, keeping an eye on the feed from Barrett's home while I sifted through the audit of the Green Valley data. The longer his flat stayed empty, the more anxious I became. But at Sentinel, I would know immediately if Vidal moved or if Jordan's patrol found something. Wandering around the city by myself, with no trail to follow, and not even a junction set of my own, I'd be blind and mute. I had to be patient. Jordan's patrol was actively looking for Kira on the streets, and I was looking for her there, in electronic space. We were doing everything we could. Jordan knew the art museum's number and would call or send a patrol officer if there was any news. I had to trust him.

David, on the other hand, wouldn't know I was here. I'd picked up a message from him that he'd left in the afternoon, which the woman at the answering service just read back: 'Any news? None on my side. Still looking. Will keep in touch.' He might be calling me at home right now.

'It really reminds us who we are, that we're made of clay,' the woman whose name I'd forgotten gushed, expertly grasping a glass half filled with white wine and a small plate laden with three bare skewers in one hand, dabbing her lips with a cocktail napkin in the other.

'Not stardust?' I muttered.

Her smile froze and she tilted her head. Then, after a pause, she said, 'That's *right*. We're not stardust – if stardust means we're all special and twinkly. That's the precise myth the soft corporations tried to sell us. The cult of individuality; tearing us apart, breaking down communal endeavour in favour of winner-takes-all competition. That's how we got to the Turn, and we must never forget. Your wonderful Fabian's collection is so important right now, when our memories are getting short. Reminding us we are clay – and, yes, *not* stardust – that we all share the same end.

Reminding us of our deaths speaks truly of our *authenticity*.'

The woman wafted off to circulate and I hurried around the edge of the vast basement space where Fabian had set up the exhibition, making towards the reception desk, where I'd be able to hear Jordan's call.

Fabian had been working on the exhibition for nearly two years, gathering death tributes, totems, funereal masks and gravewealth from museums and galleries around the world, and then commissioning local contemporary artists each to reimagine one of the pieces in whichever medium they chose. One of the paintings, of a dead baby wrapped in an Aleutian papoose, had been reimagined in a magnified pointillist style in summer colours. I remembered the dot woman whose work I'd walked into in Green Valley, her originality vampirised by exploitation, advertising and kitsch. I wondered if she regretted staying in Green Valley, trapping her imagination in formaldehyde. If she'd had the choice, would she have preferred to come out into the real world and expose her vision to collectors and patrons like these?

Another of Fabian's colleagues was coming at me with an aggressive smile. I turned, pretending I hadn't seen her, scanning for a hiding spot in one of the closed galleries, when someone *ting*ed a wine glass self-importantly.

The audience quietened and turned to the first landing on the main staircase, where a microphone was set up. Marc Fernando, the museum's director, handed his knife and glass off to a young assistant. 'Welcome to the Stanton Trust Museum's new exhibition, *Mortality Reimagined*! Gathered here tonight are the city's most far-sighted benefactors and the museum's most loyal and supportive friends. You know how much we appreciate your continued efforts, often against the tide of public priorities, to keep art and heritage essential lifelines of our communal lives. I know you're all keen to get back to looking at these marvellous pieces. Aren't they wonderful? But let's offer a minute to the curator of this incredible show, Fabian Tadic.' He raised his glass and an urbane cheer went up, along with the wine glasses of the audience. 'Fabian, will you say a few words?'

Formidable and elegant in his black suit and sea-green tie, Fabian took his place behind the microphone. He scanned the faces looking up towards him, and when he located me, favoured me with a public smile and a half-wink that, despite my preoccupation, warmed me. This was a room full of Stanton's political elite, the cream of the party and Omega, and Fabian had sought my eyes out and favoured me.

As he spoke, paraphrasing his introduction to the exhibition catalogue, the metal on his wrist flashed with each expansive gesture and his fingers shaped gracefully around every flourish. I watched him without listening, recognising how his confident stance held the room, and how the assembled power brokers angled their faces towards him, as if to a soft autumn sun. *This is Fabian*, I thought, *the man I go home to each night. He can hold this room in deference as well as he holds me; they feel as safe in his command as I do.*

Someone was watching me, a man, glaring at me from the other side of the room. Without taking his eyes off me, he nudged the woman next to him and side-mouthed something towards her. She fixed me with an equally spiteful look. I recognised the man: he'd been in Fabian's apartment a couple of times, at the Omega strategy meetings he'd hosted there. One of the group's core funders, an odious religious Luddite called Daniel Jameson. Jameson muttered something to his partner, pasted a thin smile on his face and started walking towards me. I couldn't bring myself to make small talk with that man, no matter how much Fabian would appreciate it. I shielded myself behind a passing waiter with a tray of canapés, and turned and hurried up the side stairs, leaving Jameson frozen at the end of his run, watching me leave.

By the time I slowed down, I was in the museum's administrative wing. Fabian's warm and spacious office would be a good place to hole up for a few minutes. I could use his phone to call Jordan, see if there was any update at the station, check if there were any more calls or messages from David. Passing along the dimly lit corridor, only a faint glow smudging through the frosted glass panes of the offices as I went down towards the staff bathroom, I heard the deep thrum of photostats churning out brochures for the museum and Omega material in the print shop.

Because I was upstairs, nobody found me passed out on the bathroom floor. I pushed myself up to a side-legged squat then hauled myself up by pulling on the lip of the basin counter. I stood there for a minute, leaned over, testing my legs, trying to piece together what had happened. When I finally lifted my face to the mirror, I could still see the dark, matted shape clearly, behind me, sinking back into the narrow gap between the last toilet cubicle and the wall. The lights it suggested and the imploding lives it projected shimmered faintly around its scabrous pelt. I didn't want to turn again, fall again, but it raised its head and demanded my attention, and for a second I saw a reflected flash of yellow eyes, but then they were sucked into the swirling smudge of its face. I could sense it behind me, and I turned my head to look at it, but it wasn't back in the shadows now.

It had come closer, I told myself, even as the memory was fading like a dream. I had seen some of the lives it wore. It was taunting me, dressing itself in surveillance feeds of a thousand crimes, a thousand ripped lives. It was just a hallucination, a vivid daydream. Just exhaustion.

· · ·

'How can you get into bed with people like that?' I asked Fabian.

'They support our work.' He turned to me, stopping halfway in the intricate procedure of removing his cufflinks and tie-pin and placing them in the box on the dresser. It was meant to be my dressing table that he'd installed along with me all those years ago, but the notion of sitting on a soft stool in front of angled mirrors was foreign to me. I pulled off my armful of cheap bangles and flopped them over the arms of the fanciful maquette on the dresser, twisted my arms around my back to unzip, my muscles aching, a bruise blooming on my shoulder, and stood beside the bed as the dress fell.

'Your work? You say that like it's some sort of profound mission, but as far as I can tell, the Omega group is just a bunch of disgruntled ex-intellectuals who can't move with the times.'

'If "moving with the times" is allowing us to get sucked back into complacently giving our freedom away to a corporate-technological tyranny, then yes, we don't want to move with the times.'

'But there's so much potential, Fabe—'

'Potential that continually and repeatedly becomes corrupted. That's what happens to unchallenged power.'

I sat on the edge of the bed, trying to soften my stance, trying to get him to understand me rather than offer me freshman lecture notes. 'I saw something yesterday, in Green Valley, that reminded me. There's so much we can do with the technology that would allow us to evolve. When people like Daniel Jameson are involved in Omega, it can only mean that you're working to stop our evolution. He'd like nothing more than to bring back slavery and have his church write the laws.'

He sighed and shook his head. 'It's more complex than that.'

'You're not comfortable with him, I know it, Fabe.'

He didn't rise to the bait, only turned back to the dresser mirror. 'Let's not do this now. It's been a long night and you must be exhausted.'

The petulant teen in me wanted to snap back – *Don't tell me when I'm exhausted* – but I was more self-aware than that. *I'm a highly regarded professional too,* I reminded myself, instantly remembering David's plea: *I'm important here.* All of us, every single goddamn one of us, preening and proving in front of some invisible audience. You could take away the social networks, but our will to compete and compare, our craving for affirmation, would always remain.

'I am,' I said.

I had a shower and went to bed, curling my back to Fabian as he read himself down. I was only intending to rest and listen out in case the phone rang, and I felt like I'd hardly closed my eyes, but when I woke again, at half past two, the room was dark and Fabian was snoring softly beside me.

My mind was racing with false images speeding and merging with reality, and sleep tried to drag me back down, but I fought it and pushed up from the bed, my bones still aching. Padding towards the study, I turned back at the bedroom doorway and looked at Fabian's body sprawled in a slant of light from between the curtains. Like this, he was fragile; just a body. After closing the study door, I unpacked my satchel and turned on the portable monitor I'd requisitioned from Sentinel. Having the tech in the house felt as much a betrayal as sneaking a lover into our bed.

Vidal Barrett's sitting room was still and quiet. I flicked through the feeds to find him in his bed, on his back, one bare leg sticking out from under the comforter, bare shoulders above its hem and his arms folded neatly across his chest. The scattering of books on the nightstand had been joined by a tumbler of water and a pair of glasses. In the next room, the girl lay in her top bunk. As if disturbed, she flipped over with a flail of limbs and fixed her eyes straight into the angle of the cornice where I'd set the fibre camera. I knew there was no way she could sense that I was there, but for a moment she stared at me with eyes rendered blank and glassy by the infrared sensors. Then she lay back and curled on her side under the quilt and went still again.

A creak in the hallway and for a second I was ripped between both apartments, incapacitated by the confusion. I stashed the monitor under a pile of papers just as Fabian opened the door.

'Are you okay?' he said, squinting at me groggily.

'Yes, sorry.' I made a nonchalant show of skimming through the pages. 'Can't sleep.'

He frowned and rubbed the back of his head where his silvering hair was tufted up.

'I'm trying to do some work,' I continued, 'but I'm worn out.'

'Come back to bed,' he said. 'Try to sleep.'

'I know I won't. I'll just disturb you. I'll just stay up a while, if you don't mind.'

He shrugged. 'Why should I mind?' But of course he did. 'I wish you wouldn't...'

'What?'

'Nothing. Never mind.' He turned and closed the study door behind him.

12 Vidal Barrett whisked eggs and poured them into the pan. They didn't seethe like they should and he realised he hadn't let the butter warm up for long enough. He scowled as the mixture grudgingly started to heat up and congeal, then started scraping it with a spatula. It'd have to do.

He was still getting used to this, looking after someone other than himself. When Sofie was small, he'd left the domestic stuff to Dierdra, and she'd left the responsible, rent-earning, adult-being, getting-dressed-into-day-clothes stuff to him. Then they'd split up and Dierdra's impressive lawyer argued successfully that he'd been negligent, using his time sheets and caseloads during that period as evidence against him, and she'd won sole custody. Somehow Sofie had become sixteen and still alive and funny and smart and warm-hearted. Then Dierdra had gone and fucking died.

He slid the pan off the heat and stared at the coffee machine as it dribbled a mugful out for Sofie, stretching his arms over his head and hearing his joints crack. He rotated his neck a few times in half-hearted homage to the exercise he really should be taking, then took the mug through to Sofie's room.

She was bundled up on the top level of the kiddies' bunk bed he'd bought for her when Dierdra split, naively imagining it would have more use than the odd occasion that Dierdra needed him to babysit when she had a big night out. Now that Sofie was here full-time he really should have bought her a proper bed, but she said she didn't mind, that it was comfortable, that it reminded her of home. She'd told him she always felt safe when she came to his place, like her little bed was a nest in a safe cave; it was quiet and calm and never disturbed.

Sofie'd been up too late the last few nights, and Vidal stood there wondering if he should wake her at all, whether she should just skip school today; but when she smelled the coffee, she worked her body over from its wallward curl to face him, half-open one eye and smile. God, she looked nothing like her mother. Where had this angel even come from? She protruded one arm from under the cover and made a gimme-gimme motion with her hand. Vidal passed her cup and rubbed her head.

'Did you get any sleep, sweetie?'

'Enough,' she said, pushing up to sit against the wall and squinting her face awake before taking a deep slurp of the coffee.

'Did anyone see you?'

'I don't think so.'

Vidal looked at his daughter, apparently so calm and businesslike, while he was waging a hectic battle with the panic in his chest. *How could you allow your daughter to get mixed up in this?* someone was screaming in his head. But it wasn't really his voice; it was the voice of society or propriety or Dierdra or something. When Sofie came back to him, all alone in the world, he knew he would keep no secrets from her, and when she found out what he'd decided to do, she wanted to be involved. As far as Vidal was concerned, his daughter was an adult, a partner, and his only job was to guide her and protect her and not to stop her from doing what she wanted to. Unless that involved harming herself. And he'd noticed it – being involved with the children was the one thing that had kept her mind off Dierdra's death. God knows what lives in a sixteen-year-old girl's mind, but she seemed to be thriving in this project, rather than circling deep inside herself.

This project – right. It had turned into an utter mess, and they were both on the verge of getting into serious trouble. The only thing in their favour at the moment was that the kids were from Green Valley and, as Vidal knew from his years of legal experience, Green Valley was a judicial and enforcement blind spot. People who had chosen to stay in Green Valley, and their wards and offspring, were invisible to the law outside. He'd worked on several cases that proved the state's utter indifference to issues inside the wall. There were more of them eight years ago when the treaty sealed them off: families cut in half, contracts breached by a few yards of concrete, unsettled divorces, pending criminal cases. They were all shut down and made to disappear, every police and judicial palm greased by Zeroth's exit fund. Though the cases had dwindled to a trickle over the past years, Jamie Egus still had an active and effective palm-greasing fund – there was still no way to reinvigorate old cases or start new ones. So Vidal had adapted, exploiting the blind spot in his little import–export sideline, and so far it'd been lucrative – hey, he'd had to up his earnings since he'd become a family man.

Involving Sofie was intended to help her heal; the plan was meant to be harmless. More than that: he'd intended it to be *heroic*.

What a fuck-up.

Sofie had been drinking her coffee, staring out of the window for so long, Vidal thought the conversation was over. He was about to rouse himself and go back out to the kitchen, but now she spoke again. 'Rainbow and I washed him. We dressed him.'

'Who?'

'Cisco. The boy,' she added, in case Vidal had forgotten.

'We thought it would be... kind. Respectful.' When Vidal didn't answer, just fixed her with a frown, she said, 'Do you think that's a problem? A mistake?'

But he was frowning for another reason, maybe because his heart was cracking. 'No. It was kind. Are you up to school today?'

She shrugged. 'If I don't go, I'll just have to catch up. What's more,' she announced in a sudden radio voice, 'it's Thunderous Thursday. Chilli in the cafeteria. Yay.' The disjuncture between the fake jovial tone and her deeply thoughtful look unsettled him. If she could act so well, how could he know the real her? *You can trust her and shut up, that's how,* he chided himself. *Don't even go down that road.*

'Well, I've made some eggs you can fill up on.'

'Yay.'

'I'll make you sandwiches if you prefer.'

She laughed, releasing Vidal from his anxiety. 'It's okay, Dad. It's all good.'

Vidal pushed back into the car seat, watching Sofie walking into school, cutting a straight line through the cliques and the clusters in the front yard. God, he'd hated high school, and he couldn't imagine what it was like for a girl who'd just lost her mother. Those animals would kick you while you were down if they saw any weakness, grind you into the filthy concrete. But as he was thinking this, Sofie stopped at a group of kids, flipped her hood and shared a couple of hugs. She pushed her hair away from her face and laughed. The kids looked wholesome enough; a bit of colour and a bit of shaving in their hair, a bit of metal in some of their faces, lots of white in the teeth. And they weren't spitting on his daughter; they were welcoming her into the circle.

So he watched, hunkered down in the seat, as if this would

stop her from noticing that his car was still parked fifty yards from the gate. He watched to see his daughter being happy, to bank a bit of confidence that everything was going to be all right. Some part of him was still waiting for something to give; she was too fine, carrying her sadness with such grace. But every morning he watched her, and every morning she got a day away from the trauma. Somehow, she was surviving.

Then he drove to the wall, parking in a derelict niche outside the liaison office. Going around to lock his briefcase in the back, he couldn't help remembering the dead children who'd been carried in this trunk. The third one they'd lost, the little girl, was so thin Sofie could have carried her under one arm. Sofe didn't need anyone's help.

This goddamned wall was like an iceberg, sending out frigid wafts of dead air and killing everything in its shadow. He hurried through the shade and pushed the buzzer on the liaison door. After a Gina-length delay, the door buzzed. Vidal pushed it open, but hesitated on the threshold. Every time he came in here, he had to gird himself, and rather than getting easier each time, it got harder, his body resisting the electronic parasites, his mind rebelling against the voodoo fuckery he was forcing on it. Now, his back was almost in spasm as he stood, casting one nostalgic glance at the soupy grey light over the wasteland outside. But it was business – good business – and he had to meet his client. It wasn't like Jamie Egus could come and see him at his office, meet on the terrace, have a normal cup of coffee in the sunshine. Could he? God knows what Jamie Egus was any more, what was left of him under all the video games.

'Oh, close the door, Vidal,' Gina snapped. 'The light's killing me.'

'What light?' he said, but he pushed himself in and closed the door.

'They turned me into a vampire,' Gina intoned, as if

she'd been reading too many gothic novels. 'And now, here I am, stuck in the half-life, half-world with Martin. Oh, woe is me.' She pressed the back of her hand against her brow.

'How is Martin?'

'Dead.' Vidal was surprised at the lack of emotion in Gina's voice. The two liaison officers hadn't had much in common – vivacious, broken Gina and fusty, nerdy little Martin – but they'd worked together for a long time.

Like Gina, Martin had been damaged in the Zeroth testing process. They'd both been handsomely compensated and sent to semi-retirement in this office, shuffling papers around for busywork to keep them on the payroll. Martin had loved to travel, and all the exotic touches in this office were his, from real-world journeys, before he became a virtual Odysseus.

'I still have his template,' Gina went on. 'They run a simulation for me to keep me from going completely insane. It's pretty effective. He talks to me sort of in the way he used to.'

'What happened to him?'

Gina tilted her head, as if tuning in to some information she'd requested on him, but Vidal knew she was the last person in Green Valley who'd do that; the only person who wouldn't – she was allergic to tech or something. 'You know, I think it was natural causes.'

'Hm,' Vidal said. 'Good for him, I guess. Are you all right in here? Alone.'

She frowned at him and pursed her lips, saying nothing for a moment. Then she breathed out. 'So you're here to see the wizard?'

'That's right.'

'You know what to do.' She nodded towards the changing room. 'Though I don't know why you don't just keep the rig in. It would save us both a lot of effort.'

'No fucking chance in hell.'

13

Through The I, the Zeroth campus was always sunny and always green, and Vidal had never got used to the bone-knowledge that he was walking on cold concrete in a murky warehouse while he could also feel the soft give of the earth, smell the just-watered richness of the turf, and sense the warmth of the sun on his skin. His mother would have called it Satan's evil and left it at that, but then again she'd never been one for modernity. Still, the core of him couldn't avoid superstition whenever he was in this place. He'd hurry in, see to business, and hurry out.

He walked through the front gardens of Zeroth's head office, passing through a birch glade over a sylvan bridge that was meant to provoke serenity. Ducks with iridescent green and purple sheens stayed neatly on their pond to his left, and lithe-necked swans circled opulently in their territory on the other side of the bridge. *They would be expensive creatures if they were real*, Vidal thought as a birch leaf artfully detached from a branch and elegantly deposited itself on the water, rippling the water self-consciously.

Before the low office building, squatting against a wooded copse in an attitude of environmental harmony only wealth could allow, was a defunct turning circle. For a few years well before the Turn, partners would spin their Lamborghinis and Maseratis showily outside the door, as if they thought that would motivate and inspire the software engineers inside: one day, this could be you. But then Jamie Egus, crisply attuned to the popular mood before even the populace was aware of its own feelings, banned cars from Green Valley and provided sustainable transport for everyone. Where 'everyone' was a card-carrying Zeroth dependant. What turned in this circle now? Under this projection of Green Valley captured twenty years ago, far darker things lay.

See to business, and get the hell out of here, Vidal reminded himself, deliberately shunting the images away – or was The I helping him? – and repressing an icy clutch of fear about what was really crunching under his feet.

The lobby was all matte-white finish and glass, the sun and the natural colours from outside painting everything in a luscious, shifting tone. It was perfectly warm in here, amniotic.

The pretty woman in a tight sheath dress behind the reception desk smiled at him and he looked back at her, not wasting the muscles in his face because he knew she was not real. Checking his reflection in the mirror behind him, he neatened his hair. He always used the same avatar in here. It was an image he'd spent hours customising on his second visit, back when it seemed to matter, and it bore a fair resemblance to him, but idealised – smaller nose, rings lightened around the eyes, the pockmarks and blemishes and freak hairs removed for a smooth finish. He went through the redundant act of putting his thumb on the scanner to check in and taking the visitor's tag, and the receptionist stood and showed him past the subtle security barrier at the end of the lobby. He watched her walk back to the desk in her needle-heeled slingbacks, the muscles up her legs and in her thighs and her ass working the material of the dress. He'd always *assumed* she wasn't real.

What would sex be like in here? It could be anything you could imagine, or the sloppy wank of a bad coder, failing in every respect to match a real, warm body.

When she'd settled back into her chair, Vidal turned

through an open-plan assortment of workers, climbed up a wide stairway and walked along the upper-floor passageway, skylit and art-hung. He made his way towards the office at the end, past the shaded frost-glass doors of the under-wizards, towards the lair of the wizard-in-chief himself. But he hadn't reached the end of the whitewashed corridor before he heard someone's soft tread behind him.

Vidal turned to see an avatar in a Bugs Bunny mask holding up its hand – *wait*.

'Hi,' he said, emoting neutral politeness and hoping his avatar was accurately representing it. 'Are you in the meeting?'

'No. I need to talk to you.' Bugs's face bent unnaturally as it spoke, the lips moulded static around the mouth hole.

Bugs ushered Vidal through a sliding glass door into a skylit atrium, planted with palm trees clustered artfully around a Japanese-style bridge over a patch of mangrove where jewelled carp lolled. If this was anywhere other than Green Valley, run by anyone other than Jamie Egus, this would be a smoking room and the carp would be growing tough and edgy on their nicotine habit.

Bugs glanced around to check for company. 'I've located a few more children who need our help.' A chunk of data reached Vidal on his private ID, with map coordinates and details. 'Here, here and here.'

'Are you sure Egus can't see this?' Vidal asked.

Bugs ignored the question. 'Listen, Barrett. Why are they dying?'

'It's the withdrawal,' he said. 'It's worse than we realised. We thought when Rainbow made it through that we'd found the solution, but I guess she was an anomaly. We lost another one yesterday.'

'I know.'

'Then you'll also know that we're trying our best.'

Now the bunny's rubber face did something that creeped

Vidal out. A plastic thing, warping like it was slightly too hot. One thing on a cartoon; another in real life. Fake life, whatever the fuck this was. Like a goddamned zombified doll. 'You can't keep dumping them out in the open,' it said. 'They're attracting attention.'

I shouldn't have brought Sofie into this. Trained as a lawyer, used to trying to read real people, he looked into Bugs's dead, painted eyes, and in response they started to roll back, and they didn't stop, falling back into their sockets and away.

'You have to make the bodies disappear.'

Vidal looked into the mask's eyeholes for longer than was comfortable, trying to recognise something in the blankness. He looked until his balance tipped, as if he might fall into the void. Then he dragged his gaze away. 'All right. It won't happen again.'

Outside Egus's office, the windows opaque and the door closed, Vidal presented himself to a personal assistant he'd never seen before but who was possibly a real person's avatar, given her practical outfit of slacks, low heels and a light and soft-looking emerald sweater. She was checking a quaint analogue appointment book when she glanced up and over his shoulder. David Coady was coming along the corridor.

'Oh, David. You in on this meeting?' Vidal asked.

'Yes,' David Coady said in his evasive tone. 'Jamie asked me.'

Vidal zipped his lips. Coady – fussy and uptight compared to Egus's fascinating nuttiness – sometimes appeared in their meetings, though God knew why. Maybe to give him some illusion of responsibility, since he was still officially a director of Zeroth and there was precious little need for marketing or product evangelism, as far as Vidal could tell. The woman showed them into the office and followed them, the appointment book changed into an electronic tablet in her hand. The door closed itself behind them and Vidal took in the simulation of Egus's wide desk, with just a couple of slim and elegant screens, a stylus and a tablet positioned on it. Egus wasn't here yet, so Vidal parked himself on one of the comfortable visitors' chairs, its pads of luxury imitation leather and ergonomic steel frame pushing back perfectly against his weight.

Behind Egus's chair was a wide window taking in a vista of how this sector of Green Valley used to be, how it would have been at this time of year; the trees on the hills just about turned, mostly brown against a pale blue sky, but with a sparkle of red and yellow leaves shivering in the breeze. He swivelled on his chair and looked up at David, who hadn't sat yet and was hovering in the centre of the room beside the assistant, who looked like she was ready to take a coffee order. Vidal never ate or drank in this place.

'Why does he do it?' he asked, the question so idle he hadn't aimed it at anyone in particular.

'Why does he do what?' David said.

'All of this. Meeting rooms and offices, receptionists and jobs. He could just as easily take his meetings sitting on top of a giant mushroom, smoking opium. Why does he choose to pretend to work in an office building, when his choices are unlimited?'

Vidal got more of David Coady's opinion than he'd expected, expressed in the persuasive tones of his public voice. 'This building, the campus, Green Valley – he made it all before the outsiders turned on him. It's real, where we're walking – Jamie Egus built it. It's his legacy and he wants to hold onto it.'

'He wants to carry on believing it's real,' the assistant added from behind them. Vidal turned to see her thousand-mile stare out of the window and into the hills. 'He doesn't want to let it all dissolve away.'

'I wonder if he misses it.' Vidal gestured towards the window.

'I don't,' the assistant said, coming around the desk to sit on his chair. She spun halfway towards the window and pointed out of it. 'It's all out there still. And it's all in here,' she said, tapping her forehead.

Vidal straightened, annoyed at having been caught out by such a childish prank. For a churlish moment he resisted respecting the great man, but remembered that he was there to do business and decided to stand. 'Oh, uh, Mr Egus. Good to see you again.' He put out his hand, and as Egus shook it with his borrowed soft, slim fingers, David came to sit in the chair beside him, smirking at Vidal's discomfort.

Egus sat back in her – his – chair. 'Someone new I'm trying,' he said, twisting from side to side in the chair with the energy of a bright, bored kid. 'As you say, why should I feel constrained? That's what we do here. We delimit communication. We revolutionise identity, change the way you think about it. Don't we, David?'

'Yes, that's right,' Coady uttered slavishly.

'We don't like to feel constrained by traditional methods, but I don't see that as any reason to go floating around on clouds or sitting on mushrooms or swimming with dolphins in bubbles of water on a daily basis. I happen to love this office. I always have. We designed it with love and intention and respect. So I stay here.'

'I get that,' Vidal said.

'Perhaps you'll be more comfortable if I change my body?' Now he became the younger Jamie Egus, who the world had seen on magazine covers twenty years ago, in the lime-green hoodie and jeans he liked to wear. 'Or this?' He immediately aged two decades, his hair mostly silvered, much longer, thoughtfully unkempt, with a trim greying goatee.

'I really don't mind,' Vidal said. 'I'm not at all

uncomfortable.' *I really don't give a fuck, more to the point,* he thought. *Let's just get these documents out of the way.*

Egus steepled his fingers under his chin. His eyes were more expressive than most avatars', giving too much away, shifting between sharp, intelligent scrutiny and a dull interior stare. *Nothing is an error,* Vidal reminded himself. Despite the demise of his empire and his obsessive clinging onto the scraps, Egus remained the man who had almost taken over the world by consensual coup.

'So you'll have copies of the new contracts,' Vidal said. He'd scanned and forwarded them from Gina Orban's office a couple of days before. 'I'll just need your signature to extend the contracts for another six months and to continue the payments to the suppliers.'

'And your commission, of course,' Egus said.

Vidal nodded and smiled, but inwardly grated. His commission was a fact of the transaction; it went without saying, unless Egus was somehow implying that Vidal was making undue gains. Perhaps it was a sign of increasing desperation in Green Valley that Egus should seem, for the first time in his life, to be worrying about money.

'The farmers are still on board?' Egus asked. 'I hear there's drought out there. Will they still be able to supply the nutrients we need alongside their other demands?'

'The farmers I have contracted supply Green Valley exclusively.'

'Even in a drought?'

'Even then.'

'Good. You're certain there are still no animal by-products in it? Nobody taking shortcuts? I won't become part of that particular social disease.'

'Yes, I'm certain.'

Egus called the document up on his screen. 'You'll have noted our reduced requirements for both nutrients and materials. You've reflected that in the new contracts, I see. That's all good.'

Vidal had noted the reduction: thirty per cent less foodstuff and fifty per cent fewer materials. Every order had been slashed and he knew this gig would be up soon. 'Mr Egus...'

'What's on your mind?'

'We need to talk about an exit strategy. The way these orders are declining, it may become hard to keep even one farmer exclusively bound. Maybe you just want to wrap it up?'

'So you're going to leave us on our sinking ship? Go sniff out richer scraps elsewhere?'

'That's not what I meant. I'm happy to arrange supplies as long as you need. I just wonder how long that will be.' Vidal bristled at being called a rat. From what he'd seen, Green Valley had sunk a long time ago, and it was only Egus's delusion that was shoring up the pretence that it was still working in any form. He bit his tongue and focussed on the bottom line. This wasn't just selfishness; he had his daughter's future to worry about. 'Maybe your plans are changing.'

Egus's eyes cycled through an opaque moment. 'I'll let you know.' Even the jovial old wizard's voice he'd chosen couldn't disguise the cold, sharp glint of steel in the words.

'And are you sure,' Vidal was compelled to ask Egus again, like he had every time they'd met, 'that they can't overhear us in here? That the Stanton police, the NSA, the authorities, whoever, aren't following your every move and your every conversation?'

Egus barked out a scornful laugh. 'There is no way those dullards could ever break our layers of encryption.'

'You sound very confident.' *Too confident, maybe*, he thought.

'People like me wrote every line of code they used for their surveillance systems. We're the only ones who understood it. We built in some useful vulnerabilities.'

'Do you think they have a clue?' David added in his evangelical tone. 'We built it all. And then they tore it down. We check every day, like *Homo sapiens* scanning the sky for intelligent life, but there's nothing but dead air out there. They're still grubbing around in their caves with their clubs and wall paintings. Do you think those Neanderthals could even rub two sticks together to make fire?'

Vidal would leave Coady and Egus to their smug celebration. Surely they knew the truth – there was no way they couldn't be aware of what had become of Green Valley under its roof – but the awareness was buried under too many layers of denial and delusion. He changed the subject.

'Is the nutrient mix still working for you? You're all getting what you need?'

'We're getting by.'

Not what he'd seen, not by a long way, but he was increasingly anxious to be done in here. This place started to work at your nerves if you hung around for too long. 'Great. So if I can just get those signatures, we'll be good to go.'

Egus picked up his stylus and signed the electronic documents. 'I'll see you again, Mr Barrett. No doubt when your money runs out.'

Vidal stood and went to the door without answering. He'd had enough of this shit.

'Hang on.' A woman's voice, Egus as assistant. She came up behind Vidal and he could smell her shampoo and her citrusy deodorant. She put her hand on his shoulder and leaned into his neck, her breath warming his skin as she spoke. 'By the way, you have a tail. Out there.' She extended a finger towards the window of fake landscape, but Vidal knew where she meant: beyond the wall.

'What?' he said.

'You're being monitored by the police. Electronic, the whole primitive routine. Like it's 1984.'

He shook himself away from the drape of her arms and turned chest-on to face her. 'No, you're wrong. They don't do that any more. We rejected this' – he swept his hand around the entire facsimile – 'this bullshit.'

Egus laughed, a pretty trill, the sort of amusement Vidal would normally yearn to cause in a woman. 'They do. And they are.' Egus turned to David. 'You might like to know who's after him. It's your sister-in-law, David.'

'How can you know that?'

'We left a tracer in her, of course.'

14 Checking his rear-view mirror, Vidal noticed no movement in the sterile shadow of the wall as he pulled away and headed back to the city. He puffed out his cheeks and tried to blow out his anxiety. It was possible that Egus was just a raving paranoiac, but just as possible he was telling the truth. Taking the kids behind Egus's back, even lifting Coady's own daughter from his own home, had been safe – or so he'd thought. Once he'd got them outside the wall, there was no way they could follow him – or so he'd thought. But if Coady's sister-in-law, here in the real world, was a spook, and if she was onto him, that changed things – she had more personal stakes in the case than any of the other spooks: she would want her niece safe. Egus had said she was *monitoring* him, and that word coming from his (fake) mouth implied that she had access to electronic surveillance. True or not, he had to activate his contingency plans.

Vidal unlocked the high chain-link gate down the alleyway into the small lot behind his office building, got back in his car and parked. He'd spotted a uniformed patrol officer hanging around on the street opposite the office's front door, and while street cops weren't especially common in this part of town, they weren't a complete rarity either. He never used to be the sort of person who would get infected by other people's paranoia, but the thought of Sofie getting into trouble sent ice through his veins. Coming out of the alley and rounding into Ocean Street, Vidal scanned the sidewalks. It took a moment to spot him, but there was the patrolman, staring into the window of the pharmacy a way down the block, much too idly.

Crap, Egus was telling the truth.

Vidal had naively thought the cops wouldn't waste a second on dead Green Valley kids. It was Sofie's idea to place the girl in the bakery. Something the kid had told her about her family. Vidal liked to think he would have dealt with it more cleanly, just weighted the bodies down in the canal and be done with them, but faced with Sofie's kindness, her humanity, he'd gone along with her decision to honour the kids in some small way. But that cop was still sauntering back and forth in front of the kebab place; he knew it was a mistake, and it mustn't happen again.

He unlocked the security gate at the front door of the office and walked inside. *Barrett & Sanders, Family Law*. If anyone asked, Sanders was an uncle who had died, but Sanders never existed; Vidal had thought two names would make his practice sound more like a firm, less like a flimsy one-man show. When he'd opened, Dierdra had surprised him with a plaque of the yellow rooster that was the firm's emblem; that was back when she'd loved him, when she'd bothered to do things like that for him. The yellow rooster, Upright Gallo, was a character in a running joke they used to share when they were lovers. The plaque, cemented next to the sign behind the reception desk, used to make him smile every time he saw it, and now still burped a tiny bubble of warmth up him, like a conditioned response. He'd made something of himself, he'd benefited from Dierdra's partnership for many years, and there was still something to show for it.

The three clients in the waiting room were also glad for his efforts. He did his best for them, better than they could normally expect from the justice system, and he wasn't out to cheat them – which is why he could absolutely justify his peri-legal excursions to himself. He had never intended any harm.

'Afternoon, Tertia,' he said to his paralegal plenipotentiary at the front desk, then smiled at the old couple waiting deferentially at the edge of the seats, as if they couldn't presume to make themselves at ease here, in the face of the awesome monolith that was the law. Their seven-year-old grandson Peter was caught up watching the pneums racing in and out through the transparent tubes he'd installed just for fun. 'I'm sorry to be late, Mr and Mrs Alvarez. Peter, come get a soft drink and we'll start.'

When Sofie knocked at the door later that afternoon, Vidal was shunting a tube with documents from three cases into the pneum to the civil court. Tertia got up to let her in and Vidal invited her into his office, closing his door.

'Coffee, sweetie?' he said.

'Nah. What's up, Dad?'

'Listen, Sofe, you can't come here any more. You must go straight home after school.'

'Why?'

Vidal wanted to lie to her, to protect her, but he remembered his promise that he would never bullshit her. 'We're being watched by the police.'

She straightened and turned in her chair, staring at the door as if she could see through it. Her face hardened and Vidal thought back to the Green Valley masks; looking at the flesh-and-blood face of this real girl, he could read her mind. Defiance, pride, anger, grief.

'So?' she shrugged. 'Let them.' She raised her voice, as if they could hear her, or as if she suspected they were listening in on their conversation with some electronic device, and she wanted them to know she was not afraid.

But what would she know about bugs? She was only a little kid before the Turn.

'I didn't mean to get you into this but you need to stop, right now.'

She glared at him, sneering at his mortifying attempt at parental authority. Christ, how would he be able to stop her doing what she wanted to do? It would be his fault if she got into trouble. Openness, honesty, talking to her like an adult would be his only chance.

'Sorry. The truth is, I just expected the police to turn a blind eye to these kids. They've always treated people from Green Valley as invisible. Despite anyone's personal feelings about the terms of the Partition Treaty, what Zeroth did was legal. As a corporation, they hadn't been found guilty of any crime. All along, they had been incorporated as an independent town council, and they were within their rights to administer their town as they saw fit. Stanton PD's got a lot on its plate, much more to do than concern itself with our newly independent neighbour.'

'But building that massive wall, that roof,' Sofie said. 'Surely that would need special planning permission?'

The girl was following right alongside him, sharp as a tack, Vidal thought with a swell of pride. Maybe she could be his Sanders in times to come. 'Yeah, that's the other side of it. They still had a lot of money, and they spent it to help their plans along, just as they had to fast-track the incorporation of Green Valley years before. The mayor, councillors, senior police – it was all in their interest to keep quiet and leave Green Valley alone. And the way the treaty was pushed through so quickly, before anyone had a chance to understand it. I'm sure they're still getting paid off, but of course nobody can prove anything. That's why I'm surprised anybody's showing any interest in the kids. Officially, they don't exist, and they're certainly not in Stanton's purview. Why would they upset the status quo now?'

'Maybe it's because they were found here, in Stanton's jurisdiction?'

'I don't know. Before Green Valley was sealed completely and after the wall went up, a few people living there came across, to buy supplies and visit family. They'd be targeted, mugged, a couple were murdered. The cops never flinched. Not their business.' He paused, thinking what had actually changed, then repeated, 'The kids don't exist. Even if the cops investigated for whatever reason, and they found their deaths to be suspicious, it's a crime on nobody. These people were no longer citizens. Why would they want to add ghosts to their list of unsolved deaths? That's what I don't understand.'

Sofie nodded, frowning.

'There must be some new element,' Vidal said. 'Something new complicating the mix.'

At that moment, they heard a thumping on the ceiling, a muffled scream. Sofie started out of her chair and was on her way out of the door already.

'No, Sofe. You can't be involved any more.'

'I don't care!'

Vidal tailed her down the corridor to the back of the office suite, not shouting, not running, not wanting to make a scene in front of the clients, past the bathroom and the kitchenette and to the locked steel door barring the back stairs. He'd painted it turquoise to make it seem less out of place, shunted into the back of the office with its adobe-lite decor. Sofie was using her keys to unlock the door, and the second she opened it, a half-naked, skinny little kid bowled her way out, knocking Vidal over. He whacked the side of his head on a steel filing cabinet and bit back the moan of pain as Rainbow and Sofie headed past him, chasing the kid, who was howling her head off in the reception area. He picked himself up and ventured carefully to the scene, trying to smile in a comforting way at the middle-aged couple in the waiting area. They were the Williams divorce, and they were unconsciously huddling together, Franco grasping Melissa's thigh and Melissa with her arm through her husband's. Nothing like the soul-scream of a banshee to melt away marital strife, Vidal noted fleetingly.

But now he stopped, watching the two older girls squatting down near the scared little one, hands up and arms out, ready to take her in. He knew that a grown man like him was the last person who would be able to calm this particular child down, and he left the teens to it. Together, they folded her into a soothing embrace, Sofie allowing the child to wipe her snot and tears and filthy hair into her sweater.

This was why Sofie wanted to be involved. This was why she needed to be involved. This was why what they had done was right.

Eventually, the girl was calm enough to go back towards the stairs, Rainbow following behind her saying, 'I won't make you. Promise. Only when you're ready.' Melissa and Franco had shifted a yard apart again, and Vidal collared Sofie as she passed him.

'What happened?'

'Rainbow tried to get her in the shower.'

'Christ. How did she get through the security gate upstairs?'

A complicit look darted between Sofie and Rainbow. 'We left it open by mistake. Do you still want me to go home?' Sofie said to him.

He suddenly realised what he had to do. He shouldn't have left it so long. 'Yes, in fact,' he checked his watch. It was nearly four. 'We both need to go home now.'

15

'I don't know what more you want from me,' Jordan said, his Adam's apple bobbing as he sucked on his cigarette, slurping the smoke down like it was oxygen. A dense thunderhead was blotting out the sky, bringing night down early and making the lights in the buildings opposite glare across at us where we stood on the precinct's rooftop terrace. Squalls of wind kicked dust and pigeon feathers into a noxious whirl with Jordan's smoke as he exhaled. 'I put the patrol on Barrett's office, and I'm already getting stick from upstairs, asking me why. I can't waste resources on unregistered kids.'

'They're dead, Jordan,' I insisted. 'You've got yet another dead child on your books. This is not just about me and my family. It's not just personal.'

He gave me a doleful *yeah-right* nod. Fuck him, but he was right – this was too personal for me; professional impartiality was out of the window. I'd assumed Kira was safe with David in Green Valley; I'd let her slip from my mind, but I had grievously failed Odille. I should have done more. There was every chance that my niece was undernourished and diseased just like the other dead children, next in line to turn up in the morgue.

I searched Jordan's face for his real feelings. I couldn't believe that I was the only person in this entire city who gave a damn about dead kids turning up out of nowhere. If these were Stanton kids, especially from North Harbour or Sunset Drive – rather than, say, Claymarket – the police commissioner and the mayor would be in their waders dredging the sewers personally for clues. I knew who was moving these kids, even if I couldn't prove yet that he had anything to do with their deaths. You'd think Jordan would be glad to have a lead at last, but here he was, giving me his thin-shouldered shrug.

'I have to provide compelling reasons why Barrett is a suspect,' he continued, gladly abdicating any involvement in a messy situation – just like I had when Odille died. 'So far, I have nothing. We broke into his apartment and saw no evidence, apart from that he seems to be a responsible parent with neat habits.'

'I'm telling you, I know it's him. I just can't tell you how. There is evidence, though. Can't you trust me, Jordan?'

He turned his angular face towards me, his eyes sunken even further into shadow than normal by the gloom and backwards slant of the floodlights lighting the rooftop. 'No, I'm not sure if I can any more.' He said it sadly, and his words hurt me.

The truth was receding as fast as the light, I knew. Soon, it would be dark and I'd never find Kira. So I decided to tell him; I'd deal with the fallout from Sentinel when it came. 'Okay, here's what I've got. It may sound trivial, but it's one undeniable, direct link between Barrett and Kira. I accessed his dossier, tax records, company filings – his corporate logo is a yellow rooster.'

'That's all?' he sneered, starting to turn away.

'The same rooster, Jordan. The exact same rooster David showed me when I was in Green Valley. The abductor left it behind at the scene.'

'He left a rooster at the scene?'

'Sort of. Residue, an electronic fingerprint of an old digital calling card.'

He shook his head and stubbed out his cigarette, puffing

out his last breath into the wind so it doubled back and hit me in the face. '*Accessed his dossier.* That's some intrusive shit you've got going on in there.'

I was growing tired of his stubbornness. Why couldn't he see? 'It's called police work, Jordan. Do you remember? That's what the police used to do. They'd find criminals.'

'Yeah, but not by spying. Not any more. That was in the bad old days, and we're pretty sure we don't want to go back there.'

'For Christ's sake,' I sighed. 'You have to admit: if you had that chain of evidence, you'd consider it at least enough to make him a person of interest, worth a look.'

Jordan lit up another cigarette, cowling his shoulders and lean fingers around the flame.

'Wouldn't you? Isn't it?' I pressed.

Then he narrowed his lips in an approximation of a smile. 'Yeah.' I knew that deep down he was impressed or envious. If I got him drunk one night, I bet I could get him to admit he wished for resources like Sentinel's. But he'd never be able to state that on the record, not as an officer of the consensual peace.

'So?'

'So what?' he said.

'Can I get a patrol on the girl's school? Get a twenty-four-hour monitor at the apartment? Get eyes in the office?'

He shook his head. 'I'm not going to help you break into his office so that you can bug it. Never, so get over it. Ask your spooky friends if you want to do that. All you have is footage that doesn't officially exist, and a "digital calling card" that you can't show anyone.'

I strode off to the other side of the terrace, grinding my teeth and balling my fists, my nails digging hard into my palms. 'I like the way you're a stickler for the rules all of a sudden,' I mumbled. He shot me a warning look, and I knew I'd gone too far. 'Sorry. Forget it,' I said, as I made for the stairwell door, knowing that I'd blown it. Nobody else would help me. It was done.

'Wait,' he said, and I turned. 'You misunderstand me. I'm with you on this. Like you, I do care. I want to know what killed those kids as much as you do. Do you think it's fun for me to take snapshots of dead kids and be told to file them away as if they didn't exist? There are people up there' – he pointed upwards, meaning *upstairs*, in the police and city hierarchy, but all he was pointing at was the bruised and swirling storm clouds so it looked like he was talking about some ancient, all-powerful deity – 'who strongly and aggressively *don't* care, and get very upset if people care when they're told not to.' As if punctuating his point, a bolt of lightning gathered and belted down somewhere close by, and fat raindrops were shaken out of the cloud. Jordan hurried behind me into the stairwell. On the first landing he said, in a low voice, 'I don't think your methods are good detective work. Snooping and drawing prefabricated conclusions from the comfort of your office. That's not the way to find the truth. I'll be able to get you the patrol at the school tomorrow, and we can ask around. But we need to go carefully.'

He dropped his cigarette butt on the floor and ground it out. 'All right?'

'All right,' I confirmed. 'Thank you.'

16

'You made it,' Fabian said, coming from the kitchen and wiping his hands on a dishtowel as I walked into the apartment.

For a second I thought he was being sarcastic, still bitter from our argument the night before, so I answered defensively. 'I had to wait out the rain; it was—'

But he approached me and kissed me warmly on the cheek, moving his hand to my back and pulling me in for a moment. 'I'm glad to see you,' he said. 'Come get some wine when you're ready. I'm making pasta.'

I was grateful to him for breaking the ice between us; I didn't want to fight tonight. I wanted, somehow, to dial down my mind, which had been whirring at a burnout pitch ever since David had called. I showered and dressed in better clothes, then joined Fabian at the kitchen counter. I downed the glass of wine he'd poured then refilled it. I poked at the fresh herbs decorating the pasta with my fork. I couldn't eat. How could I? How could I even sit in this luxurious, glossy room while Kira was lost and afraid, waiting for help, Jordan's team coming too late? Or worse… Something like a sob lurched out of my chest and I pushed my plate away, hiding my face from Fabian.

'You're not okay,' he said.

'No,' I said. 'I'm sorry, Fabe.'

'Please,' he said, 'don't say sorry.' He looked at me in silence, clearing all the space in the room for me to talk, and for him to listen.

'I really thought Kira was all right in there. Odille loved David, and trusted him. They wanted the best for their child. Of course they did.' I glanced at his face and he looked back, all patience and receptiveness.

'I didn't want to bring her in here. I didn't want to bring my ancient, grubby history into your home. But now...'

'What's happened?'

'She's missing. David can't find her; he says someone's taken her. And I shouldn't be speaking about it, but...'

'Go on.'

'Green Valley children have been turning up in Stanton, dead. Three so far, and I'm so scared that Kira's next. David can't find her,' I repeated, willing the statement to prove itself false. 'The police are looking out here, but there's nothing. I feel so fucking helpless.'

'Is there anything more you can do? I mean at... your work. Do you need to go somewhere and do it? Can I help you?'

Even now, even while Fabian was being the perfect, gentle partner, I couldn't trust him enough to tell him the truth. I didn't trust him to love me more than his principles. So I said, 'There's nothing for me to do but wait. Jordan's got good officers out looking for her. They have a lead, but I sit here, just waiting for him to call, to tell me that they've found her, and every minute that goes by I think I should be doing something more, but there's nothing more I can do. I'm useless to my only remaining family, Fabian.' I pushed away from the counter, the stool scraping on the tiles and tottering. 'I don't want to just sit here and eat your lovely pasta and pretend that everything's fine. I wish it was, but it's not.'

I lay next to Fabian and waited for him to fall asleep, and I must have gone under myself, because it was 3 a.m. when I pinged awake, the fervent noise in my mind quick out of the traps. It was as if I was living in a different time zone and I thought for a minute of all those people, thousands of miles away, who were eating breakfast legitimately, seeing sunrise out of their window after a night full of sleep. I couldn't remember when last I'd slept a whole night through. I'd sleep again when this was over.

The bed was so comfortable, I lay in a stupor for a few minutes, battling the swirling lists in my head and willing back the oblivion, but Fabian had pulled up the mohair blanket and its tickle on my nose was what finally encouraged me to move. I got up to pee, and then closed myself in the study again. If I couldn't sleep, at least I could watch other people sleeping.

Flicking through the camera angles on my monitor and adjusting the earphones to a low volume, I settled back in my chair and watched. Vidal and Sofie Barrett were doing what normal citizens do at three in the morning, and observing them was a meditation. For the first time this week, I had a chance to think about everything I'd seen, my mind gradually grinding it into some sort of processed material. I spent hours like that, looking at them sleep, shifting only when it became uncomfortable. The sky was already beginning to lighten when I noticed it.

A glow at the window, around the rim of the blackout curtains in Sofie's bedroom, followed thirty seconds later by a double flash. Sofie sat up for a second, then turned and went back to sleep.

I rewound and turned the volume up. There. An answering rumble of thunder.

I looked out of the window at the washed violet sky, the last morning stars flickering out against the approaching sun. There were no clouds out there; that storm had run its course last night.

Jordan had dragged on some track pants and a dressing gown before answering my hammering knock. When he saw that it was me, he stepped back and widened the door.

'What's the matter?' he slurred.

He ground his eyes with the heel of his palm, the gown angling open. I couldn't help but see the scattering of hair over his sunken, bony chest. He scowled and tightened the gown, leaving the door open for me to follow him inside.

It was the first time I'd breathed the cigarette-and-cheese funk of his apartment. The stubby hall led to a poky kitchen-dining room with an uncurtained window looking at the back of another block. Peering into his bedroom, I saw a barely ruffled three-quarter bed crammed in beside a neatly stacked desk. His apartment was about the same size as the one I had grown up in; at least this was in a decent building, in a better neighbourhood than Claymarket, but still I felt guilty, having rushed here from my five-star lodgings to batter him awake.

'I'm sorry,' I said, as he carried a bundle of clothes past me to the bathroom. 'I waited until I thought you'd be up.' The petty lie and the apology rolled off my lips.

He nodded at me wordlessly.

'Something urgent's come up. I need you to come with me, and there's no time to wait. We may already be too late.'

As we got past the security guard and up the stairs to the landing, I signalled Jordan to stop. I took my tablet out of my bag and showed him the feed. On the screen, Vidal and Sofie were still in bed, just where I'd left them, and for good measure, just in case I was wrong, we padded silently along the corridor. As we rounded the turn in the corridor, we surprised a neighbour heading out early and locking her door. I startled back towards the wall, trying to look innocent, but Jordan proceeded with besuited authority, nodding at her once. The woman gave us a quizzical glance, but kept her questions to herself like a good citizen.

When we got to Barrett's door, I pulled out the tablet and checked the screen again – no change, they were still in bed inside – and Jordan unholstered his pistol, finally allowing himself to check on the feed. I smirked at the minor moral victory, but he kept a stony face as he hammered on the door with his fist. 'Police!'

I killed the monitor screen and slipped it back in my satchel. 'They're not here,' I said.

'But your machine...' he whispered, gun still at the ready. 'It shows them right there, in bed.'

I shook my head. 'We're too late.'

This time, Jordan insisted on entering legally. It took a while for him to persuade the guard to call the landlord for authorisation. The little man stood at the threshold as we trailed through the apartment. It was pretty much as we'd last seen it, except this time all the dishes were washed and packed away, the fridge had been emptied of fresh produce. There were gaps and empty hangers in the closet, and the toothbrushes and some toiletries were absent, along with Sofie and Vidal Barrett.

In Vidal's bedroom, out of sight of the keyholder, I showed Jordan the screen. Vidal and Sofie still fast asleep, no sign of us on the feed. 'What's the matter with it?' he asked, wilfully feigning ignorance. 'Can you fast-forward to now?'

'This is the live feed. He's put it on a loop.'

'You knew that all along.'

'Yeah, but I hoped we had a chance to catch them leaving. That's why the early wake-up call.'

'How did you know?'

When I'd discovered the loop, I'd scanned through the last several hours of buffered footage. It had taken a while to isolate the flashes at such a high speed, but eventually I found them, three hours and ten minutes before, six hours and twenty. The same rhythm, *rumble... bang, bang.* Sofie sitting up and turning over.

'They knew we were watching,' he said. I noticed the 'we' and banked it.

'Yeah.' I glanced at the invisible installation I'd made in the cornice, and then at Jordan. 'Someone must have told them.'

17

I might have read it as guilt, or it might have been because he was telling the truth when he said he cared about the invisible children, but Jordan threw himself into the investigation that day. He knew as well as I did that the longer Vidal Barrett was off our radar, the less chance we'd have of ever finding out what happened to those kids. He blew off all his other cases for the day, prepared to deal with the captain's flak for spending all his man-hours on helping with a non-existent case.

We drove straight to Barrett's office, which was in a tenement on the edge of Claymarket, two blocks from where I'd grown up, but showing more signs of the changes that had come over the city. The brickwork had been acid-cleaned and repointed, and the ground-floor windows of the office suite reframed in wood. On the same stretch of Ocean Street, down from the office, was Suds Ease, the ancient laundromat my mother and I used to take our clothes to when the machine in the tenement's basement was broken, and Sweet Times, the candy store that had been there for ever. I noted that they were offering *Artisanal Drops and Bespoke Gums Made on Premises* for five times the price of the same thing at the supermarket, while an expensive hair salon pushed its chest out from the storefront in between, reminding me of Main Street, Green Valley.

While Jordan went to stake out Sofie's school, I waited with Berna Danielewski, the patrol officer on the one-to-nine shift, drinking coffee at the counter across the front window of the diner opposite Barrett's office. She'd seen nothing unusual overnight, and Vidal Barrett hadn't come into the building. We watched Barrett's receptionist unlocking the office at twenty past eight and workers rushing their kids to school before catching the bus.

'You've been with the force for a long time, haven't you, Officer?' I said. Danielewski looked around seventy, though she had to be younger than sixty, the mandatory retirement age; sucked towards the ground, grey and sagging, by her beat. She winced when she got off and on the stool at the counter, and I wondered why she'd stayed in uniform all this time, never made it to detective or an office job.

Her eyes were still trained on the building opposite. 'Retiring soon.'

'You've been a cop all your life?'

She glanced at me for a second, and shrugged. 'Not when I was a kid.'

'So you were on the beat before the Turn?'

'Sure.'

'It's hard to meet people who were, you know. So many people from before seem to have been swept away, under the rug, changed jobs afterwards. It's hard to remember what things were like back then, like we're not allowed to think about them.'

'If you talked like that, I probably pepper-sprayed you on your university campus back then.'

I couldn't help laughing. 'I wasn't exactly an instigator back then, but still, I never dreamed I'd end up working for the police.' So much had changed in the last twenty years since I was in college, but nothing had. One sort of protest had been replaced by another. Officer Danielewski's life had turned out just as hard as it would have if the Turn had never happened. Claymarket was still Claymarket; people still grinding away at a grubby, difficult existence. Maybe we hadn't evolved at all. It all made me nostalgic for Zeroth's false promises – at least they offered a vision.

Next to me, Officer Danielewski spluttered, derailing my train of thought. I thought she was choking for a second, then I realised she was laughing. 'I can tell you're a bit of a square peg.'

'How so?'

Danielewski just shook her head and drained her coffee, eyes trained on Barrett & Sanders.

I scanned the building, a squat, unadorned brick cube of four storeys. While the blinds came up and the lights went on in the windows below, nothing stirred in the three storeys above. The thick drapes never twitched. 'Surely someone lives there or works there. You don't think it's suspicious, the very lack of movement?' *The very...* I cringed at myself. Next to this old-school Claymarket woman, and milk-fed in Fabian's Museum District apartment, I'd become a hollow poser. Of course someone like her could see right through someone like me, the person I'd become.

'Maybe. Or maybe it doesn't mean anything.'

Officer Danielewski's relief arrived, posting himself outside the diner's window, and she eased herself off the stool and hobbled out, offering me a nod. I watched her go, feeling like a fraud. Wouldn't it be great if we could switch between avatars at will? My problem then, I guess, would be choosing who the hell I wanted to be.

To my relief, Jordan came to rescue me from my mood before too long. 'Up, up, Detective Lucie,' he said, apparently over his gloom of earlier. His morning stimulants had evidently kicked in. 'The daughter didn't go to school today. We've got work to do.'

The first work we did was cross the street. Jordan rattled at the law firm's door handle until the receptionist peered through the pane, frowning. I noted the steel bars slotted behind the new-wood frame, the double-thick, security-laminated glass. Trustful cottage gentility hadn't quite completed its invasion of Claymarket yet.

'Do you have an appointment?' the receptionist asked as she retreated behind her desk to look at the large-format appointment book. The firm's offices were neat and tidy, with an off-the-shelf anonymity of design, as if Vidal had paid someone to decorate the office and never looked twice at the result. The vase of sticks on top of the receptionist's filing cabinet was silvered with dusty cobwebs, a redundant intricacy the cleaning service wasn't paid to handle. Behind the desk, screwed into the pastel-purple wall, the firm's name and logo: a yellow rooster, the stylised rooster David had found in Kira's bedroom.

Jordan introduced himself and me to the woman, who said her name was Tertia Pineira and that she'd worked for Barrett & Sanders for four years.

'Mr Barrett's not in yet,' she offered.

Jordan checked the clock on the wall. 'He usually come in this late?'

'No, not at all. He's usually here before me.' She paused, perhaps considering that she might be implicating her employer in something. 'But he often has meetings, then he comes in.'

'Did he tell you he had a meeting this morning? Did he log anything?' he asked, bending his long frame over the desk in the direction of the appointment book.

As Jordan and the receptionist talked, my leg started shaking and I looked down at it, as if it was someone else's, but along with the judder came a flush of panic, my chest filling up with lead and stopping. 'We're wasting time here, Jordan,' I said. 'None of this matters.'

But he seemed not to hear me, trading chitchat with this woman who could tell us nothing useful. My eye was drawn to the rooster, and I would swear that it spoke to me, if that didn't sound crazy. 'Are we going on holiday?' it said.

I wandered away from the reception desk, goose bumps rising painfully over my skin, past a row of chairs in a waiting area and down a narrow side passage with a sign indicating *Toilets*. Maybe that's where my leg wanted me to go. I was feeling nauseous, the bitter diner coffee churning with bile in my growling stomach. Cold sweat was pricking on my brow and a stream of saliva was washing my mouth.

I tried to make for the bathroom door, but my right leg dragged me further down the corridor towards a heavy, steel-riveted turquoise door at the far end. Then it stopped me there and the quivering moved from my right knee and into my arms, and the neurons in my head zapped as I waited. I knew I should move, but I couldn't. My body had planted me there, and I had to wait.

Everything stopped but the palsy of my muscles. The world around me disappeared, and there was only the turquoise doorway and the quaking periphery.

Someone was bowling downstairs, somewhere beyond the door, hooves clacking like gunshots against the concrete.

The door smashed outward, and I saw the yellow slits of his eyes and the foul gnarl of his horns and smelled his breath before he ran right over me, belting me to the floor, crushing my shoulder against a waste bin as he went. As I fell, I caught a flash of the inside of the stairwell, a pair of small, bare feet pointed through the railing, a trail of blood running over the toes and lazily following the black ram's course before the grey sheen over my eyes became too thick to see through.

When I could push myself against the wall and open my eyes, the turquoise door was closed and there was no blood on the floor. But my shoulder still throbbed and my gut was still swirling and the muscles in my back had seized up.

'Where've you gone?' I heard Jordan calling, and desperately pulled myself upright. I didn't want him to see me like this again, but it was too late. Although I had managed to stand up, I was still leaning woozily against the wall and I guess my face looked as ashen and clammy as it felt because as he came to me, the receptionist trailing a couple of hurried paces behind him, he muttered, 'Again?' I was relieved that he didn't make more of it in front of the woman.

'I'm just having a look around, if you don't mind,' I managed, pulling my jacket straight. 'Where does that doorway lead?'

'Up to the apartments above, but it's permanently locked,' Tertia said, her eyes darting almost out of her head.

'Who lives up there?' Jordan said.

'Tenants.'

He waited but she added nothing else. 'How do they get into their apartments?'

'Through the back,' she said.

'Will you show us?'

She led us back out onto Ocean Street, then into the access lane on the side of the building, and stopped in front of a weed-strewn lot that was closed off by a double-tall chain-link truck gate, which in turn was topped by a loop of razor wire.

'Doesn't look that easy to get in,' Jordan commented.

'The tenants have keys to the padlocks,' Tertia said, warming to her lie, indignation creeping into her voice. She pointed out the two heavy chains that secured the fence.

'Does Mr Barrett have keys to the padlocks too?' he asked.

'Yeah, of course. He parks here. When he's at the office.'

Jordan moved to the fence and threaded his fingers though the links, staring up at the tenement's windows, just as dead as the ones at the front. 'It's very quiet. How many people live here?'

Tertia shrugged. 'I don't know. I need to get back to my desk.'

'Sure. Go ahead.'

I watched her go, and didn't even have to tell Jordan that I thought she was lying. Something flickered at one of the windows on the second floor; I glanced up to catch the motion, but everything was still again. Maybe it was a pigeon or a cat; maybe not. The growl of the traffic from Ocean Street funnelled into the alleyway, making it impossible to hear any small sounds over the rumble. The scent of diesel smoke and piss and dirty drains wafted in the swirling breeze with cooking aromas and refrigerant from air-conditioning units – the back end of any building in the city. 'It would be good to get in there, wouldn't it?'

'We'd need cause,' he said. 'And a proper warrant.'

So instead we plodded about the neighbourhood, asking shopkeepers and barmen when last they'd seen Vidal, if they'd seen him with any small kids – no, not his daughter, but younger ones, maybe a bit dirty, in clothes that didn't fit them? We took out our sheaf of photographs, asking: did either Vidal or Sofie Barrett purchase new clothes, sneakers like this, hair ties like this? Had anyone overheard anything about missing children, any children who needed to move anywhere?

The first hit was at the Bayview Bookstore, where Sofie had bought a pile of markdown kids' books. The old guy on the counter recognised her from her picture and remembered her because she was 'pretty cute'. 'She's sixteen years old, you know that?' Jordan said, the poison in his eyes making the bookseller shrivel.

The supermarket manager, for his part, didn't have a clue: 'Lots of people buy lots of stuff here.'

'You remember, don't you, Jordan?' I said, as we clanked the security gate shut behind us and headed up the street.

'What?' Jordan stopped and curled himself around the cigarette he was trying to relight. An old woman with a wheeled shopping basket came past and tutted, presumably because he was lighting up over a tray of fish on ice outside a general store.

'Closed-circuit TV. Aren't you ever nostalgic?'

'Don't start,' he sighed out with a mouthful of smog.

'Imagine being able to rewind and get a photo of Barrett from the screen. Hey, remember computerised stock records and transaction details? You could see exactly what was bought at that till at that time, and the method of payment. Name, address, all that handy information.'

'I said don't start.'

'What's that saying again? We threw out the baby with the bathwater.'

He darted his eyes at me and lowered his voice. 'You shouldn't speak like that.' He let out a stream of smoke.

'Why not? It's a free country, isn't it? Isn't that what all the blissfully ignorant citizens fought for? Freedom?' Less fighting than simple dismantling, I sometimes thought. It's much easier to tear things down than build something. Much easier to go back than forward.

Jordan was scowling. I was ruining his cigarette break, so I decided to let it go, and walked on.

He caught up with me and matched my stride. 'The baby was dead, Lucie. The spies, the corporations, those people we trusted to look after it – they killed it,' he said, grinding his cigarette butt out on the ground before pushing into Sweet Times. 'Then we threw it out.'

The bell tinkled, and a man in a full beard shot through with squirls of green came out from the kitchen area behind the counter, wiping his hands on his striped apron. I felt like I'd walked onto a stage set, but the warm, syrupy smells from deep in the store were real enough. I saw a row of candy presses on the back workbenches, like brass pasta makers.

Jordan showed him the pictures of Sofie and Vidal and asked if he'd seen anything.

The candy-maker bent over towards the photos and raised a pair of glasses to his eyes, leaning awkwardly over the counter and peering at the pictures.

'You want to take them?' Jordan asked.

'Sorry, my hands are sticky. But maybe the girl looks familiar. I remember because it looked like a lot of sugar just for her. Yeah, yeah. It was… two pounds of gum snakes and a wholesale jar of jelly beans.'

'Are you sure it was her?' Jordan asked.

'I couldn't swear on it. I see a lot of kids.'

The cashier at the pharmacy remembered Sofie buying some hair ties and quite a lot of pain medication. 'I remember because there was some paediatric syrup along with several tubs of paracetamol. I asked her if she knew how to use it, that she shouldn't give tablets to children under six. Yeah, she said. And there was something so sad in her face that suddenly I remembered who she was. The lawyer's girl – her mom died just recently. Do you think she's got younger brothers and sisters that she has to look after? That would explain the little-girl stuff she was getting… She also bought two packs of panties with ponies on, some undies for little boys – cowboys and trains – and some little hairclips and Strawberry Fairy shampoo and I wondered why, I thought it was a bit wrong, somehow, you know. But, jeez, it just makes me want to cry. The poor kid.'

'You know what this means, Jordan,' I said, as we pushed out of the pharmacy.

'Yeah,' he said. 'They're holding other kids.'

'This is enough for probable cause. We have to stop messing around.'

I took Jordan's car and drove back to the precinct,

hurrying through to the Sentinel offices.

'Come with me,' Barbra demanded when I got in, angry enough to storm out of her office in the middle of a meeting with some important-looking people and down to me in the pool. She hustled me into the corridor towards the bathrooms. 'I gave you special clearance to work on your case – *two days ago*, while we were waiting for the data. Then I called you back. I need your full attention on this.'

'I'm sorry, but this case with the children' – I used the word to try to appeal to some emotion in her – 'the suspect is getting away.' I watched her face ease, then added, 'And we think he's got more children with him. More are going to die. Every minute we don't find him, he's getting further away, and the children are in deeper danger. I've been asking around with CID but it's so damn slow. All we're getting is confirmation of what we already know.' I paused, steeled myself. 'You know what I really need?'

She did. But she said, 'The children are from Green Valley, right?'

I stiffened. 'They're kids, Barbra!' I was yelling at my boss and I didn't care. I'd had enough of politeness. All I could see was that unclaimed, unwanted girl's colourless little face. She'd been killed and nobody was looking for justice. Every hour that passed was condemning Kira to be next. In my hot eyes, Kira's face merged with Odille's, with my own, when I'd had only myself to count on, nobody to look out for me. 'I don't care where they come from. They're children. We have to save them, for Christ's sake!'

When the red mist had cleared, I saw Barbra holding her hands up, pacifying. 'I get it, but keep your voice down, Lucie.' She waited for me to take a few deep breaths then continued, in a low voice barely above a whisper. 'You know as well as I do the official policy on people from Green Valley. The jurisdictional boundaries are perfectly clear. I happen to think, though, that dead children in Stanton, wherever they come from, should very much be our concern.'

I tried not to widen my eyes at what was close to a treasonous admission.

'I know you want live data on the suspect,' Barbra continued, 'but let's go one better. We need someone to test the capabilities of the hardware as we have repurposed it using the new data streams, and finding your suspect may be the ideal exercise.'

I followed her up to the labs, where Schindler passed me the lens I had smuggled out in its little box, and explained how they had adjusted it.

'We want it back by five today,' Barbra said. 'And no more bullshit, I'm warning you.'

18

It was embarrassing how easily I tracked Vidal and Sofie, after all that. No, more than embarrassment – a deep clot of guilt congealed inside me as the Sentinel-enhanced lens showed me Vidal's devious route and his car's current location on a map laid over my eyeline. It was apparently parked in a barn on a farm on the other side of Green Valley. For all my cant about progress and my private belief that the Turn had betrayed our potential, I felt like a heartless super-predator, gliding towards my unsuspecting prey. Vidal was a canny shrew, scuttling to a hidey-hole where the other shrews couldn't find him, but I was an eagle with the intelligence of a million processors wired in. When this sort of tech was unleashed on us, the sneaky little shrews – the citizens of Stanton – wouldn't stand a chance.

But today I couldn't allow my sensibilities to slow me. I found it hard to correlate a teenaged girl who bought sparkly hair ties and pony underpants for children being a murderer, or working with one. But what did I know? Vidal Barrett would know where Kira was, and that was all that mattered.

I raced eastwards towards the farm, chased by the ram and pulled by the memory of Kira when I last saw her, dozing in her papoose on David's chest, so content. I was already halfway around Green Valley's wall before I wondered if I should have asked Jordan to come. It was too late now. If I managed to find a callbox to phone the station and ask a patrol officer to tell me where Jordan was, and if he drove out here, even if he could help me, even if he wanted to – even if he could stomach the idea of me getting a live surveillance feed beamed into my retina – it would be too late by the time we made it to the farm. Barbra wasn't joking when she said she wanted the device back by five. Getting fired wouldn't be the least of my problems then – I could be prosecuted for stealing classified property, espionage, treason. I wouldn't put it past Barbra if I crossed her again.

When I finally rounded the wall and made it beyond Green Valley, the road spooled out before me into an undulating basin bounded on both sides by ice-grey mountains. The rich soil of the valley floor was a patchwork of fruit and grain farms and rolling pastures. Elegant signs advertising guest cottages hung before many of the farms' entrances. They were popular with weekenders and tourists, who must have felt the same as I did out on this road, lighter once they'd pulled away from the dark gravity of Green Valley's monolithic wall.

But The I was taking me beyond the last of the picturesque properties and told me to turn down a dirt road into a shadowed nook in the hills, where warehouses and rundown farm buildings squatted together, out of the holidaymakers' sightline. A few hundred yards away from the arrow on the map, I crunched to a halt, out of sight of the low assembly of anonymous grey warehouses and workshops beyond. I checked my watch. Half past two already; I'd have to hurry.

I called up the file on the property and skimmed it, scrolling through it on The I. The land belonged to someone called Roger Basson, sole proprietor of Misty Vale Farm. The farm, a large swathe of diversified land, had almost been repossessed for unpaid arrears on a development loan, but had been bailed out by an investment from a company called Blank Slate Holdings six years before. Now, scanning through Misty Vale's and Basson's tax returns and lodged contracts, I noted that its only source of income for those past six years had been a lucrative contract for 'sundry supplies', paid quarterly from Blank Slate's account. All of the paperwork, though deliberately vague, seemed above board and correctly processed.

According to the consolidated Sentinel dossier on Basson, he had no criminal record, was still comfortably creditworthy despite the near-insolvency. He subscribed to *Stanton Times*, *Farmer's Weekly* and *Men's Choice*. He held loyalty stamp books at Homepride supermarket and Builder's Mart. He was unmarried but had lived with a woman called Naomi Reiffel, now deceased. He was a registered member of our ruling party. So far, so clean – but if I needed to, I was sure, I could find something to compromise him. But later; there wasn't time now.

I cross-referenced Blank Slate's other dealings, and noted that six other farms in the valley, along with a timber yard further into the hinterland and two industrial supply factories over in Racino, had been exclusively contracted for supplies to Blank Slate, although only two of the companies showed an active income stream, decreasing substantially from the previous year's figures. I tried to call up Blank Slate's company ownership structure but was referred to a trail of two other holding companies, which hit a dead end with a corrupted record for a Girded Cloud CC. In just this brief bout of research, I'd become so used to getting the information I needed immediately that the sudden dead end was annoying. I didn't have time to dig around any more, though, and I was sure that Sentinel resources would eventually show me who Basson was working for.

For now, though, I stepped out of the precinct's unmarked pool car, making sure it couldn't be seen from any of the buildings on the property. I was aware of how conspicuous I'd look, a woman in city clothes strolling up this worn-out industrial road in the middle of the rural hills. As I approached, walking alongside a long fence of spaced wooden slats, a battered white truck with no logo reversed away from one of the warehouses at Misty Vale and turned a groaning circle in the dust before pulling out of the gate. I hid behind a tree and set The I to record as it came past, zooming in on its licence plate and a glance at the driver's face through the window as it passed.

A man came out of a small prefab building at the fence and pushed the gate closed, and I watched him go back inside before scanning the lot for further movement. White steam plumed from a pair of high smokestacks at the far end of the warehouse, and the wind whipped it fitfully down from the mountainside, replacing the familiar starchy odour with grassblood and mud from the ploughed fields across the road.

Aware of my dwindling time with The I, I set it to infrared and heat-scanning modes, noting three adult figures inside a barn behind the warehouse and three in the warehouse itself. The heat scan showed no sign of any children – no living children, at any rate. Magnetic resonance threw up the shadows of a couple of pickups, three more trucks, and a sedan, shaped a lot like a Toyota Camry. The way it was parked, at the back corner of the property, I'd have to go past the gate and the guardhouse and down the neighbouring drive to get a straight-line view of the car. Calculating how much time it might take – The I offered me an estimated walk time of thirteen minutes – I considered running back to the car and driving up the next farm's drive, but if there was a closed gate, something I couldn't see from this angle, I'd have to reverse back, raising as much suspicion as hiking past the guardhouse in my city flats.

As I was deciding which was the better of two poor options, I heard a yapping sound piercing though the distance and saw a small, shaggy white dog bolting away from the obscured doorway of the barn, springing up on its back legs then squatting on its haunches, yapping excitedly. A tennis ball followed it, and the dog launched off and rounded on the ball in a tight circle, pluming up dust from the lot. Then Sofie Barrett strode out, calling to the dog, slapping her thighs. I jolted as Sentinel's version of The I started speaking in my ear: *Here, Pika. You're so cute. Good girl.* The words broke up and were filled with a neutral machine voice which merged and flowed with Sofie's voice. It took me a moment to realise that now the target was in line of sight, the tech was integrating long-range auditory signals with lip-reading software to produce an almost real-time play-out of what she was saying.

The dog delivered the ball, darting away each time Sofie reached out for it. Finally, she bent down and caught hold of it, fluffing the fur around its head and giving it a kiss before throwing the ball again.

I watched on the infrared feed as the two remaining adult-sized figures moved around the barn, stopping, squatting and stretching every few yards, methodically measuring up the space. Every few moments, they came together to consult what was probably a notebook or plan, and then moved away, measuring segments of the periphery again. Finally, one of the figures moved away from the middle of the barn and towards the doorway. I followed his form out the front and then it conjoined with my real vision as he emerged from behind the warehouse and stood in the lot.

'—get the generator to you in the next hour and you can start,' he was saying to the heat signature that had stopped at the threshold.

He paused, listening to a reply.

'Yeah, it's a shitload.'

The second heat-shape moved closer to the doorway, and then he was out, and The I captured and instantly matched his features to the pictures of Roger Basson that Sentinel had on file. The enhanced I locked into the sound waves and the motion of his face and rendered a digital voice for him. '—completely secure,' he was saying as he stepped out. 'There's no way, is there?'

Vidal replied, 'I know. They *shouldn't* be able to find them; there *should* be no way. But that's if they're playing by their own rules. Which I now know that they're not.'

'How so?'

'Egus told me I've got a tail.' My gut clenched and I froze, as if he was talking right to me.

'Jesus.' Basson lifted his arm to wipe his hand over his brow, blocking the signal for a moment. 'That'd… breach of trust. If that came out…' He muted himself again by wiping his mouth, the most cutting-edge tech defeated by that ancient gesture of evasion.

'Yeah. Massive. My contact inside has been watching and is still a hundred per cent sure Stanton PD isn't tracking me and isn't interested in the kids, just as we hoped. I don't know if Egus is just messing with me, or what this tail might want. From what my contact sees, it doesn't seem official, at any rate. All the same, we have to get ready to move them. But it's dangerous. So we need to get the biome up and running, before we even think of transferring them.'

While Vidal spoke, Basson went back inside, into the sound-shadow, turning back into an infrared shape.

'Thanks,' Vidal said. 'You're a lifesaver. We have to move quickly.'

Vidal stood watching his daughter. I shifted slightly to make sure I was out of sight, too far away to make out the subtleties of his expression, but my overactive mind filled in the blanks between him and me. I knew I was being stupid, but my eyes started prickling as I watched him watch Sofie; a man with silvering hair with one object of devotion. A man who would change his life for his daughter.

Then I snapped myself out of it. I knew nothing about this man, except that his car was delivering dead children to a Claymarket bakery in the middle of the night and that he was deliberately evading the authorities. I hardened myself. I had what I needed, and it would have to do for now.

As I stepped back towards the car he must have noticed the flicker of movement, and although he was far away, attuned only to gut feelings rather than priceless surveillance equipment, he turned to look at me. Into my eyes. I was certain he couldn't be seeing me for what I was, half-obscured by the shade of the tree and the slats of the fence, and I knew he could never pinpoint my pupils at such a distance, but he held my gaze while I stood, frozen like a rodent in the grass in the glare of a predator's scrutiny, trying to manage my breathing.

Ten seconds, fifteen. Then a frown, and a sigh, and Vidal Barrett turned his attention back to his daughter.

V

19

Three months before, Vidal might have chosen to run; he might have chosen to toy with the investigator, play a losing hand just for the hell of it. It might have been fun, to see just how long he could evade her, even though she clearly had technology on her side – technology no state agent should be using.

But that was three months ago, before Dierdra had died. Now, Vidal's priority was getting Sofie to school on Monday and he couldn't drag her around the countryside playing cops and robbers, and he couldn't leave the Green Valley children to look after themselves. The time he'd bought by tricking David Coady's sister-in-law with the tape loop had been enough to get the contingency arrangements in place with Basson, and to avoid being pulled in for questioning and leaving Sofie alone in the apartment.

So he let Sofie scruffle Basson's dog goodbye, then packed her back in the car.

'I wish we lived out here, Dad,' she said as they pulled out of the yard.

'Really? It's in the middle of nowhere.' He noticed the immediate fall of her expression and chided himself. The parent's trick of subtly deflating kids' hopes before they even knew they were inflating – he was learning quickly. *No bullshit*, he reminded himself. *No manipulation*. He'd promised himself when Sofie had rejoined his life. He changed his tone. 'What do you like about it?'

She regarded her hands, mucky from a paste of

dog-slobber and dust, her chewed nails flaked with chipped polish. 'I don't know, really. It is pretty far away from everything.'

They drove on for five minutes, and the longer the silence went on, the heavier it became, so Vidal broke it. 'You liked that dog, didn't you?'

No answer. Sofie just stared out of the window at the subliminal glower of the mountains and the lamplit signs of the orchards spinning by like fireflies in the darkness.

'What was his name again? Pookie?'

She let out a snort of laughter. 'Her. Pika. She was cute.'

'It would be nice to get a dog, wouldn't it?' he said, manoeuvring past a farm truck. 'We could get an apartment with a garden, a cute dog like Pika. That'd be fun, wouldn't it?'

In his peripheral vision, he noticed her turning to him, but could only glance at her face once he had clear roadway ahead of him, and when he did and a car swept past in the opposite direction, illuminating her features, she was fixing him with such a pitying look, he almost wrenched the car into the gravel. 'What's wrong?' he said.

'Dad, I'm… you know. I'm not going to be around for ever. I don't even know where I'm going to be next year, never mind in ten years when that dog is still going to be sniffing around your duplex.' She stared at his face. 'Christ, Dad, don't look like that.'

'Like what?'

'You know. Needy, I guess. Bereft.' Vidal was fixing his eyes on the road ahead of him, because it was hard enough to concentrate on the driving itself at this stage, but he could hear her sniffing. 'You've helped me, and I'm grateful. But I'm not the five-year-old you left. I'm not your baby and you can't expect me to be half of you.'

I didn't leave you, I never wanted to leave you, he wanted to tell her, but he just nodded, his hand clenched on the wheel and his eyes on the road, the dark grey mirage of Green Valley seeping up from the horizon.

When he got back into Stanton, Vidal left Sofie with Rainbow at the shelter, parked around the corner from Lucie Sterling's apartment, found a shadowy alcove, and waited for her. The main Museum crawl was busy with cars offloading patrons in suits and scarves, groups walking home from dinners and private viewings and theatre shows. Above him, rich yellow lights from the lofty apartment blocks looked over the broad sidewalk, waiting to welcome their owners home.

It was close to ten when they came along the sidewalk. It wasn't particularly cold tonight, warm winds sweeping in from the mountains inland, but Lucie was folded into herself, her arms crossed, talking seriously to the man next to her. Even without Bugs Bunny's intel, Vidal would have recognised him – Fabian Tadic, the renowned privacy crusader. He'd fronted so many class-action suits against old corporates that every Stanton lawyer knew his name. Barrett & Sanders had tendered for a spot on one of his counsel teams years ago, when Vidal was naive enough to imagine that Fabian Tadic would spend a second of his time with a two-bit – make that *one-bit* – outfit like his. The Omega group, self-styled guardians of the Turn, the powerful lobbyists keeping Stanton government on the straight and narrow, only played with the big boys. It was a little surprising, then, when Vidal discovered that Lucie Sterling, currently using illegal tech against a Stanton citizen, was involved with Tadic. Only a little, though, because in Vidal's experience, the higher up the power went, the less holy the alliances.

Did Tadic know that Lucie Sterling was a reanimated version of a bad-old-days cyberspook? If so, he was a fulsome hypocrite. If not... Vidal would love to be a fly on the wall when he found out.

He crouched back into the shadow, an incidental stranger, as they approached the front door of their apartment building. They pushed through the glass doors into the bright, marble-lined lobby, Vidal trailing a few yards behind. There were enough people coming through the lobby on this busy Friday night, and Lucie and Tadic were so wrapped up in their low-toned conversation that Vidal was invisible to them. He positioned himself next to the potted ficus opposite the elevators, a casually dressed middle-class man, drawing no special notice from the concierge, who was busy signing in a group of five loud students heading up to a party.

Vidal glanced around before approaching Lucie. She sensed him coming and turned, but her face froze and then cycled through confusion before she locked him with a complex, suspicious gaze.

'You were looking for me?' he said.

'I think you know why,' she said.

'Who is this?' Tadic asked.

Lucie and Vidal ignored the question. 'Do I?' Vidal said.

'I'm not in the mood to play games. I know what you've been doing and I need you to tell me right now: where are the children?'

Vidal felt a bump of relief. If she didn't know that, she didn't know anything. She was fishing, and she was working alone. As he'd suspected, the whole Stanton police force and the city's black ops were hardly interested in him. He could control the way this played out.

'Is this *him*?' Tadic asked.

'I want to show you something,' Vidal said to Lucie.

20

Vidal checked the time on the dashboard clock as they drove closer to Barrett & Sanders. Past one. They'd be offline at the moment, but it should be okay.

God knows what exactly Lucie had said to Tadic or what he thought of it, but she'd made Vidal wait for hours in an all-night kebab shop in Claymarket, until he was uncomfortably full and had memorised the backlit Perspex menu and had earmarked the Monday-night doner, fried chicken and chips special for a father-daughter date night of his own with Sofie.

'Listen, Lucie,' he said, keeping his eyes fixed on the road in front of him. The Toyota's brakes were stiff and its tyres were smooth, and the denizens of Claymarket were prone to lurching out into the foggy road from its underlit sidewalks. 'Do you mind if I call you Lucie rather than *Special Agent*?'

She pulled her eyes away from the battened shopfronts rolling by in the mist-washed dark, and towards him. 'Go ahead, *Vidal*.' He couldn't read anything on her silhouetted face, and although his name dripped with bitter sarcasm from her lips, he liked the way she said it. She pronounced it like his grandmother would – soft *d*, long *a* – but he could also imagine her whispering it in his ear, the languid drape of the last, long vowel, the curl of her sharp tongue on the *l*. This line of thought was inappropriate in the context of everything that had happened over the past few days, and proof that Sofie was right – he should get a life, instead of fantasising about some orange-and-spice-smelling stranger just because she was within touching distance of him in his humid car.

Besides, as she'd got into the passenger seat, she'd made a show of removing a can of mace from her bag as she dropped her keys into it, and pocketing it. The look on her face made him wonder what other ordnance she might be carrying.

'Since we're being honest as judges with each other, I need to tell you something,' he said.

'Yeah?'

'The reason I'm talking to you, the reason I'm taking you inside my building, the reason I'm telling you anything about my business, which mostly – until recently at least – has been all strictly legal, which is more than I can say about your activities—'

She rolled her eyes. 'Jesus, get on with it.'

He drew to a stop at a red light. 'The reason is all the same. I need you to stop bothering my daughter. She's been through a rough time and she needs a normal life, not to have spooks watching her sleep, not to have plods watching her when she goes to school. She's not stupid. In fact, she's the smartest person I know in this world, and she can see you, and she'll begin to doubt whether her ethical instincts are right, and she doesn't need that in her life, not right now, and not ever. Her instincts are a whole lot purer than any of the filthy scumbags who maintain law and order in this city, you and me included. Do you get me?' To her credit, Lucie didn't sneer or shrug or groan or say anything sarcastic; she just nodded. Vidal watched the pattern of the rain on the windscreen while he spoke. He glanced at her as the light changed all the droplets green, and he pulled off. 'So the quickest way I can get you to understand what I'm doing here is to show you, even when I know that most of our friends at the police wouldn't understand. But for some reason, I think I can trust you. I don't think you're *them*, if you know what I mean.'

'I just want to know the truth. It's personal for me, too.'

He rounded into the gap beside Barrett & Sanders and pulled up the handbrake, checked for any miscreant youths lurking down the dark end of the alley, but it was raining and they'd have moved their bottleneck-smoking to some warmer alcove. He got out, the odour of oil and piss and old beer being spirited up from the concrete by the rain, unlocked the two chains around the back lot's wire fence, got back in, and parked the car.

'Will you give me some privacy?'

'You mean, get out of my own car in the rain?'

'Yup. You can wait for me inside if you want.'

He stared at her, saw that she wasn't joking, fiddling impatiently with the strap of her satchel, some spooking in mind that didn't involve him. How had he let this dynamic emerge? Ah, well, he hadn't brought her here for a fight – the opposite. He opened the door and got out, accidentally on purpose nudging his rear-view mirror as he reached back for his jacket. 'O–kay, I'll just be…'

He wandered to the far side of the next car and swivelled its side mirror so that it lined up with his rear-view. Craning, he could just about see a third of what Lucie Sterling was up to in his car.

Lucie had opened the satchel and drawn out an electronic tablet, a gleaming, sleek little device that was a couple of generations on from the ones Vidal had known before the Turn. It glowed like a window to the universe in her hand, uplighting her face as she powered it on and started tapping commands into it. Even though she'd ordered him out of the car, she was being hazardously indiscreet by doing this in front of him – a suspect in multiple murders, no less – but he could tell she didn't care. She wasn't doing this for admissible evidence. She was telling the truth on that front at least: this was personal, not an official investigation. For now, and from this quarter, at least, he and Sofie were safe.

Vidal observed through the mirrors as she worked the screen: this is how she'd monitored him and Sofie yesterday. He strained to see her pan across what might be a surveillance shot of the building, a heat map, by the look of it. It caused a hollow sink in Vidal's chest to see his building so easily violated, but as far as he could see, she wasn't accessing any internal camera feed that might have been set in the offices; there were no eyes on the rooms upstairs. The deflector panels and interference broadcasters were aimed at keeping Egus's prying eyes out, but if they worked against the Stanton cops too, all the better. Lucie Sterling he could handle, but a whole snoop force with access to pictures from inside his business? That would have been another proposition.

Finally, Lucie killed the screen and shoved the tablet back into her bag. She peered up at the building's blinded back windows for a long minute before stepping out of the car.

'What were you looking for?' he said.

No concern that he'd seen what she was up to. 'Checking the building, of course. That you're not leading me into a trap. I wouldn't want to bump into an army of your goons.'

Vidal couldn't help laughing. *Goons*. 'And what does your device say?'

'So far, so good. Nobody inside.'

For a heavy second, neither of them made a move. But she had wanted to know the truth; it was too late for doubt.

'So let's go,' she said.

He didn't say anything as he watched her step out of the car into the brackish sea-blown mist; he knew too much about conflicting interests.

He locked the car-lot gate behind them and she made him walk ahead of her around the corner onto Ocean Street. As he unlocked the office's front door, he noticed Lucie glancing over her shoulder at the darkened windows opposite; he knew one of her patrol officers was looking back, maybe that stolid old woman who'd been keeping the late watch, no family to go home to, just an empty flat and a lonely retirement waiting for her. Vidal in a decade or two, if he didn't manage to keep Sofie close to him.

He turned to deadbolt the door behind him, but she told him to leave it open. He led her through the reception lobby and the waiting room.

Now that they were here, he was hesitant. This could bring a lot of shit down on him. He went behind the reception desk and turned on the kettle, spooning instant coffee into his mug. On his message spike was a yellow notelet from Tertia: *Police came asking Qs. I let them in. One interested in door.* Tertia's inimitable objective brevity. 'Can I get you something? Coffee? A cookie?'

'No,' Lucie said. 'You brought me here. Just show me what you want to show me. Whatever it is, I doubt it's going to be enough to stop me bringing the cops in.' But was it all empty bluster? Her voice had trailed away and her face had dropped fractionally as she'd spoken. Maybe nobody in Stanton apart from her was really interested in these kids. They may have sent a half-hearted officer out to check up on him, but that was the sum of it. If they had wanted to raid his office, they would have done that already. Or maybe he was being too complacent.

He waited for the water to boil, considering whether to turn around and throw her out right now, but as she paced behind him, he realised that just as she had her personal reasons for wanting to know the truth, so he had his reasons for wanting to share it. It was why they'd decided to leave the bodies out in the open, instead of burying them in some faraway woods or weighing them down in a lake. It was why Sofie had used his car – she'd *wanted* them found; they'd both wanted someone to care enough to ask who they were and how they died. He wasn't a criminal – he was only trying to help. Someone was showing an interest in what was happening to these children at last; maybe somehow he could get her onto his side. It was a gamble, but he considered himself a good judge of character. Her primary interest was the safety of the children, otherwise she wouldn't be here.

'All right,' he turned, grabbing his coffee mug. He stuffed a cookie into his mouth and proffered one to Lucie, who bared her teeth at him in response.

He led her to the stairwell door and unlocked it, flicking on the low-wattage timer light as he went. She picked her way up the stairs, trailing him cautiously, and Vidal unlocked the security gate – glad the kids had remembered to keep it locked – and let her through, leading her into the corridor which looked even dingier now that he was showing a guest around.

'It doesn't look like—' she started, but stopped talking when she saw the small figure of Rainbow step out of her doorway and stand with her hands folded behind her, awaiting them like a polite host.

Vidal had bought the four-storey building lock, stock and barrel for next to nothing as part of an insolvent deceased estate. After spending all his money on renovating and converting the lower floor to an office suite, which was more than big enough for his practice, he'd left the upper three floors more or less as they were, promising himself that he'd do them up when his ship came in. The old transitory tenement of one-room flats with a shared bathroom, utility room and kitchen on each level had frozen where they'd died with old Robert Marx. The years had slipped by frighteningly fast before he'd had to come up here again, a thin layer of dust had settled on every stripped, knobbled and stained mattress and every creaking floorboard; lightbulbs had yellowed, window latches had seized with salt rust, and insects had started eating the walls from behind the wallpaper. He'd done his best to make the place habitable with his severely limited budget. Got a deep-cleaning company in – a client's payment in lieu – bought in a batch of flatpack beds and cheap and cheerful bedding with prints of football pitches, hot-air balloons and dolphins. Even so, he'd had no money or time to repaint or make it more homely than that. Kids shouldn't feel at home in a place like this, but Rainbow was; she seemed to glow softly in the dusky space, and gently, carefully, allowed the stagnant air to start circulating again.

Lucie stared at the girl: her clean black hair tied with glittery elastics into pigtails that hung over her new purple hoodie and neat-pressed jeans. The toenails on her bare feet were painted with a fresh coat of sparkling strawberry-pink polish. Behind her, the austere room – just a bed, office desk and chair – was washed by two bedside lamps in a warm yellow that spilled out into the subterranean gloom of the rest of the floor. Unlike the rest of them, Rainbow liked the light. Hers was the only window on this backside of the building that they'd blanked with curtains rather than a plywood board.

'This is Rainbow,' Vidal said. 'She's why we're not giving up.'

'Hello,' said Rainbow, her eyes not settling on Lucie's face.

'How is she not showing up on the imager?' she asked Vidal. 'Are there other children in here?'

'We need to take this one step at a time. Say hello to Rainbow first.'

He watched her fighting her urges and organising her impressions before speaking. 'How old are you?' was what Lucie chose. Of all the possible questions, it was also the first one that had come to Vidal's mouth when they'd met. Judging by her height, Rainbow might have been nine or ten, but her voice and her bearing were unsettling – there was a self-possessed confidence in them, a clarity and directness. The impression had been even more uncanny when Vidal had first picked her up. Her skin had been dry and mottled like an old woman's; gratifyingly, it had already regained much of its elasticity, and there was warmth and colour in her cheeks.

Rainbow glanced at Vidal, and he nodded. 'It's okay. Lucie's a… friend. Tell her, sweetie. It's okay.'

'I'm fifteen.'

'Oh,' Lucie said.

'Sofie told me I don't look like fifteen, out here. Back there I… I guess I was any age I wanted to be.'

'Do you miss it there? Do you want to go back?'

'No,' Rainbow said, darting an urgent look at Vidal; and before allowing Lucie to manipulate Rainbow any more, he interrupted.

'So you're ready to turn them on soon?' he said. He walked into Rainbow's room and squatted down to check the relay servers and router hub. The small lights flashed rhythmically between orange, red and green in that cheerful, chattering way of theirs.

'Where did you get all this equipment?' Lucie asked. 'What are you doing with it?'

'You'll see in a few minutes. It will make more sense if we show you.'

Rainbow glanced back into her room, where an alarm clock with flipping digits sat on the side table. 'We'll turn them back on at two o'clock, yes?' She flinched, as if worried she was getting something wrong.

'Yes, that's right, sweetie. All set.' He watched Lucie staring at the rig, tracing the bundles of cable that ran along the skirting and up and out through the corners of the room. She still hadn't worked it out; she thought they were talking about the routers. 'You're doing a great job.'

Rainbow's eyes darted downward over her shy smile, then she went back to her breakfast – late-night snack, whatever it was; the girl was eating a lot to make up for lost years, and it was doing her good, but with her teeth and gums as messed up as they were, she still wasn't managing anything solid.

'We'll leave you in peace,' Vidal said to her.

As they turned to leave, Rainbow shucked off her hoodie and threw it onto the bed. Lucie stopped and asked, 'Where did you get that T-shirt?'

Rainbow frowned. 'My mother made it for me. She makes things.'

Vidal hadn't really taken note of it before; he'd just assumed it was something Sofie had bought, a cool and arty sort of shirt any teen might wear. But now that he paid attention, it was more worn than the new supermarket sets, fraying a little around the neck, and it looked handcrafted. There was an oddly defiant-looking panda bear set on a bright cerise background, and the panda was made with a sheen of coin-sized polka dots, appliquéd tightly like fish scales or sequins.

'Your mother's an artist?' Lucie said. 'In Green Valley. She stays at the Edges?'

'Yes,' Rainbow said, her voice sounding very young. 'Have you met her?'

'I think so.'

There was a frozen moment as Vidal watched Lucie watch Rainbow staring into nowhere, and Vidal had to break it. 'I'm just taking Lucie upstairs, then we'll come back down and help you, okay?'

Rainbow retreated into her room and Vidal strode back towards the stairwell.

'Stop, Vidal,' Lucie said, and he waited for her in the thick gloom of the landing. 'That girl, she came from Green Valley. Tell me: are there others here?' There was a malicious focus in her face, and Vidal could tell she was ready to gut him if she scented a lie.

'Yes,' he admitted. 'I'm taking you to them.'

Lucie shoved past him and hurried up the stairs. When she reached the heavy metal security gate locked across the top landing, she rattled at it. 'Open this gate, right now.'

'Wait,' he said softly, coming up behind her with a slow gesture of his hands. 'You need to stay calm. You cannot go barging and banging around them. I'm taking you in, that's the plan, but you have to promise to be calm. Okay?'

Lucie took a deep breath in, and he could see her face blooming in the low light, the anxious twist of her body, but she was trying to contain herself, gripping her messenger bag to her front like a shield, or a weapon. 'I scanned the building,' she murmured. 'There are no heat signatures, no sign of inhabitants up here.' She paused. 'Not even the girl downstairs.'

'That's because I'm protecting them.' He unlocked the door and led Lucie down to the far end. He'd been up here so often that he'd become used to it, but as Lucie recoiled and choked as the soupy hone of the place got richer, he remembered that it wasn't exactly the freshest. 'Don't blame us,' he said, leading her along the corridor. 'They don't let us open the windows. They don't like fresh air. You'll see.'

'Why's it so dark?' The pale orange glow of the safe lights was swallowed by the far heavier darkness.

'They don't like light, either.' He turned on the small flashlight that hung on his keychain and continued to gabble. The truth was, these conditions gave him the fucking heebie-jeebies too. 'Well, it's not so much they don't like it than they're not used to it. It frightens them. We're trying to acclimatise them to living normally: a bit of air, a bit of light, clean clothes, trying to get them to wash, but it's slow. It's hard. Harder than we imagined.'

Lucie started walking along the corridor, following the

narrow trail his penlight was picking out of the gloom. 'How many are there?'

'There are thirteen left. We run a small local network of The I here for the kids. They'd die from withdrawal without it. It's a slow process, so we're starting by teaching them to sleep without the signal for short bursts. That's why Rainbow's watching the time carefully. She's the only key we have to helping them.'

Lucie just shook her head. 'Show me. I want to see all of them.'

There was, finally, nothing more to do or say. Vidal knew that however much he could explain, this was still a goddamn horror show. Nothing would prepare her, just as he could never prepare himself every time he looked in on the children. This was why it was so important that Lucie Sterling understood that he was saving these children, and why she must not get in his way. There must be no threat that they'd ever be hauled back to Green Valley.

He showed her into the rooms, one by one, two kids on single beds in each one, the windows blocked and boarded, the faint orange glow of the power-out strips from the corridors the only light they could bear. It made him look bad, the way they clung like abandoned puppies to some scrap of clothing they'd come out with, or a filthy toy. The new toys he'd bought them lay rejected on the floor. Lucie surprised him by going straight for the beds, squatting close down beside them and scrutinising their ruined faces as if looking to find something.

She spoke softly to them, but they just stared straight ahead with those terrifying, jammed-open eyes that never seemed to close. They never talked to him either, but sometimes, when they didn't know he was outside, he'd hear them murmuring to each other, nothing he could recognise as language, but more like a song on a scratched record, drowned at the bottom of the ocean. A rhythmic hissing crackle from their throats that seemed to comfort them more even than the loose shrug of the rags they wore and refused to take off, or the catatonic rocking of their bodies. They were unplugged, that's what they were: inoperable.

By the third room, the third pair, Lucie was crying and calling to someone, not to him. 'Where are you?' Then, when she noticed him trailing her, she rounded on him. 'They're all dying.' Vidal backed out of the room into the corridor as she advanced on him. 'You don't have any idea,' she gritted out, speaking softly in deference for the sheer enormity of the wrongness in here, but her rage even sharper for her taut delivery. He'd bumped into the wall, but she still advanced, pushing him with the flat of her hand, as if wanting to shove him through the wall. 'You have to send them back.'

'No.' It was a voice behind her, a girl's voice, but firm, carrying a lifetime's weight in that short syllable. Vidal looked over Lucie's shoulder. It was the little one with the knotted hair, the one Sofie called Merida, though God knows what her real name was. This was the first time Vidal had ever heard her speak. She was awake, moving around, talking, all without being connected to the rig. That was good—

Lucie was turning towards the voice behind her, and it was only then that Vidal understood, seeing them in the same frame. This little girl and Lucie Sterling were flesh and blood.

But Lucie wasn't listening. A sound was getting ripped out of her, not loud, not a shout, but a strangled moan.

At that moment it must have turned 2 a.m., because Vidal felt more than heard the thrum of electricity in the air as Rainbow powered the rig back up.

The little girl stiffened as she came online, the punch of overstimulation as she booted.

Lucie, tipping over, reached out for the girl, her knees buckling.

The girl gasped, her eyes opening too wide.

Lucie sprawled, her arms still reaching, not protecting herself from the floor as she fell, chest and chin and elbows crunching down into the splintered wood.

The girl rode the wave of the boot-up, breathing it out as she settled. She looked curiously at the woman writhing in pain on the floor, who was gibbering something, pointing towards the dark end of the corridor – 'It's here!' – clarity emerging from the convulsive gasping – 'Run, Kira. Run away!' – still reaching for the little girl.

VI

21

I fought Vidal as he pulled me away from Kira and wrestled me downstairs, but the ram's incursion was weakening me. I was still struggling against him, batting him away, screaming to be taken back to Kira as we reached the floor below. Rainbow was waiting down there. She handed Vidal something, then I had nothing left as he got me down the last flight of stairs and slammed the heavy steel door behind us.

It all stopped.

The ram was gone, vacated my cortex the moment I crossed the threshold of Vidal's I.

'We need to get that tracer out of you,' Vidal said, pressing an electronic wand to my back. 'But this will help for the moment.' A vibrating, crackling sensation radiated outwards from my spine; there was smoke in the middle of my brain. He handled me back into the stairwell and slammed the door behind us again.

Now that the electronic panic had cleared, and the ram had ceded control of my systems, I had my strength back and ran up the stairs and to where I'd seen Kira. Vidal knew not to try to stop me. As I passed the bedrooms, I saw the children had been reconnected to The I. They were sitting on their mattresses, their faces relaxed and pacified, staring into the middle distance. Nothing like the moaning and fitful grinding I'd seen a minute ago. In the last room, Rainbow was propping Kira up on her mattress, as docile as a rag doll.

'She's gone out,' Rainbow said to me.

'She was standing there a minute ago,' I said. 'She was talking to me.'

'Yes,' said Rainbow. 'She's getting better. But she's gone out now.'

Vidal had caught up with me. 'I won't be able to do the extraction here. I'm already worried that they'll have seen you.'

'I'm staying with her,' I said.

Vidal frowned, glancing between me and Kira. 'I had no idea. Honestly. Who is she to you?'

'She's my niece. Her name is Kira,' I said, going over to her bedside, sitting down at the edge of the mattress and rubbing the hair back from her brow, a carbon copy of Odille's. My motions were stilted. I didn't know how to act maternal; I didn't know what to do with this mess of protective rage inside me. Kira didn't respond to my touch, but her breathing was deep and calm.

'What...' Vidal started, then decided against asking anything. 'Oh,' he said again, ruffling his scalp. 'You'll need an explanation, then, won't you?'

'Yes,' I said. Potboiler-aunt might have stormed up to him and grabbed him by the collar, shoving him into the wall and demanding to know what the hell he was doing with her niece, but I just sat there, holding her limp hand. What Kira needed, more than bravado, was peace.

'Okay, so,' Vidal started, approaching carefully, and keeping his voice low, 'it looks bad, I know, but the first thing you need to know is that we're trying to help them. This, without a doubt, is the best thing we can do for these children.'

'You mean kidnapping them?' I said, the menace clear in my level tone. 'Taking them from their parents and their homes?'

'No. Freeing. Rescuing. They're not well there. They're not healthy, they're not safe. I want to reintegrate them into normal society.'

'And this is a decision – what? – you made all by yourself? To take these children from their families?'

'No, not by myself. There are others involved.'

'Who?'

'Others who have their best interests at heart.'

'That's bullshit,' I snapped. 'Someone who has their best interests at heart would call the police, social services.'

'They wouldn't have a clue how to treat them, Lucie.'

'They wouldn't be dumping their bodies.'

He shook his head. 'You don't understand.'

'No,' I said. 'No, I don't. Tell me this at least: why are they dying?'

He looked down and paused, knowing that a glib answer wouldn't be good enough. He sighed, and I could tell he wasn't pretending. 'They're so damaged by that place… it's so damn hard for them to adjust, especially the born-ins. And the slop they've been feeding them isn't designed for growing children. I wish we knew how to help them better. It's so fucked up in there. That's why I brought you here. I needed to show someone who cares, so you can see them, what's happening to them, why they have to come out of there.'

'Still, she shouldn't be here,' I said, looking around at the dingy interior of the room. 'These children should be in a hospital. They should be with their parents.'

'They can't go back and they won't,' Vidal said.

I'd almost forgotten Rainbow, standing as a silent auditor in the corner of the room. But now she spoke. 'She's getting better,' she said, glancing between Vidal and me, tears welling in her eyes. 'We're all getting better. Please don't send us back.'

'But surely,' I said to her, 'being at home is better than being here?'

'No,' she said. 'We're working so hard,' she begged, as if it was my decision to make. 'Please don't let her,' she said to Vidal.

'You still think it's fine in there, don't you? There's only one way you're really going to understand,' he said.

22

'This is going to be a bit uncomfortable.'

I'd heard those words too often in the past week. We were in the back of a Misty Vale delivery truck, surrounded by strapped-in pallets stacked with forty-gallon vats of Green Valley's potato-yeast starch. The driver was Roger Basson, who I'd last seen talking to Vidal at the farm. Close up, he was a paunchy, red-faced man with a narrow ring of hair and narrower lips, and he'd jumped down from the cab and unlocked the back of the truck for me and Vidal without a word, only a side-eyed glance. On the drive out to Green Valley's delivery bay at the far end of the wall, I'd got used to the funky stench of the foodstuff. I lay face-down on the scratch-fibre carpet that lined the back, hearing the growl of the truck on the road and the squeak of the chassis and the cargo belted onto its shelves. The cheap carpet smelled like a teenage boy's sheets, and I shuddered as Vidal squatted down next to me and opened a metal-clad briefcase of electronic equipment.

I'd wanted to stay with Kira, watch over her, but soon I'd realised that Vidal wasn't lying when he said she'd be in her digital coma for the whole day. Rainbow and Sofie seemed to understand her better than me. Reluctantly, I'd let him convince me to leave her in their care. 'Just a couple of hours, and you'll know everything you need to know,' Vidal had said. He was right. If I wanted the truth, and I did, I had to go back to Green Valley.

In the truck, I remembered that I should have told Jordan

that I'd found Kira, and I wondered if I should have told him where I was going, but it was too late now. I'd fill him in when I got back. Seeing Vidal Barrett with the children, I knew I could trust him – this wasn't a violent man, and he was being honest with me. It was before dawn on a Saturday, and I hoped he'd be fast asleep or, for all I knew, entertaining someone he'd picked up in a bar. As it was, I'd only tried Fabian from Vidal's phone. It had just rung, so I called my answering service. He hadn't tried my number and had sent no message, so I simply asked them to tell him I'd called.

Vidal seemed at first to be gentle. He swabbed my skin with alcohol where the pinpricks left behind by Gina Orban's intrusion had just about healed, but when he started digging into my lower back with what felt like a screwdriver, I was scoured through with pain. Vidal was leaning over me, my arm braced between his knees, and whatever he was doing to me had paralysed me.

I was letting a lawyer operate on my spinal cord with a screwdriver, some morbid part of my mind commented. I strained to coordinate the muscles in my throat to yell out for him to stop, but he pre-empted me. 'Don't worry. It's temporary. I'm not causing any damage.' He shifted and brought a small spike, like a dental pick with a tweezers end, into my eyeline. The truck jerked again. 'This is all I'm using. It's not as bad as it feels, and I've done this before.'

I squeezed my eyes shut and pressed my face into the rough carpet as the truck jerked and bounced along. I clenched my jaw, wishing I had something to bite down on, and trying not to think of what would happen if the truck bumped at just the wrong time.

Vidal moved on to my mid-spine with a, 'Hmm, okay.' By concentrating on the ebbing throb in my lower back, I found I could ignore the new sear from the middle as he picked and scraped. *Oh God, get it over with.*

'You must be very important,' he said cheerfully after another minute or two, and he went on picking at the third site, at the base of my neck. I was forced to grunt for him to explain what he'd meant. 'They left three tracers in you. One's usually more than enough. It's almost as if they were worried you'd have help getting them out.'

When he was done, he rubbed the wounds with antiseptic and stuck small, round plasters on them, like the type you put on an inconvenient pimple. He handed me a blanket, a pastel-teal supermarket fleece, and turned away as I pushed myself up. I draped the floral-scented blanket around my shoulders. Under the material, I rubbed at the plasters I could reach, feeling them spaced evenly down my spine, the deep throb and sting of the wounds beneath.

'What does that mean?' I said. 'How exactly do these things work?'

He turned back to me and held out a swab on his palm, where three miniature metallic discs like little sequins lay, still covered in a coating of blood and yellowish flecks of what I didn't want to think too hard about, that came from my body. For a moment I felt exposed and a pre-cortical shame, but I told myself to get over it.

'They're RFID chips. Based on the old-school tech people used to use to track their pets. You remember?' I nodded. 'But with lots of added goodness. That's why you have to check yourself afterwards.'

'You say it like everyone should know that. Like it's common practice, just popping in to Green Valley.'

'Gina must've put them in when she installed The I, under orders from Egus, I guess.'

'You know Gina Orban?' I said.

'Of course.' He shrugged. 'She's the liaison.'

'It's weird. It all seems so small-time. Even though there's not much traffic, you'd think there'd be enough visitors to warrant a slightly bigger staff.'

Vidal frowned, a dark look, almost of pity, clouding his face. He muttered a small word under his breath, then after a pause, 'So, it's clear Egus wanted to keep track of you after you left.'

'Is that all these things do?' I asked. 'Keep track of me?'

'No.' He bent over a large kitbag and removed what looked like a shirt wrapped in thin plastic. 'Because they're linked to the Green Valley ecosystem, they can affect your physiology and your psychology like a limited version of The I.'

A sick bolt cramped my gut. 'You mean they can control my moods and my reactions?'

'We're not sure,' he said. 'There's probably not the full mood-altering capability on these little things.'

'Who's "we", Vidal? Who are these others, who apparently have my niece's best interests at heart.' David had said someone from inside was probably helping; whoever had faked Kira's beacon and corrupted the playback. 'It's someone inside, isn't it?'

He didn't answer, so I went back to questions he seemed keen on answering. 'So, these tracers? Could they make me see things?' I asked instead. 'Hallucinations?'

Looking over my shoulder, focussing a little way behind me with a look of caution, as if he saw the ram standing right there, as if he knew precisely what I was talking about, he said, 'Yeah. That's likely.'

'Okay,' I said.

'I'm guessing you've seen a black ram, right?'

I felt a jolt through me and I crackled with focus. 'What is it?'

'It's someone in Zeroth's twisted vision of a Green Valley cop. For one thing, it checks on visitors and makes sure they're following the rules. They're big on rules there, you may be surprised to know.'

'No. I'm not.'

Vidal was setting up other equipment as we spoke, tidying away the tools of the operation – like he'd done this a hundred times before. What exactly did I know about Vidal? Was I right to trust him? He may well have just put something else in me, and just be pretending to help me. But I'd never allowed myself to give in to formless paranoia. If I didn't trust anyone – if I didn't allow myself to trust my own instincts – I might as well stay at home for ever, waiting for the knock. I remembered his concern for Rainbow and the children. I believed he was helping them, at least.

'Listen, Vidal,' I said. 'Can The I make things real? I mean, can it make things materialise?'

His hands froze when I spoke. After a second, he recovered himself and said, 'There are rumours they were working on that before the Turn. It would have been the holy grail. They never managed.'

'I think they've done it. I saw the ram in real life, not just a projection or residue.'

'Outside Green Valley?'

I nodded.

'No, never. They weren't close to it, even in the environment. It would have been impossible for them to just magic things up wherever they liked. Laws of physics. It would always be reliant on the infrastructure.'

'I saw it. It was real. It attacked me.' I pushed the blanket away from my shoulder, showing him the bruise.

'Not possible,' he said. 'It's a biodigital projection like the rest of The I's environment. It reached you through the tracers. You must know how convincing it can feel.' But he didn't catch my eye as he said this, afraid either of looking a madwoman in the eye or lying to my face.

So, feasibly, signals from the mirror network Vidal had set up in his office had caused me to see the ram outside

Green Valley, that was all. Maybe I wasn't going crazy. It felt good to have a rational explanation to hang onto, no matter how tenuous – but still, I didn't like how The I could make such a fool of me.

'Anyhow, you won't be seeing the ram any more,' he said, the three metal tracers rattling as he dropped them into a canister. He carefully opened the seal along the top of a plastic ziplock bag and removed the folded navy blue material from it. It was a shirt, long-sleeved, thin material, like a thermal undershirt, but as Vidal unfolded it, he exposed a nest of wires in the middle of the parcel. 'The next step,' he said, passing the shirt to me, 'is to get you on our interface, the safe version. The open-source one, let's say.'

I almost told him to stop there and take me back to Stanton – I didn't want anyone installing anything into my body ever again – but I had to know for myself whether Vidal was telling the truth. Were Kira and the other children better off inside or outside Green Valley? There was only one way to find out.

Vidal turned away in another show of courtliness, which I thought was redundant since he'd already been poking around in my flesh, digging out parts of me. I dropped the blanket behind me and pulled the shirt on. It fitted quite closely, but with a bit of droop in the biceps and around the chest; I wondered who had worn it before me, as I worked the wires out of the back and flipped the close-fitting hood over my head. Had he brought Sofie into Green Valley?

'So, I'll be able to access The I's feed with this, just like with their implants?'

'More or less,' he said, as he adjusted the wires running along the shirt's spine and up over my skull, clipping transponders into the studs there. 'There are some differences. For one thing, this is a shitload less invasive. You can take it off any time, or you can turn it off any time. For another, there's no aversion control.'

'So why bother using it? Why not just go straight in without any interface?'

'You want to see what they see, remember,' he said.

'Yeah. Makes sense.'

He stopped reeling the wires and looked straight at my face, his eyes flickering between my eyes and my mouth. 'Remember, Lucie, I'm taking you in today to see what Green Valley really is, because you want to know. But that reality is something nobody should ever have to see. The I's illusion is what makes the place... bearable.' He handed me two fresh I lenses in a case.

'What do I need these for?' I asked.

'You still need to see the simulation. But you'll be seeing our version, and it won't be controlling your mind.'

The truck slowed and I could hear the crunch of gravel below us. Vidal zipped himself into his own electronic vest. 'If you're ready. And remember, you don't have to do this.'

'Let's get on with it.' I stood up, moving towards the truck's door.

'Uh-uh,' Vidal said. 'We're not just going to stroll in. We have to get in here.' He lifted the red lid of a white plastic skip, like a hospital laundry trolley, strapped to the truck's wall, and half-hoisted himself over the lip before turning to me. 'You need a hand?'

I pushed by him, flipped myself into the skip and squatted into the base. At least it was clean.

'Thought not.' Vidal wedged himself in beside me. 'I usually do this alone. Sorry.' I peered through one of three small holes drilled under the skip's handle, trying to ignore Vidal's shifting and grunting behind me and the press of his limbs on my back as he adjusted his body in the small space.

Basson reversed the truck to a stop, then came around and opened the rear door. Light glared from outside, despite the fact that it was only a textured expanse of wet grey dawn beyond the truck's rear doors.

'You're a good man, Roger,' Vidal said.

'Yeah, we both know I'm not doing this for the benefit of my eternal soul,' Basson said bashfully, patting his pocket.

'Nonetheless,' Vidal said.

It took a moment's adjustment to identify the delivery bay set into the shadowy windward side of Green Valley's shell, barred by anonymous steel roller doors; the only marking apart from years' worth of rust, dents and hurried patch-up was a faded sign, stencilled in Zeroth's corporate typeface to the lower corner of the roller shutter: *DS-793 A-F.*

Climbing a metal ladder to a chest-high concrete lip in the wall, Basson entered a code into a keypad to the side of the roller and raised it up. Two seconds later, an intense waft of pungent garbage fingered its way directly into the skip with us. 'Jesus,' I gagged.

'Yeah,' Vidal said. 'Let's switch you on.' He twisted something at the back of my neck, where the shirt's hood joined the hem, and the smell was replaced by a simulation of herbs and rain that swept away the molecules reacting in my olfactory system.

Basson folded out the truck's gangplank and approached our trolley, still wordless, and with that neutral, closed-down expression that wouldn't raise any suspicion from anyone watching the delivery-bay feed – just a solitary farmer delivering his goods.

'Keep down,' Vidal whispered as Basson unlocked the straps over the trolley and unclamped the wheels, reversing us with a solid pair of bumps onto the rust-streaked and stained concrete floor of the delivery bay.

Except, it was softer than that, more undulating; we were being wheeled over a quiet gravel pathway in an overgrown corner of what looked like a suburban park. Through the trolley's eyehole, I saw a grove of silver birches, leaves perpetually gently turning in the warm sunlight, and then we were parked halfway into a verge of purple buddleia and berry-laden brambles. Then we were alone. Vidal flipped the lid open and stepped out of the trolley, and I stood up and looked around. Vidal's avatar was a plastic-skinned, crop-haired, fake-muscled GI Joe in Hawaiian civvies – irony or wish-fulfilment, I wouldn't guess. Intra-ocular lines of text, just like The I's familiar readout, scrolled to the side of my sightline. My body knew I was still standing in a concrete delivery bay, but my mind was asserting the fragrance of crushed leaves and seed-blown autumn flowers, insisting that fecund wasps and bumblebees were drifting in the space in front of my face, that the muddy ground was spongy beneath my feet.

When I caught the sight and sound of humans passing along the road just beyond the stand of shrubbery, my stomach lurched. My mind knew they were not real, and it knew at the same time that they needed to be engaged with and assessed on a full cerebro-social level – a swell of bile rose in the pit of my stomach, searching for equilibrium, then hacked its way out on a wave of retching. This is what it would feel like to see a horde of ghosts; I'd stumbled into Gina Orban's uncanny valley. I folded double and retched out the contents of my stomach into the wood-chipped bed at the base of the shrubbery.

'There's no aversion control on our interface,' Vidal mused as he stood a few discreet yards away from me, 'so it isn't as comfortable as Zeroth's. But the flipside is that they don't know you're here unless they're physically watching you, which they wouldn't bother to do. They've grown lax, since The I does it all for them.'

I stayed in my doubled-over crouch, hands on my knees, and scrutinised him with red and stinging eyes, bruised by the force of my nausea.

'Their aversion control is an integral part of their biometric monitoring system,' he continued, 'that charts every resident's movement, emotion and inclination, so—'

'Yeah, I know,' I interrupted him, wiping my mouth on the side of my hand and forcing myself up. 'I'll trade a bit of nausea for personal freedom. Let's go. You wanted to show me something.'

He shrugged his blocky shoulders. 'Okay, let's ease in by going somewhere familiar.' He started off through the undergrowth like a robot, crackling right over saplings and through swathes of heavy-leafed branches as if they weren't even there. They weren't, of course, but still, the branches snapping back at me as I followed stung me just as if they were. 'We'll get to the town square this way. It will be safer to disconnect there. It's more… It's better.'

'I'll get used to it,' I said. 'I think I've had the worst of it already.'

'There are different kinds of aversion.' He came around behind me and touched the plastic toggle sewn into the base of the hood, attached to a transponder on my cervical spine. 'Feel here?' I moved my right hand behind me and touched against his as I felt for the knob. 'You'll just twist it a quarter-turn clockwise and you're disconnected. Easier than extracting your soul from Zeroth, right? But I wouldn't do it here. Really.'

A few paces on, he pushed his way through the foliage and onto the pathway, where a perfect jogger in purple togs and with a small, acid-green music player strapped to her arm ran by. To our left, a toddler followed a duck, offering it a bunch of willow leaves, an exhausted-looking mother trailing them watchfully a few paces behind. Were these people real, or environmental detail in the program? I couldn't fight the perverse impulse to check, and the scene seemed safe enough despite Vidal's warnings, so I turned the dial and the world switched off around me; my stomach hit the roof of my mouth like I'd just teleported into a plummeting lift in the final second of its fall. Squeezing my eyes shut as my knees quaked, it was all I could do to stay upright. When the ground solidified, I looked around me. I was standing in a cavernous and dusty delivery bay filled with wooden pallets and a stack of the forty-gallon barrels I'd seen in the Misty Vale truck. Deep mounds of trash decayed into seeping puddles, a landfill with no ground to rot into; mountains of waste receding from the gloom into full dark a few dozen yards away. The silence was sudden: I hadn't noticed the birdsong and the buzz of insects, the clink of bicycles and electric trolleys around the Green Valley park, the chatter of children playing, until they were gone. A cold, sterile quiet broken only by the unnatural echoes of my footscrape and my breath, which in this space sounded like gasping.

And underneath, the hessian must of the starch barrels, replacing the herb-and-soil fakery – the deep, sweet rot of a mountain of overblown carcasses in the prime of their ripeness, so thick it held up the concrete roof. Wheeling around to try to locate the delivery-bay door, I stumbled over something dense and yielding on the floor beneath my feet and could swear I heard it squelch and crunch under my boot as I struggled for my balance. Willing myself not to look down, I hurried back towards Vidal where he – his real body – stood beside the dust-caked plastic wrap and cardboard piled haphazardly in the unloading area near the door.

Eager not to gag again, I clutched at the back of my neck, ignoring movement in the piles of waste, squeezing my eyes closed and twisting the knob a quarter-turn back. The fresh smells wafted back in. Only when the rot had cycled out of my lungs and my nose did I open my eyes, to see the sunlit grove and the butterflies, and Vidal watching me, the text readout helpfully telling me the time and the temperature and that I had zero messages and zero likes.

'Fuck this place,' I managed.

23

I wasn't certain that Vidal deliberately lost me, but as we approached the familiar lines of the town square, he disappeared. I hadn't been looking at him every second of our walk, so couldn't say when he'd gone, but one minute he was walking beside me, and the next, he wasn't.

I figured at the time that he was playing some macho game with me, like an asshole father throwing his kid into the deep end to teach her to swim, so I spent only a few minutes searching among the avatars and the decorations walking around the square before seeking him on the interface's contact list. He wasn't listed on the directory. I knew I wouldn't find him in there if he didn't want to be found, and I had no intention of hanging around waiting for him, so I called David instead, to tell him that I'd found his daughter.

I'm dialling David's number, I thought to myself as I scan-typed his name and eye-touched his picture as Zeroth had taught us to do all those years ago. In here, there was no dial, and no number, and I was filled with an absurd longing for Fabian's green plastic telephone with its analogue wheel, the way the digits under the plastic circles were increasingly worn from zero all the way down to one, the whir of the rotor, like the living purr of a cat, the notch in the finger guard; the double kink in the coil of the wire and the way the tone would affirm its life to me as I picked up the phone. The earpiece of his handset smelled of Fabian's cologne and the mouthpiece of the mint and orange essence of his breath.

In Green Valley, the false smells were thin, a patina of

sensation masking reality, and seeded no memory behind them, leaving only a ghost-whisper of what they signified. As the green *Calling* halo throbbed around David's avatar's image, I imagined that he'd become a ghost himself, drifting and detached, nothing to anchor himself on. I wondered if he regretted that irreversible decision he'd made all that time ago, whether he ever dreamed of being rescued from this place and rehabilitated like those children in the shelter, back home in Stanton.

David's avatar throbbed along to the digital tone for a few more moments, then glowed red. 'Call failed,' Clara's electronic voice said in my ear, without giving me the option to leave a message or request a call-back. That must be Vidal's touch – calls didn't *fail* in The I; Zeroth had never admitted the word 'fail'. I'd once read an article on their lexicon, years ago, Jamie Egus and his Communications Director explaining that we can 'actuate positivity by our lexical choices'. I remembered the phrase verbatim, because it had become a running joke in the office for weeks afterwards, someone even making a full-sized poster of a ginger kitten in a coffee cup saying 'Fuck You', and underneath, romantic hand-stencilled script in rainbow marker pens reading 'Actuate Positivity By Your Lexical Choices'.

The computerised voice pronounced that unfamiliar word bluntly and, it seemed to me, with a vaguely malicious satisfaction. Tech firms had always offered the illusion of choice to their end-users, but now Clara was only offering me a dead end. As if it knew I was trespassing and didn't deserve the same platitudes it offered to its paying customers.

It couldn't know, Vidal had assured me. The alternative was worse – had David been disconnected from the system? Would he even survive disconnection?

I tried the call again, two times, three, as I hurried through the town square in the direction of his house. Pushing past the avatars on the street, I followed the arrow on the map towards his address, dodging down unfamiliar side roads as the sky started to lower with heavy slate storm clouds. Angry skies had never been advertised in Zeroth catalogues.

The cursor led me along a narrow footpath wedged between the backs of two rows of houses. As I hurried, my counterfeit I struggled to keep up with my pace, rendering the path into virgin panelled fencing and overhanging shrubbery a few metres ahead of me from a blur of pine-brown and foliage green. The solid sidewalk asphalt became patchy and pitted until it gave way to rutted mud. Vidal's I was creating this route as I went, and I knew I should go back, but still the destination star, set over where David's house should be, pulsed only a little way away on the map. I wanted to trust that this was a legitimate shortcut, so I did, and I followed the path which narrowed further, funnelling me into a wedge of backyard fencing and low-hanging branches. I came to a stop where the path became too overgrown to follow, the surrounding detail taking advantage of my pause, manically filling itself in. I pushed at the skein of hedge that had grown across the path. My arm sticky with spider webs, willing myself to remember that nothing The I was generating could really bite and poison me, I shoved my head and shoulders as far as I could into the overgrowth. I'd have to shuffle down and crawl through a stretch of around ten metres to get through to the other side of the funnel.

Or I could turn back. But when I reversed from my squat in the hedge and stood and turned, the path behind me had closed in with equally heavy growth. When I took two paces back the way I came, Clara voiced in my ear, 'No route found to destination. Turn around where possible.'

I turned again, trusting only in the beacon throbbing above David's house, and flicked on *Try again* as I got onto my knees and started to crawl under the hedge and through the muddy tunnel. The *Calling* halo throbbing over David's portrait, just beyond me, always a few metres away, dragged me on, through the muddy tunnel, which I could imagine was made by dogs or children or small animals, not by a deranged businessman's artificial intelligence. As I crawled, sharp stones bit into my knees, and the mud squelched between my fingers. *This isn't real, this isn't real*, I muttered to myself, in time with the throb of David's halo; *I'm just crawling along a dry warehouse floor*. Because thinking too hard about what was real and what was not, about what could be coating the floor of a concrete dome where three thousand people had been locked for eight years and who kept an untamed, festering mountain of garbage at the only door where they received slop for food, was not a viable option.

The crawl lasted too long, David's image ever backing away out of reach, the undergrowth thickening when it should be opening up, the sting of brambles and nettles – *they're not real, Lucie* – starting to scald my skin and seize my muscles, a reek of shit and rot starting to emerge from beneath the fresh-earth veneer of the mud. I pushed on and on, driven by the rhythm of the throbbing halo, the *call failed*, the *try again*, David's fake face always retreating from me.

When the pattern shattered and the halo went green, glowed solid. *Connected*.

'What do you want?'

'Da—'

'You're pretty fucking persistent, aren't you?'

I came up off my hands and knees and found a space to sit on my heels. The image of David's face didn't resolve into a video feed. 'Is that Eloise?'

'Who else would it be?'

'David,' I said, my teeth gritted. Like when you've been on hold for an hour and you want to tell the call-centre agent exactly how you feel, but you don't want to lose the call. 'I'm trying to get hold of David.'

'He's not here.'

'What do you mean? This is his personal number… user ID, whatever you call it.'

Eloise just sighed. 'He's in a meeting. Hush-hush, no comms.'

'With who? About what?' I asked, as if it would help me understand anything.

'Wizards.'

'Why are you answering his calls?'

'Because you were calling and calling. I was busy minding my own business, but all I see is the flicker of *Lucie Lucie Lucie*. Calling from nowhere. Very interesting. Or not, depending on your angle. I wouldn't have bothered. But after twenty, a hundred, a thousand calls, I kinda know you're not going to go away. So what do you want, Lucie Lucie Lucie?'

'I want to see David.'

'He'll be back soon. Maybe.' I could almost hear her shrug. 'Come by.'

'That's the problem. I'm lost. This map has sent me—'

'The map? You're following the map? When you're visiting unofficially? Jeee-sus.'

I took a deep breath, understanding that if I said what I wanted to say to Eloise, I might be adrift in this imaginary sphincter for ever, or until the whole of Green Valley lost power, whichever came first. Then I remembered: I had an off switch. I could disconnect any time I wanted. But, shifting my weight in the slop I was kneeling in, the mud oozing between my fingers and getting under my nails, I was pretty certain I wasn't ready for that. And besides, I might not be able to find David or Vidal on my own here, in the dark. 'Can you help me?' I said.

'There they are. Some of the hardest words for us to say.'

I ground my fist into my thigh, but I couldn't plug my mouth this time. 'Christ, Eloise, stop being such an asshole. Will you tell me how to get to your house if I'm not supposed to use the map? I don't live in this stupid dump, I don't know its rules and I don't give a crap about them. I just want to see David, if that's okay with you.'

She snorted briefly, a sort of impressed half-laugh, then said, 'Here's a beacon, *entre nous*, no snoops. Follow it. I'll clear your path a bit. Give me a sec.'

She dropped the call without another word and within a few seconds, the undergrowth and the overgrowth and the fences and the mud were dissolving away, and replaced by a yellow brick road through a kids' cartoon candyland, towards a diamond floating off in the near distance wreathed by a cartoonish neon sign flashing *Lucie Lucie Lucie* with a theatre-light spangled arrow pointing downwards from the blue heavens. To my left, a unicorn grazed on a marshmallow bush.

24

Eloise's graphic attempts at irony might have cost her energy or, more likely, she simply may have lost interest in goading me, because soon the cartoon-candy shell of the path she'd devised fell away to be replaced by the familiar veneer of suburban Green Valley. Perhaps she'd gone off to get another beer. And the thought set me wondering whether The I had the capacity to make you drunk on imaginary alcohol. Could you sit there sucking at a bottle of potato slop and feel a beer-buzz? Or perhaps Eloise had access to a store of real alcohol – fermenting alcohol from organic matter was one of the most basic technologies of any human settlement, no matter how straitened. I wanted a drink, but more, to be drinking red wine with Fabian on his couch in our apartment, feeling the mellow blur and the heightened touch, something deeper than the skin. I longed to be back home with an aching stretch across space that was too deep and sore to account for the fact that in the real world, I was standing fewer than ten miles away from that warm apartment and that anchoring man. I wished I'd never heard David's voice again, never seen Odille's face reproduced on the little girl in the shelter; I could have turned away, complacent and complicit, from all those dying, invisible children.

I could already recognise how the sterile superficiality of this place made me crave touch, and yearn and ache and regret, and it was a sign that Vidal's interface was working, that rather than having the anguish erased by The I's nano-suppressors, I could feel that craving now, in here, both connected to The I and removed from it. That remove from total immersion in Green Valley, I thought, would help protect me from the worst of the aversion.

But I couldn't be comforted by the familiar concrete sidewalks with their lawned edgings and the white-panel houses set back in their mature front gardens, knowing now that it could all turn, in a twist of malicious imagination, to a psychotic nightmare tunnel, a maze devised by the wizards to torture the creatures stuck in this trap. The ground was unsteady beneath my feet, able to fall away at any moment, and the depth of my skull and the pit of my stomach began to throb with a sort of psychic motion sickness. Yearning for the solidity of hard, real concrete under my feet, I moved my hand behind my neck, touching the toggle there, but I couldn't bring myself to turn it off. For one thing, I'd lose sight of Eloise's beacon, still floating, though less ostentatiously, above the position of David's house; but more than that, I was afraid of what I'd see.

So I walked on, the scuff of my footsteps too loud on the sidewalk, echoing off the walls of the houses that leant in like silent witnesses to an atrocity. It was a strange thought to come up with here, among the motionless trees and the temperate flowers of this catalogue street. How many people lived along these roads? And where were they? All holed up, attached to their devices, like Eloise? Or somewhere else?

The stillness had become so pervasive that I was startled when a bright-blue bird flashed across my path, followed by another pair from a high sycamore bole threaded with Spanish moss, down across the road, and camouflaging themselves on a hydrangea bush in front of an unexpectedly shabby house. Then another blue flash followed, and three more, five, eight – until it was a silent swarm of blue squalling across my path. *Locusts*, I thought for a moment, as the haze expanded towards me, and only now – as the blue shapes whirred past my face and around me, sheening in iridescent waves as they tilted, the individuals still too fast to examine, but the mass taking form, like a swirl-school of paper fish balling and sliding around me – did I hear the slightest whisper of their speeding arc through the air. I had to strain to hear, but a voice resolved out of the wisping hiss, in time with a tickle on my skin like a tiny feather of down travelling over my limbs: 'You want to feel someone, but here is nobody to touch.'

Then the blue stopped and fell, coating the ground where it died, feathery flakes like the dust of a butterfly's wings, in royal and cobalt and indigo and electric oil, coating every surface. The whisper died off into utter silence again, and the colour settled. It was less a sound of a shuffle that brought her to my attention then, than the feeling that I was being watched – by something more intense than these houses, or the presences behind The I. In the static air, the sensation of being scrutinised by a warm-blooded intelligence was so focussed, it had a heft, it almost buzzed in the vacuous space. I glanced to my left and saw her standing still in front of the shabby house, which was cladded in a rusted sanatorium green, a mottled and diseased colour that made me think of the morgue where I had seen the little girl. As the blue powder dissolved, the front lot of the house stood out in mortified contrast to its lush and exemplary neighbours: all that was left of the hedges and shrubs in the front garden were dead twigs poking out of ashy, leached soil and hard nubs of grass roots, pale like maggots, as if they were scrabbling in the dark towards some distant light, knotted between clumps of dogged weeds where a lawn had probably grown.

The woman stood on the bottom step of the house's porch that was flaked and weathered, and as I looked – as The I detected me focussing on the detail of the rotting wood – I smelled a less animal waft this time, a smell of damp decay. A shattered lamp on the porch sputtered with a watery brown light, flickering the artist in and out of silhouette. Like before, she was wearing a long dress, this time in the shimmering blue of today's emotion, all the way to cover her feet, and her long hair, black painted through with silver, hung loose over her shoulders and down her back.

'Welcome to my house,' she said.

I did my best to smile, wondering for the first time what body I was wearing on Vidal's interface, and how I appeared. 'I saw your daughter,' I said, not knowing any more delicate way to raise the issue. Any conversation in this place was tenuous. There was no time to skirt.

She frowned, and the colour seeped out of her dress like water draining from a tub, the blue revealing a monochrome grey in its wake. *Ashen*, I thought at first, and then I saw the colour drifting off in an eddy of breeze that had picked up around the woman. 'My daughter is gone,' she said, and her face slowly cycled from the smooth, iconic composition to a weary, drawn and lined mask. *Not a mask*, I told myself. *This is her real face; this is the mother in mourning.* 'I think she's dead,' she added, as her knees gave in and she crumpled to the ground, her head bowed and her back rounded over the emptiness she cradled in her lap.

I came towards her and squatted down in front of her, afraid to touch her, but reaching out nonetheless, and finding that beneath the rough sackcloth she was both firm and malleable, both warm and touched with the ice of death. 'No,' I said. 'She's not. I saw her yesterday. She is alive, and very brave. She was wearing the shirt you made her, with a panda made of dots. I remembered the dots you showed me when we met last time.'

The artist looked up at me, a jaundiced yellow around her black irises, the lids rimmed red. 'Where is she?'

'Outside. In Stanton. You know where that is?'

She nodded. 'She's alive?'

'And doing good things. She's helping other children survive when they get out of Green Valley.'

She looked back down at her folded arms, the invisible bundle she nurtured there. 'Good. Don't bring her back here. They cannot live here. Nobody should live here.'

'Why don't you leave?' I said with a confidence I didn't believe. 'Rainbow knows how to wean people off The I. Maybe she can help you too.'

'I can't live here. Or there,' she said. 'People like us can't live anywhere.' *Us?* I opened my mouth to ask her what she meant, if she was implicating me too, but my voice died as her sackcloth dress started to twist around her torso, tightening around her arms and twisting them around, tighter and tighter, the audible crackle of her joints ricocheting in the still air, until she was locked in a straitjacket. She looked up at me with a vacant stare, and a line of drool escaped the corner of her narrow lips and I had to watch it sliding down to her chin, hanging on her jawline, and then stretch and fall. I watched where it landed in the barren soil, a pointless little bloom of moisture in the stagnant earth, and when I looked back up at her, the dress was restored to its free flow, but the woman inside it had disappeared. All that remained was her voice, a fading echo: 'There is no home.'

25

David's house appeared as I'd last seen it, the neat, colonial bungalow elegantly matching the subdued opulence of its neighbours. The Spanish moss and subtropical foliage, too lush to be native to our part of the country, looked as Zeroth had imported it when they'd established Green Valley twenty years ago: the integrated, healthy campus town they imagined everyone working in once all workers had been freed by Zeroth technology from the shackles of heavy industry and the grinding commute. It had been a seductive vision, and even I had to credit them with the audacity and hope that having a motivating vision required, no matter how it had been corrupted.

As familiar as the street was, though, the empty windows glaring across at me were discomforting. I could feel the vacancy. I was walking through nothing more than a photograph of what Green Valley once was. Beneath my feet, around me in the dead air, was the real Green Valley, and I was still too afraid to look at it. Without The I's aversion control, I couldn't quell the feeling that the houses around me were all empty, that where once there had lived a thriving and hopeful population, pioneering into a limitless virtual realm, there was now only a cold void. It would have been some light relief to see a jogger or a cyclist like those installed at the town square and the park, or to hear a dog bark. But here in the suburban expanse, it was almost as if the simulation wasn't trying to impress me; the sky was a uniform, sullen, yellowing grey, and the only sound I could hear apart from my own footsteps echoing on the concrete and my breathing too loud in my chest was a groaning creak from the trees' branches, and a tight and rhythmic tap against the wood. *Deathwatch beetles*, I thought, and wondered whether it was Eloise or Gina Orban, Vidal or Jamie Egus himself putting on this morbid show for my benefit.

I went up the porch steps, and as I swiped my hand over the wooden railing, a splinter jagged and bit into my skin between my thumb and forefinger. I yanked my hand back and turned to catch as much of the gloomy light as I could, then picked at the throbbing wound until I found where the dark splinter had gone in. Sliding my thumbnail under the sharp end of the splinter, I drew it out carefully, as a swelling bead of blood welled up out of the tunnel. I put my hand to my mouth and sucked the blood away before approaching the front door and knocking.

The door budged open as I knocked. I pushed it wide and stepped into the entranceway that led through to the sitting room I had seen before. This was David's home still, the place where I'd seen him four days ago; for a deluded moment, I allowed my tight shoulders to relax and the familiar veneer to comfort and anchor me. Then I noticed it: the cheese sandwich on the green ceramic plate at the corner of the coffee table. Three perfect half-moon bites, the sprig of tomato leaf balanced on the edge of the plate. The single tiger-striped sock lying in the middle of the pristine dove-grey carpet. The red-and-blue wooden truck on its side, four building blocks spilled out, spelling Z, K, A, S.

Vidal's interface didn't suppress the icy scrawl that shivered over my skin. 'Hello? Eloise? David?'

All I heard in response was a white-noise hush. I paced a few steps further into the living room of this catalogue home and bent to inspect the toy truck. I righted it on its chunky wheels and drove it over the carpet, feeling the smooth finish of the wood as I pressed it into the lush pile. Had Kira played with this toy? It felt real. I picked the K block up and turned it in my fingers – Ks on all six sides. The other blocks too – only Z, A and S. I dropped them into the back of the truck, deliberately making a noise to test the simulation, wanting to catch it out in its lie, half expecting them to disappear silently as I dropped them, proving their fakeness. But they clacked together with a convincing echo. I held the K block for last, turning and turning her initial in my fingers. Kira. The reason I was here.

I dropped the block, hearing its echo die in the waiting silence.

Then, a sudden waft of air and a scream.

A child.

A shriek, joined by another, and more: laughter.

As if tuning into another frequency, the house brought up the sound of children playing nearby. I stood and walked through the living room into a wide, open kitchen, furnished with unmarked stainless steel and polished granite, unsullied cream tiles on the floor.

The sound of the children was louder now, as if they were in the back garden outside, through the French doors from the kitchen. But there was nobody out in the mist-shaded garden, a small patch of immaculate lawn bounded by newly varnished wood-panel fencing. A slam and a scream, running feet and a thump. Right past me; right *through* me. A bursting balloon. Another series of children's shrieks. Nobody was here, but they were freezing my blood.

Although I might have explained it away as some programmer's whim, my primitive brain knew I was in the presence of ghosts. Taut with fear, I felt the sweat rise on my entire body, physically repelling me from the kitchen and making me run across the living room, through the hall and to the front door. I'd only feel safe when I—

'Lucie.'

Eloise was standing on the turn of the staircase, wearing a naked man's body, like she had before. Her sickly-pale, yellowish mottled skin patchy with wiry smears of black hair, her ribs showing, her dick shrivelled atrophically into itself. Somehow, this mottled authenticity was the most trustworthy thing I'd seen today. I scrutinised her for a while and, feeling the ghosts flee, glanced back into the living room. The toy truck I had righted was on its side again, the blocks reset into their spilt pattern. Z, K, A, S.

When I looked back at Eloise, she was coming down the stairs, covering her genitals with her right hand in a nod to decorum.

'Thanks for the directions. I was stuck in some sort of thicket.'

'Yeah,' Eloise said, skirting around me and leading me towards the strange room where I'd seen her last time. 'That happens sometimes.' I looked at the sagging skin on her butt as she walked, the spine and shoulder bones jutting – Eloise's avatar appeared to be starving.

She turned into the room, and I expected to see the psychedelic meadow with its rainbow-gushing unicorn, but when I turned in, there was Eloise, now clothed in jeans and a plain green T-shirt, greying dark hair scraped carelessly back into a ponytail, sitting on her office chair at a plain white desk in the middle of a small study carpeted in navy blue. *Is this you?* I wanted to ask her.

She indicated the chair at the head of the desk. My legs were tired, but I didn't sit. 'Can you tell me where David is? I need to talk to him.'

'A drink? Anything?' she said.

'No,' I said. 'Where's David?'

'I told you. At a meeting. Why are you here, Lucie? I can understand coming in once, for jollies. Gawping tourist.

But not again. Don't take this the wrong way, but you don't belong here, and you should go home.'

I stepped towards her. 'I have something important to tell him about his daughter.'

'Which one?'

It's The I, I told myself; *it's The I that's blunting her.* I needed to talk to her carefully, or I'd never find David. 'Kira, of course.'

'Oh, Kira,' she said. 'Yes, she's gone too.'

Her voice had taken on that vague blur that I'd heard in David's, so I slapped my hand on the desktop to try to snap her out of it. I'd trusted David; and he'd trusted *this woman* with Odille's daughter. 'Kira's the little girl you've been looking after as your own daughter, Eloise. You must remember her, or else she'll be gone for ever. You don't have any others.'

'Is that what David told you? That we didn't have other children?'

'What are you talking about?'

'The triplets. He told you they were fake? An animation?' Coughing as she exercised her atrophied voice. 'A primitive subroutine? He told you that?'

'Yes, I—'

But she slammed the chair back and stood, grabbed my arm and dragged me out of the office.

'Let me go,' I said. 'Take your hands off me.' But she was pulling me up the stairs. I let her draw me upwards, drag me along the corridor, past the bedroom David had shown me, the bedroom where Kira had been abducted, and through the next door along into another bedroom. This one had three little beds lined up along one blank wall and an expanse of brown carpeting leading to them. The carpet was vacant, making the room lopsided, as if the beds had been stashed to the side and the other contents cleared – it was more like a storeroom than a bedroom. But lying in the middle of the carpet were three pieces of paper with coloured scrawls over them, and I remembered the triplets drawing at the table in Kira's bedroom. I stepped closer and squatted down to the pages. Three identical drawings. Black rams, yellow eyes, hanging head-down from a hook, blood spilling from the gash in its neck.

'I tried to be understanding,' she said as she watched me recoil from the images. 'I tried to forgive him for his negligence, forgive him for his unforgivable sins, because negligence was my sin too. Together, so caught in the simulation, we left them to die. I gave him time to work through his mourning. Grief can fuck you up. But he disappeared, Lucie, somewhere I can't get him back.' Now, in the bedroom, at the foot of that bed where the sheets were sweat-stained and crumpled, she stopped and turned to me. 'If you want to remember his children, remember them all.'

She reached to the back of my neck, gripped, and pulled.

A foul smell hit my face and rocked me back at the same time as darkness blotted the world; the background hum of life disappeared, replaced by a small, regular drip in the corner of the room. My eyes were squeezed shut, limiting the sudden onslaught of information. It was too much for my mind to analyse the new threats or locate and estimate the dripping sound, the keening groan emanating from the floor. My instinct told me to clasp my hands over my ears and curl foetal on the floor, block it all out until I could deal with it, bit by bit. Still, despite my spasming back and the shake in my knees, I stood upright. It wasn't bravery that kept me standing – it was terror of falling into what was covering the floor. Because the ground was soft, shifting with my weight, a sticky pull slurping as I stepped backwards.

The rasp of distressed lungs close to my ear. 'This is what he wants to deny. This is who he's trying to forget.'

Her voice hitching. Then, when I didn't move, she barked, 'Open your fucking eyes, Lucie!'

And I did. God help me.

In the gloom, resolving, the three blackened, bloated, sundered little corpses, neatly aligned, dissolving into a mould-caked bedspread.

26

I turned then and ran, Eloise calling after me. 'Their names were Zara, Anya and Sabine. Add them to your list of the forgotten.'

I ran down the disintegrating stairs, tripping on the water-eaten, dark-stained carpet, landing knee and elbow first, tumbling over when the banister gave way as my head and shoulder smashed into it. Numb to the pain, I rushed on, casting only a glance at the waste-strewn floor of the living room, the rug blackened with blooms of mould and animal smears, back through the cracked and smeared plate glass of the kitchen doors, pale tendrils of some subterranean ivy reaching through shards towards feeble points of brown electric light. Outside the windows, it was cavern dark.

Flinging the front door back so hard that the rusted top hinge gave way, pulling a shard of the door frame away with it, I ran out through the benighted gravel and dead sticks of the remnants of David's real garden, and into the road.

The street was still a street, potholed and cracked, gutters flooded with dark ooze. But the solidity and familiarity of a solid road, lit every fifty paces or so by mouldering brown light, settled me enough to stop gasping and take some air in. I had to connect my I and contact Vidal, and he had to take me out of here.

As I hurtled along the road in what I thought was the direction of the centre, I grappled with the switch at the back of my neck. I lifted the hem of Vidal's electronic top to cover my mouth and nose, but then I couldn't breathe, so I had to run on without a shield, letting the foul rot into my lungs. I worked at the switch; the stupid thing would not turn. Then I felt the wires. Two little points of sharpness, dangling, and now the smashed casing of the switch, and I knew I was alone and unsheltered in Green Valley.

I caved then and fell to my knees on the relatively sterile strip of roadway, fighting the image of those denatured, mortified little girls, still lying there on their melting bed, physically evicting the sight until I got my breathing under control again.

Get it together, Lucie.

I couldn't allow myself to collapse in the middle of a dark road and cry helplessly.

But three thousand lives around me… *Get it together.*

Two things came to mind. I could walk straight until I reached a wall, and then skirt it until I found an exit. Easier said than done in this poisoned bell jar. But Eloise was alive after eight years, and David, I tried to tell myself; the air wasn't instantly toxic. Stumbling on in the dark remained Plan B at best. Plan A, then: try to fix the switch on Vidal's interface, turn it on and get hold of him, or Eloise, or anyone who would lead me out of Green Valley – I'd even give myself up to Gina Orban. First, though, I'd need light to assess the damage.

The road ahead was lit with low, sulphurous light from every third lamp post, like the emergency strip lights in the corridor of a disaster-stricken office building. I realised that's what they were – emergency lights from years ago, still drawing power from the solar-fed batteries installed when the place had been built. It made sense that Zeroth wouldn't waste energy on real lights when everyone was living through The I. Green Valley wasn't designed for offline interlopers. The emergency strips were too dull for me to examine the wiring, so I wandered on, casting my eyes into the textured darkness either side of me, tracing the sagging outlines of dead houses and the spindle fingers of dead trees reaching in a final grasp for the blotted sky. If The I could control my mind with a series of small electrical impulses, I told myself, surely I could do that myself. Nothing real had harmed me in Green Valley while I was connected to The I, so nothing would hurt me now.

But a scurry and a rustle to my left stopped my breath again. Something small. I peered between the dead growth towards a flickering point of brown light, my eyes picking up more detail in the gloom. I was looking down what was once a neat pathway up to a neat little Green Valley house, but the garden's shrubberies had been left to overgrow and then die and now they formed a shield of thickly knotted twigs across the front of the porch. A low, narrow tunnel was carved through the twigs – this house was occupied by someone, or something, living.

I weighed up the potential danger from whatever could shimmy through that narrow gap between the branches against my urgency to repair the switch on Vidal's interface, then ducked towards the brittle hedge and plunged into the gap before I could think too much about what could be living in these dark branches, or beyond, drawn like a moth compulsively towards that throb of light.

This time, the wooded tunnel didn't play tricks on me; it was as wide as it appeared to be, and I swatted my way only a few steps through thick cobwebs, violently slapping the sticky webs out of my hair and off my skin as I emerged on the other side. Three paces from the slumping front porch, I paused. Green Valley's concrete roof loomed over me – no fake sky, no simulated breeze, no false colour. Whatever had become of this place and the people in it, I was seeing what Green Valley really was. It had an edge; it had an end.

Taking the three groaning steps up to the porch, I

ignored the symbolic twig construction nailed to the green-painted door and pushed my way through. I made towards the glow in the front room without looking up or down or to the sides, already unzipping Vidal's top and shucking it off my shoulders, ready to scrutinise the switch's wiring as soon as I reached the light.

When I got into the front room, though, I was forced to a halt; the word *parlour* rolled through my mind, the echo of a nightmare built a hundred years ago. *Come into my parlour...* the voices of dead children chanted in my imagination. The voices of triplet girls. The glow I'd seen from outside wavered from a coffee table that had been turned into an altar, a small twig-hewn shrine built on it. Set into the framework, dozens of pilfered emergency lights, burning brown, sulphur and ochre, undulating in waves as they jostled for control of the same hidden power source.

This was the brightest patch of light I'd come across since Eloise had disconnected me, so I squatted down by the altar and inspected the shirt. *I'm not superstitious,* I told myself.

I'd noticed a sort of pattern in the ripple of the lights, and I turned the broken switch to follow the brightest ebb as it swirled across the altar. The plastic casing was cracked and points of jagged metal protruded between them, along with the bare ends of four fine wires. Even if I had the right tools to strip and solder the wires back to the circuit, I wouldn't know which wire belonged where. Plan A was finished.

Despite everything around it, this altar room felt peaceful and protected. It struck me that this was probably the artist's purpose, and I was tempted to stay here a while, maybe just for a few minutes, maybe until someone found me. It would be a relief not to be feeling and fearing so much, to just take a rest. I was so tired; I'd barely slept for days. Just a short break. I was in the real world, safe in here, surely? The ram couldn't find me here, and that imaginary monster was all

I had to fear in Green Valley. I'd become used to the chill in the room, and maybe, if I just lay back, I'd find that the carpet that once lay here was still thick and warm and soft on the bare skin of my back.

Something crawled up my back, grappling with little hooked feet.

I sprang up, fully awake again, swatting at my skin with my hands and with the cloth of the shirt, and saw shapes drop and disappear, quick, dark blots, into the gaping black corners of the room.

My sudden motion, waving the shirt around, seemed to loosen stagnant eddies of air from dense pockets in the house, and a thick and putrid current wafted slowly from a doorway at the far end of the altar room, followed by the sound of creaking floorboards. Time for Plan B. I hurried Vidal's top back on and ran towards the hallway, where I skidded straight into the path of a dog. Eight years ago it must have been a young retriever, someone's pet, but now its hair was matted, its hackles raised and its teeth bared around something grey, tightly clamped. It growled from the depths of its chest, the low vibration making the air ripple and the hollow wood of the walls resonate; the house was alive and hungry, and I was already in its maw.

The dog stood its ground, front feet planted, tail between its legs, and I knew it was as afraid of me as I was of it. Fearful and ravenous – the worst type of enemy. Sparks of common wisdom chased each other through my mind: retrievers are friendly dogs; they don't bite – it was a formula I'd trusted on my solo walks around Stanton and through the rundown parks as a child, but just like everything else, this dog had been denatured by Green Valley. I stood still. If I left the dog alone, it might just go away.

It seemed about to do that, quietening down and turning gradually away from me, but the smallest subliminal creak on the steps made it prick its ears towards a sound up the stairs, and it started its low growl again. I was standing in the altar room's doorway with my hands up, still frozen to the spot, waiting, but the swirl of movement and sick air happened before I could even process it. A big black shape flew in a hurtling leap from the stairs onto the retriever, the growls exploding into a burst of pure need and foul odour, and before I could even step aside, the dogs barrelled right past me – through me – into and through the altar room. I hit the floor, hard shards of wood buffered by what used to be carpet and was now a mat of mould and waste.

Amplified in the wooden house, the snarls and yips of the dog fight moved further away. Gathering my breath, I rolled myself to sitting, and saw the grey object that the retriever had been carrying in its jaws. It had landed in the spread of light from the altar, and I could see the mottled skin on its three remaining fingers.

27

Plan B, Lucie, Plan B.

It's logical, isn't it? You're in the real world, with real dimensions. Just run until you find the wall, and skirt it until you find an exit.

Nothing can hurt you in here. All the damage has already been done.

Plan B, Lucie. Just keep moving. Green Valley is only three miles across.

I stopped when I came to the gatehouse that I recognised from the old brochures. The stylised Z of the logo, the bright pastel colours of the rest of the corporation's name hung artfully over the patterned face-brick building were as clean and polished as they'd always appeared in the catalogues and news reports decades ago. This gateway to Zeroth's Green Valley campus had been the ubiquitous symbol of modern, soft and environment-friendly business, and stood out in its pool of bright electric light like a service station on a night road.

Slowing my breathing, I approached the booth, half expecting to see a guard posted there, as if the putrefying wasteland around it was an illusion. Although the lights were on and the windows recently cleaned, the booth was empty, no screens or files on the desks, only the steady red stare of LEDs over the cameras posted to every angle around the building.

I felt the cameras on my back as I walked up the road, following a path of garden lights glowing brightly along the driveway towards a low building at the top of a gently landscaped hill. The building exuded a warm yellow glow from its banks of bright windows, looking just as it had in the tourist shots all those years ago, as if the Zeroth campus remained immune to the waste pooled at its foot.

As I approached the main doors, something moved across the bank of the upper storey's windows, and I froze, scanning the spot, but nothing stirred. I considered going back down the slope and out of the campus, continuing on my path to the wall, but the safety of the bright, warm light was seductive. If anyone was living in here, I could face them. Far better than going back out there, into the darkness, where there was only death.

A red-eyed sensor blinked, and the front doors opened automatically, just like pre-Turn office buildings used to, citizens never considering the price of that simple convenience as the server banks stored their movements and their moods. I wondered whether anyone was watching me enter in a security office in the bowels of the building, or whether the Zeroth computers were just digitising me for later analysis and conglomeration. I felt the corporation's clingy fingers reaching out towards me from the motion sensors and the red, unblinking eyes trailing over and through my skin.

The polished marble floors of the wide and lofty atrium gleamed, reflecting the looming shadows of three gigantic insectile shapes: three dead palm trees planted in an oasis in the middle of the space, beside the swirl of the reception desk. *Zeroth: better than first* was still marked out boldly across the wall behind the desk, but like the desk's surfaces and the steel banisters and the stairs and the seating in clustered islands in the atrium – like everything above floor level – the letters were dulled and tarnished, layered with dust. A low mechanical whine, like the keen of trapped wasps, echoed from some corner of the space, but over it I could hear the bass tones of an amplified voice from somewhere further away.

I stared down at the shining floor, for a second seduced into believing I was somewhere normal again, not in a place where corpses putrefied on beds and makeshift shelves and where pet dogs scavenged body parts. For a second, I was in an anodyne office block, plush and characterless, untainted by death. But the illusion was broken by a tangled trail of shoeprints painted in sludge from the front door towards the wide, sweeping staircase leading to a mezzanine level. Strips of this muddy pathway had been erased haphazardly by whoever had cleaned the floor. Following the voice, I trailed the footprints up the stairs and to the right, where more trails of footprints converged, muddying a broad carpeted corridor towards a double door marked *The Ingenuity Auditorium*.

The voice began to resolve from a meaningless throb to muffled speech as I approached the doors, and I made out a male voice saying '…innovative product launches of the season. The Comsec team has worked for seventeen months on the project, and I'm sure you'll be as excited by the end result as I was. Let's ask David to tell us more.'

I pushed through the doors as quietly as I could, hit in the face by a pungent waft, and shifted my back to the wall on my right. There were about twenty broad rows of seats in the auditorium, and it was dark but for a bright projection at the back of the stage, displaying swirling colours and a square, metallic device floating in front of the Zeroth logo. The absurdity struck me then. Keeping up the pretence, like it was twenty years ago. How long had this projector been shining out its images when nobody would be off The I to see it? Nobody but me. In the darkness, I could make out the silhouettes of a scattering of people occupying a swathe of seats in the middle towards the front. An old man with a white beard and wearing a pair of jeans and a casual tan jacket, who I recognised as Jamie Egus, even with the overgrown facial hair and the extra decade, limped across the stage to sit upon a lone chair, while David approached the lectern.

What struck me most about him, seeing his real body for the first time in so many years, was how much he looked like his avatar. He seemed not to have aged, even in the midst of all this decay. He trained a steady, arrogant gaze into the camera.

He began to speak, amplified and confident: holding forth with practised peaks and troughs. This was David Coady, once Zeroth's most charismatic director, Stanton's fast-track success story. A massive image of his avatar's perfectly made-up face, smooth and clean, unlike everything else in this place, was projected onto the screen behind him, bobbing and swerving in macro scale as he gestured. The cadence of his voice gripped me as I sat down to listen, and I believed what he was saying, even though I couldn't understand it.

And I tried. At first I thought I was not seeing through the jargon, but as I concentrated harder on trying to parse the syntax of David's words, I realised that he really wasn't making any sense.

'Software evangelists working with Zeroth of the most complex. Floribunda scenarios to choose the power of I-Mesh to run only selected I-Mesh devices. This number less than twelve periods.'

I tried to grab onto subjects, objects, verbs, but they were all mangled. The more I tried to focus on his words, the more the meaning slipped away.

'Where only two of the program, and in the past, now, and the first I-Mesh device, as well as the test.'

My mind twisted and cramped, rebelling like it did the moment when I tried to look into the ram's face. There was nothing there, only a chaotic void.

I tried to look away; I tried to stop listening. But when I let his speech wash over me without trying to understand it, his voice lulled me.

This is a man who lets his children die and then forgets them.

If Eloise had told the truth.

'I know, and we believe that open and for a strong case under the guise of trying to cover up the real question is: "What is the real customers, compared to knowledge?" We left a lot of the daily losses.'

You saw them, Lucie. With your own eyes.

'But it's those failing belief in the future' – he paused, as if scanning the room for me, even though I knew he was seeing only whatever glorious vision The I was projecting into his mind, and that he couldn't find me because I was not on the interface – 'those who infiltrated the organisation, trying to destroy our future generations have done honour to work.' He was talking to me. He knew I was here. 'Those are people who surely futureless.'

I glanced at the stage, at the giant image of David next to the small version of him at the lectern, but his image faded, replaced by the swirling Zeroth logo, and the lights came on. Jamie Egus was on his feet again, applauding in David's direction, looking out over the dust-caked seats with an encompassing smile, as if he were riding the swell of a standing ovation. David clasped his hands together and then spread his arms wide in a crowd embrace, now a half-bow and a gesture towards Egus, the man they should all be thanking.

But there was no sound in the room, other than Egus's clapping, and whatever rapturous applause they were hearing and seeing was being piped into their brains by The I.

David stopped and looked at me, directly at me, then turned and walked into the wings. Springing up, I vaulted onto the stage and ran across it, following him, but found only a locked door. I knew I shouldn't, but I looked back at the small scattering of the audience where they were seated in the auditorium in their once-best suits. My eyes adjusted to the subtle lighting, I could make out hands folded neatly in laps, shoes half on where not chewed away. Lank hair, matted. The heads lolling at uncomfortable angles. Grey skin, patches of purple flesh, bare bones on old corpses.

'David!' I called, knowing it was hopeless, knowing he would be hearing only what he chose to hear in his gilded fantasy of corporate success. 'David!' I yanked at the handle, the door rattling too loudly in the auditorium. I was answered by a slow handclap from across the room.

Slap, slap, slap. Languid and ironic.

'I'd buy what he's selling, wouldn't you?' Vidal stood from his seat, far corner, front row.

'Where the hell have you been? Where did you go?' I regretted the relief in my voice.

But he was looking back towards the rear of the auditorium. 'No,' he muttered in a phone-call undertone. 'Not right now… As agreed… It'll be fine.'

I glanced one more time at the locked stage door. All this time I'd been trying to get hold of David to tell him I'd found his daughter, but it finally struck me: where David was, he couldn't hear or help me, and they were all right – Vidal, Rainbow and her mother – Kira should never come back here. Now I knew what had become of Green Valley, and now I needed to leave this poisonous place. Vidal would show me the way out.

Vidal had ended his brief call and turned towards me, almost smirking in my direction. As I hurried towards him, his face changed and he rushed to meet me, reaching out towards the neck of my body suit where the wires dangled from the broken switch.

'What happened to this?' He stepped back, looking me up and down, then his face bloomed in undisguised shock.

'Holy shit. You've been in here… raw?'

All I could muster was a nod as the enormity of what I'd seen in Green Valley smashed into me and choked me.

'For how long?'

'A while. A long time. I've been looking for a way out.'

'Who did this? Why?'

But I was already heading for the auditorium's exit, trying not to glance again at the corpses in their formal array in the seats. Someone, offline, must have chosen this theatre as a mausoleum. And why not? It was a more peaceful resting place than many. Someone had tried, at least, to honour these people in their deaths. You can't bury the dead in a concrete floor. 'Just take me out of here, Vidal,' I said.

Vidal caught up with me as I pushed out of the theatre doors and was hurrying back down the carpeted corridor towards the staircase. 'Let me try and fix this.' He reached his arms around me, to the back of my neck, and fiddled with the shards for a moment. Then he shook his head and frowned. 'So you've been seeing… everything.' Again that querying gaze into my eyes, over my body, as if he expected me to explode or shatter into pieces.

Vidal's shock validated my reaction. Maybe it wasn't so shameful that I'd spent the last however long screaming and gasping in snot-clogged revulsion and terror. 'That's what you brought me here to see, isn't it?'

'Yes, but I was just planning to give you a glimpse. Just a controlled look. That would have been enough.' And when I couldn't bring myself to say anything in response he repeated, 'Wouldn't it? Are you okay, Lucie?'

'Where were you?' I didn't want to wheedle; I didn't want to shout, *Why did you leave me?* like some pathetic adolescent. We were standing at the tarnished railing overlooking the building's entrance lobby, which was being randomly patrolled by three little automatic floor polishers, whining like trapped wasps as they worked. 'You just disappeared.' The robots clunked into walls and furniture and switched direction to another random course.

'No.' He shook his head vehemently. 'We discussed it. I thought you were going to go to the town square, have a coffee, whatever.' I tried to play back the moment in the park. I was sure I hadn't made any plans with him. I'd been on my knees, vomiting into the shrubbery. 'Like any normal person would,' he continued. 'I told you I had a meeting, that I'd come back.' We were interrupted by a heavy thump, a crash in the corridor behind me that was too loud to be another cleaning machine.

When I startled and turned to look over my shoulder, Vidal said, 'Can you hear that?'

'Yes, of course.' A shadow, large and slow, was stretching out of a doorway between us and the auditorium. 'What is it?'

'You shouldn't have heard it. Not if you're disconnected.'

'What *is* it, Vidal?' I pressed, but as the shadow emerged and I saw the first glimpse of black, matted fur that was casting it, a gnarled curl of horn, hinting at the golden slitted eye that would cut into me, my body was already in motion, running down the stairs. Halfway down the staircase, my foot lost purchase on the years' layers of dust and dander and I stumbled, but it didn't stop me, and I was out of the building and running down Zeroth's driveway, into the darkness. Vidal was behind me, yammering on as if it was important: 'But you're not connected. You don't come up on my scan. You shouldn't be seeing it. You're clear; I checked you when I fitted my interface. You're completely offline.'

'Shut up, Vidal!' I called back. 'Get us out of here.'

As we passed the gatehouse Vidal caught up with me. 'Not that way,' he gasped. 'Here.' We ducked into a stand of dead birches, the soft yellow glow from the emergency lights on the road strafing through them in disorienting stripes.

The stripes were blocked out by the shadow, the stink of tallow and congealed blood from the ram's pelt pursuing us as fast as we ran. I could hear its ragged teeth grinding, spittle foaming, the crack of sticks and the slurp of mud under its hooves.

We shoved our way through desiccated undergrowth and plunged out onto a roadway again, and I recognised where we were: the town square. The shops were slumped and dust-caked, signs peeling and windows shattered, gutters overfilled with debris and failed colonies of weeds.

As we belted across the long, dry grass on the square, I ignored the scurry of small creatures and the suck of putrid mud at my boots. Past the bandstand, roof caved in and railing flaked to stagnant drifts below, past a decrepit playground and seized merry-go-round. Something, someone, shrank back from us as we sprinted, but I didn't look into her eyes, afraid that I'd draw the ram's attention to her as it passed. *Hide*, I willed her. *Hide until we come back for you.*

Then we were through the square and jogging along one of the facsimile residential streets. Vidal slowed his pace.

'Keep going,' I yelled, glancing back. 'Why're you stopping?'

'It's gone,' he said, slowing to a walk, checking behind him. I could see his gaze switching between The I's overlay and what was real. 'We lost it.'

The shadow was still looming behind us, keeping pace. 'No, we haven't,' I said. 'Come on!'

'It's gone, Lucie. It must be a flashback or something, that's all.'

And with the word – *flashback* – as if all of this could just be explained away as a bad trip, my mind wanting so desperately to believe in comfortable explanations, the shadow stopped moving. 'I saw it. It was chasing us. You saw it too.'

'Yeah, through The I,' he said, speaking softly, as if to a frightened child. 'We're close to the delivery bay. It's just through there. You've had to take in more than you ever should have.'

'Don't patronise me,' I hissed. 'I know what I saw. But what I don't know is how you can slip so comfortably in here and *have meetings* with the freaks who've done this, who've let all these people die.' And that was all David was to me at that moment – a freak, a murderer. He'd worked with Egus to build all this. I rounded on Vidal, grabbing the front of his shirt, with a fistful of hair and skin, wanting to gouge into him, but he stood passively, patiently, hands out. 'You're doing business with the fucking Devil. For what? For money? You're filthy.' I shoved him away. But I was as filthy as him, I knew, snooping for a living, just like Zeroth. I was complicit.

I trailed him in silence along the curving suburban road, until he turned left down a narrow walkway between two houses. When the way narrowed, I remembered the constricted tunnel of foliage I'd been caught in earlier, and wondered if Vidal was leading me into a trap. But that had been online.

'Could I have imagined it?' I asked Vidal as he strode ahead, half to break the unsettling silence, and half to gauge how badly I'd damaged my relationship with this ally. 'The ram?'

He took a few more steps in silence, playing my anxiety out, then relented. 'No, not pure imagining. Flashbacks can be very convincing. But I'm certain that you're clear of tracers, so there's no way you would really have seen it.'

I was starting to believe him; the fear had dissipated like a bad dream. It was as if I'd been visiting a memorial to a place where something tragic and evil had happened a long time ago. There was a still, cold stink in the air, and old ghosts, but for the moment that was all in the past. Intellectually, I could call up images of the dead triplets, all the other decay I'd witnessed that day, but my mind wouldn't let me feel it any more – my glands were spent for the day and my brain was in charge; the native chemicals in my brain were managing my emotional reactions just as effectively as The I ever could.

'How did this happen?' I asked.

'We let it happen,' Vidal said. 'All of us.'

'You're right about one thing, though,' I said, because at that moment I truly believed it. 'Those children are the only remnant of this place we can save.'

We trudged on for a minute more and I saw the end of the narrow pathway, and beyond it, the familiar concrete loading bay. The mountains of garbage to one side that had seemed so offensive to me when we'd first entered hours ago were a homely relief, like a link to the normal processes of civilisation. We were leaving Green Valley.

Vidal went through the gap first and turned right, disappearing. I followed, and walked straight into a hard, dark shadow.

VII

28

'This is why we don't advise coming in on unauthorised devices,' Gina Orban said, trying to place the flat of her hand against my back as she led me through the tunnel.

I squirmed away; I knew where to go. The tunnel led only one way: away from the loading bay in a gentle curve. In the skeleton strip-light, only one neon tube lit up every ten paces, I could see how the tunnel was moulded out of cement and lined with fat brackets of cabling just above head level. Where their coating of dust had been disturbed or clawed away over the years, the plastic sheaths of the cabling peeked through brightly – yellow, green, blue, red. Steel plumbing followed parallel with the bundles of wiring, some of the joints leaking, painting rusty smears down the light cement below and onto the floor. We were walking around the base of the wall, the functional shell that kept the illusion of Green Valley alive for those inside. The volumes of personal data churning around this electronic shell once would have outstripped the worst imaginings of the Luddites outside.

'It's a free world after all,' Gina went on in her nonchalant lilt, as if she were the last person in the world who'd defend repressive regulations. 'Visitors are entitled to come and go, but the interference needs to be managed properly, otherwise…'

She reached out again, and I knew in her way she was trying to make me feel better – she could see the state I was in – but I twisted away and faced her, planting my feet in a thin imitation of a warrior, the muscles under my ribs cramping and searing at the sudden movement. 'Don't.

Don't touch me.' I was made of shards of lead, grinding against each other, the lactic acid or the spent adrenaline from my fright, or whatever poison it was, turned to sludge in my muscles. 'Interference? Is that what you call it? There are corpses in piles in here, Gina.'

She shook her head, smiled patronisingly, but it was just a stock motion of her lips. She didn't believe herself. 'No, honey. It's just code. Bad-natured code. It's all an illusion.'

I'd walked straight into Gina just as Vidal and I were near the loading-bay door. She'd caught hold of me, feigning surprise to see me there, while Vidal slipped away like a rat into the darkness.

'Bullshit,' I spat, trying to goad her into giving something away, just a little wink that she knew what I'd seen and that she was in on it. 'You know what I saw. I saw the truth. I wasn't on any interface – *authorised* or not. You've seen it. That's what your little act's all about, isn't it? Avoidance, denial, self-delusion. You can't bear it, can you? That you're the warden of that' – I pointed at the inner wall of the tunnel, all that stood between the civilised world and Zeroth's apocalypse – 'that disease, that decay. That evil.'

She shook her head, her mask in place, turned and walked on. 'Interference, that's all,' she said. Could it be that Gina had only ever skirted the periphery, along this tunnel? I couldn't imagine any other way that she could stay so complacent. She was allergic to The I, so she would have to see what I had just seen every time she went into Green Valley. If she never had to look at those horrors, she could safely convince herself that they didn't exist. The alternative – that she was aware of what lay inside, that she was knowingly hiding the truth from people outside – was too frightening to allow.

I scrutinised her face, traced her movements for any sign of complicity, but her body remained relaxed, guilt-free.

Some minutes later, by the time she unlocked a door in the inner wall and showed me through to the changing area I recognised from my first visit here, she'd learned not to reach for me. 'At least let me help you get washed up, offer you some clean clothes,' she said, turning to one of the lockers.

But I was onto her. I was coated in filth, head to toe, and I was convinced that some of the mess was blood, some of it putrefied flesh. Some of it could even be – I had to force myself to remember, and to think the words – the remains of David and Eloise's children. 'No. Let me out of here, now.' I had to leave with the evidence intact.

I pushed my way out of the changing room, hurried across her office with the homely touches – the South American cloths and the Japanese ceramics, the battery-operated flamingo lights flickering in the lonely air – and shoved at the handle of the locked glass door to Stanton. I watched her coming towards me across the faded Zeroth carpet, trailing her hands almost ritually over the mohair throw on the back of her thrift-store sofa, a thoughtful look on her face. Something in her eyes as she approached, hard and dark, a yellow glint. Yes, a tallow stink in my nostrils, the funk of damp, dirty wool, and I could feel the ram reaching for me as Gina's arm came towards me.

And past me, to unlock the door.

'Free country,' Gina repeated with a disappointed sigh as I walked out onto the frigid street, a plastic bag swirling up in the eddy of wind to greet me. Nobody pulling me back, no demonic ram stringing me up. Not this time. It was the fake strawberry of a protein shake on her breath that I was smelling, the essential oils she'd dripped on herself.

29

The cold late-afternoon sun slanted into the concrete wall, making it look warm. I'd been in there maybe ten hours, and the day outside had passed as normal while I'd lived that endless nightmare.

I walked right through the dead suburbs and halfway to the centre of Stanton before I found a taxi that would stop for me. It was hard enough out there at the best of times, but it didn't help that my hair was crazily tufted and I was smeared in muck – not the sort of fare a cabbie with options would choose on a Saturday evening. Maybe this driver had fewer options than most, or fewer prejudices, but he still seemed relieved when he dropped me at the Stanton precinct and I actually paid him.

The weekend-shift guard at the door didn't recognise me, and he glanced through me and wrinkled his nose as I went inside. Just another victim. I went through the charge office, the officers behind the desk not raising their eyes from their glacial affidavit dictation and the photocopier conversations, and up the stairs to the archive offices as if I was invisible.

In my office, I found the overalls I sometimes used when we went into the deep evidence store, and the jacket I'd left on the back of my chair so long that it seemed part of the upholstery; I changed and bagged up the clothes I'd worn in Green Valley.

Upstairs, there was only a scattering of skeleton staff on the detectives' floor, and I was disappointed not to see Jordan jutting out of his chair, bent over case files, even though there was no reason for him to be in today. He was probably in a bar, watching a game, and the image of that cosy normality gave me an unexpected punch of breath-hitching nostalgia. A couple of the detectives looked towards me as I stopped in my tracks, steadying myself on a cubicle partition while I levelled my breathing again, but turned back to their work as soon as I moved on.

Bert Halstrom was sitting at his small table in the Sentinel lobby, filling in a crossword from the weekend paper.

'Discard the mistaken nobleman in capital city,' he said.

'Excuse me?'

'Six letters. It's after hours, Ms Sterling. Nobody's in.' His eyes shifted focus from the newspaper to where I was standing in front of him, taking in my getup of bare feet, blue overalls and corduroy jacket, the transparent plastic bag of stained clothes and the filthy boots I was holding in my fist.

'Are you sure?' I approached the inner door and made a show of pressing my ear to it. 'I can hear voices inside, people typing.'

'Office hours Monday to Friday, nine to five,' he said. 'Saturdays nine to one. As you should know, Ms Sterling. That's official policy. We follow national regulations in this office, Ms Sterling.'

'Knock it off, Bert, please. I need to see Barbra, urgently. She'll be very interested in what I have here. Very interested.'

Bert shrugged. 'I can leave her a message.'

I swore under my breath. 'Don't worry.'

I hurried back to Jordan's desk and picked up his phone. The other detectives weren't interested in what I was doing. I dialled Sentinel's number. The answering service voice: 'Welcome to Stanton Police, administrative department sixteen. Stanton PD's administrative office hours are Monday to Friday, nine to five, and Saturdays nine to one. Please leave a message and contact details outside those hours.'

'Barbra, it's Lucie Sterling.' I glanced at the clock on the wall. 'It's Saturday, half past five. I have something very important from… inside. Physical evidence. It's bad, Barbra. Worse than any of us imagined.' I hesitated before adding, 'I think you're in the office now, and I hope you'll get this. I'll wait a few minutes, but I need to leave soon.'

I left Jordan's desk extension number, then picked up the phone on the desk opposite and dialled Fabian's number. There was no answer. I pictured the two phones ringing in their lopsided harmony, vibrating the still air in the apartment. Where was Fabian? I dialled the messaging service; no messages.

I might have gone back down to my office to check the pneum box, but I remembered that the pneum in the apartment had been out of order, and I wanted to wait by Jordan's phone in case Barbra called back. I'd give her until six; if she hadn't called me in by then, she either wasn't there or she wasn't planning to humour me today.

So goddamn stupid, I started seething to myself, *short-sighted*. She'd want to know about the children, about the bodies littering Green Valley. Surely she would. Surely, despite the treaty and the official blindness, the scale of the devastation in Green Valley demanded a response from us outside.

Now I heard a clinking shuffle, and turned to see Bert approaching me. 'Ms Reeve says to leave it with me,' he said, pointing towards the bag of my clothes.

I reached for the bag, ready to hand it over, then stopped. His hand was frozen in a receiving gesture. How did I know Barbra had sent him? He could just as easily be working for someone upstairs – he might simply throw it in the incinerator. But if he was telling the truth, getting the evidence to Barbra was the only practical thing I could do, the only way to escalate the case; I couldn't refuse her.

I reached over to the bag. 'I'm just going to hang onto the boots, all right? I can't go home in bare feet.'

I studied Bert's face as he shrugged; either it made no difference to him, or he was a good actor.

But as I pulled the boots out of the bag, I got a closer look at their treads, caked with nuggets and mud and blood and ooze of Green Valley's firmament. Barbra had to have this analysed too – she had to get everything I had collected, and she had to see it now.

I looked at Bert's face, into his eyes, and decided to trust him. 'Never mind, I'll find some trainers in the gym.'

'Okidoke.' He grabbed the bag and the boots and sauntered back towards the stairwell.

'Berlin,' I said behind him.

He turned. 'Excuse me?'

'Your clue. Berlin.'

Now he smiled. 'Of course! Berlin. Good one, Ms Sterling.'

I knew I should go home and tell Fabian where I'd been, but first, I needed to hold Kira, as if my belated care could ever heal her. The only thing that could keep me sane was the hope that for all those years she was plugged into The I, there was never a false moment or a glitch when she would have experienced raw reality. I ran through Claymarket, towards Vidal's shelter.

The front door of Barrett & Sanders was locked when I got there, the blinds down. I rattled the doorknob, then glanced behind me, over the road. I couldn't see Officer Danielewski or any other patrol officer watching the building – they'd probably called off the surveillance – but still, I didn't want to draw attention to myself or the building, especially now that I knew what it was sheltering.

Instead, I went down the alley and around into the parking lot. Vidal's car was still there, but that didn't mean he was back yet. If he was here, it would mean he'd abandoned me to my fate in Green Valley and skulked to safety. I collected a handful of small stones and started pinging them into the middle-floor windows. It took nine stones and one crack for the curtain in Rainbow's room to twitch. When Vidal pressed his face closer to the window to peer down at me, his expression was so relieved that it diluted my anger.

He held up his hand – *wait there*. A minute later, he'd joined me in the lot, giving my overalls a brief once-over.

'Lucie, thank God. She didn't put anything in you?'

'You knew it was Gina?'

'Yeah. She didn't fit you with anything, did she?' he repeated.

'No. I didn't let her touch me… except… she did press my shoulder here.'

'But no pain, no stab, right?'

'No. Would I have definitely felt it? Could she have put something in me just with her palm like this?' I put the flat of my hand against Vidal's back, like Gina had done when she'd guided me through Green Valley's peripheral tunnel.

'You'd have felt it. You'd have known if she'd inserted another tracer. Unless you were unconscious. Were you?'

'No.'

'At no stage?'

'No.'

'Okay, then you're probably still clear. It looks like we got away with it last time. Bringing you downstairs, out of the perimeter, with the tracers still in you. They don't seem to have picked you up. If Egus knew we were here, we'd be fighting a barrage of intrusions, but there's no unusual traffic. We were very lucky. So if you're clear now, we should be fine to let you in. Come. Quickly, quietly.'

Without speaking, I followed him around to the street

and ducked inside, only letting my lungful of air go when we were up the stairs and locked in behind the hatch door.

'How is she? How are the kids?'

'They're all fine. Still online. Rainbow will turn them off again tonight.'

I trailed him up to the next level and looked in on Kira, who was sitting slumped against her headboard in the exact same position Rainbow had set her the night before. But she was awake, in a virtual sense, her head slowly turning as she followed the view of whatever was being spooled into her ocular nerves, a smile playing over her lips, and then a frown. Then she began to talk, but no language I'd ever heard, that static-electricity crackle, the void-tuned radio hiss I'd heard them making in the night. These poor children had become machines, bypassing the middle step of fake translation and talking directly to the system in code.

In a better world, Kira's mother would be sitting with her and watching over her in this trance, but I was not her mother and this was a fucked-up world and I couldn't bear standing idly by, unable to make a difference.

'What time is she coming off tonight?'

'Midnight till two again. They're calmer then.'

'Will she be okay until then?'

'Yes.'

'Will you let me in when I come back, so I don't have to wake the neighbourhood?'

He pursed his lips and nodded.

30

The lounge lights were still on when I came in. I imagined Fabian sitting up worried or in silent anger on the couch, so I angled straight for the bedroom, not glancing through the lounge door as I passed. I did owe him an explanation, but I couldn't take this up with him soaked in sweat and Green Valley shit.

I shucked off my makeshift outfit, had a shower, and got dressed into my own clothes, feeling like a knight strapping on armour, all the while imagining long-suffering Fabian in the lounge, pretending to read, waiting for his prodigal to return, an absurdly biblical tableau, and it was only when I stepped out into the passageway and felt the prick and crumble of a small clod under my foot that I noticed them.

The impressions in the thick pile of the cream-coloured passageway carpet were unmistakable, but still I squatted down for a closer look.

Hoofprints.

I was no farmer, but I knew they were the hoofprints of a ram, interspersed by clumps of dirt scattered along the carpet where it had walked. Not farm-mud, but the cess of Green Valley dried and caked in the clefts of its feet, or fallen from the matted skeins of its gore-soaked hair, my consciousness admitting it at last.

'Fabian?' No more than a whisper. It might still be here.

Now I was up and hurrying quietly, following the dirty spoor, pushing through the doorway to the lounge. He wasn't on the couch.

'Fabe?'

A book on the floor, the novel Fabian had been reading; a drinking glass on its side on the rug, whiskey soaked in around it, the ice long melted.

'Fabian?' My voice was too loud. I tiptoed into the kitchen. Nothing out of place, everything as we generally left it: a few dishes in the sink, a couple of mugs on the counter; nothing pulled out of place, nothing smashed, nothing spilled. Had I just imagined it again?

No. I peered back through the door into the lounge. The heavy prints, the muddy leavings trailed over the rugs in the lounge, pressed out as clearly as stencils. Unless this was a new, self-conscious form of hallucination The I was treating me to, I knew I wasn't dreaming this up. I could follow the trail into the kitchen right to where I stood, imagining that sickening clicking of its bony nubs on the white tiles, Fabian's home become that clinical slaughterhouse it had shown me.

I circled the counter on my way out and saw a smear of blood on the floor by the washing machine. My thoughts and my muscles focussed in icy precision, I went to the knife block. Someone had got here before me, and the largest butcher knife had been removed. I had to settle for the cleaver and a small parer.

Hurrying back up the passage, following the spoor into the study, I was almost gratified to find evidence of an invasion. Nothing much: just a few books flipped open on my desk, the handful of photos from my top drawer spread across the blotter, but enough to prove that someone – or something – real had been in here. As I turned, I noticed bare footprints on the carpet beside the desk – human footprints pressed out in faint smudges of blood and mud, a drag and a scuffle over the pile.

'*Fabian!* Fabian, where are you?'

I retraced my steps, bargaining with the truth despite all

the evidence: maybe it was just a common burglary; maybe the guy just had funny shoes; maybe the criminal had cut himself with a knife while he was forcing my desk drawer open. I could swear I'd left it locked. Maybe Fabian had been out when the intruder came in, I reasoned against the evidence. *He's got a life – he doesn't just sit on hold, waiting for me when I'm away. He'd go to a show, for a drink, for a walk. Maybe this mud is from the park.*

A knock now, a clink; a small shatter, and I was running to the source, the guest bathroom off the entrance hall, where Fabian was trying to pull himself up against the basin with his left arm while clasping his forehead with his right.

'Ow! Motherfucker,' he said. I almost laughed, both in relief that he was well enough to swear, and at the profanity that spat off his elegant lips. Blood was oozing around the palm clamped to his head.

'Here, let me.' I wet a facecloth under cold water and tried to pry his hand away from the wound. He was pressing tightly, as if his life depended on it, as if he'd lose all his blood, or his brain would fall out of the hole. When he eventually let go, the released pressure did send a dramatic well of blood out and over his brow and through his eyebrows, but it was only a surface wound. The skin around the gash was purple and puffy, but his hard skull seemed intact. I pressed the flannel against it, staunching the flow, and Fabian winced and leaned into my touch.

'What happened?' I said.

'It's going to sound mad, but it was…' I waited. I had to hear him say the words himself. *Please tell me you saw a black ram in our apartment.* It would prove to me that I wasn't demented, that it wasn't just flashback and residue, that Zeroth's fuckery really extended beyond and outside my mind. If Fabian had seen what I'd been seeing, it would mean everything – it would mean that Zeroth was committing crimes in Stanton's jurisdiction, and that nobody here could say it wasn't their business.

But Fabian shook his head. 'No. It was dark. I couldn't see him properly.'

'Go on, Fabe,' I said, trying not to lead him but desperate to hear him say it. 'What did you see?'

'I could swear it was…' He shook his head again, his own mental controls asserting themselves over his reality. 'I was sitting in the lounge when someone came in. He just walked in. There wasn't a noise or anything breaking. I thought it was you. I heard him moving around in your study, like you do sometimes before you come and say hello.' I blushed with guilt; it felt shameful, how offhandedly he described my coldness, but he was absorbed in his story. 'So I waited a little, but then I heard something falling, so I got up. I still thought it was you. I was so stupid. I thought you were going postal on the pneum or something.' He snorted a rueful laugh. 'So I just strolled up, and I saw him…'

'What did you see? What did he look like?'

He looked me in the eyes, and for a moment I thought I understood his appeal – *I'm not making this up; I'm not batshit; you've got to believe me. It was a giant fucken black sheep, standing on its back legs. Tall, like this.* But it was a punch of disappointment when he finally said it: 'It was David Coady, Lucie. I've only ever seen him in pictures, in publicity footage for Zeroth. He was bundled in a dark overcoat, a hood over his head, but I recognised him. I'm certain of it. He turned to face me when I came into the room. He looked like shit.'

'David? Here?' So I wasn't being tracked by some super-soldier from cyberspace; it was only David. Deflated, I went back out into the passageway and looked again at the prints and the smudges on the carpet. I'd been so willing to believe. But here they were: just shoeprints after all, my mind resketching the hoof dents I'd so fervently imagined.

'Did he speak to you? What did he want?' I said as Fabian trailed me out, taking stock of the urbane little mess trailed through the apartment.

'I don't know. He didn't talk to me. He didn't even engage with me. He was sitting at your desk, just flipping through your things as if he belonged there, as if he were the one waiting for you to come home. When he saw me, he stood up and walked past me, almost through me, to the kitchen. That's where I…'

'Go on.'

'I'd been tired and worried all day. I'd been waiting for you to come home, Luce, and I was in a foul mood. And this was David fucking Coady, Zeroth visionary… breaking into my home. It's almost as if this intrusion gave me licence to… I'm so sorry.'

'What did you do?'

'I took a knife out of the block and threatened him. I don't know which was worse, having our home invaded or being rendered invisible by this… ghost, but I was so angry. I shouted at him and waved the knife, like a complete goddamn fool, and he just ignored me. And the more he ignored me, the madder I got. So I went closer to him, and he hit me, kind of swatted at me without even looking. It wasn't so hard, but I slipped and whacked my head against the kitchen cabinet. I crawled into the bathroom, and I must have passed out for a second.'

'Oh, Fabe, I'm so sorry.' I could almost laugh. If Fabian ever got involved in a fight, this is exactly how it would go. And I loved him for it. I loved that he was so unprimed for brutality that he couldn't even get violence right. This was why I'd so readily succumbed to him those years ago: his was the gentleness I constantly searched for. I touched my fingers to the hand that was clamping his forehead. 'Are you sure you're okay?'

'I'm fine,' he said. The phone started ringing in the study.

'Did you hear him leave?' I asked Fabian. 'Did he let himself out?'

'I guess so. I didn't hear. He's not here now.'

I went to pick up the phone.

'Hello?'

'I'm too late, I know. He's been and gone.' The voice was granulated, swooping and eddying as if through a cosmic distance, denatured by the shift between there and here, but I knew Eloise was only a few miles away.

'What does he want from me, Eloise?'

'Same as you, I guess. I suppose he wants Kira back. He thought once you'd found her, you'd take her home with you.'

'But they can't go back there,' I said. 'It's over, Eloise. Green Valley is dead. Long and badly dead. Calamitously dead, for Christ's sake.'

'I know that, but they don't.'

'They? Egus too?'

'He believes the children are the future. There's a song about that, isn't there?'

'And if the children leave Green Valley,' I filled in, glancing at Fabian, who was tentatively prodding at his staunched brow as he listened to my side of the conversation with interest, 'it condemns Egus to failure.'

'Yeah. The end of his future, the end of his vision. The ultimate failure of Green Valley and the Zeroth dream. David thinks just like Egus,' she continued. 'He's even worse than Egus. For him, always, the vision is more important than the truth.' Eloise had just summed up David in one line. 'You need to protect Kira.'

'But can he even… survive outside Green Valley?' I thought of the children jolting through their fevered withdrawal.

Eloise snorted back a laugh. 'Of course. We're not like the kids. We're grown-ups, no more addicted than anyone outside used to be. We're all habituated.' She spat out this last word like a curse.

'Is it safe for you to tell me this?'

The static crackle grew into a howl again, and I thought I'd lost the connection, until Eloise's voice emerged from the swirl. 'Everything you saw in here is real. Don't let them lie to you. Nobody should have to live like this against their will. *We* made the informed choice to live here, but none of the children did. Green Valley needs to come to an end with us. You've seen what it's really like.'

'Thank you, Eloise,' I said.

'Egus will have my mind for this. What's left of it. It was nice knowing you, Lucie; you seem like a good person.' Eloise's bland words carried the weight of a profound benediction. And then her voice turned into a high-pitched grunt: 'Eh, that's all, folks,' she said, before the line cut. I remembered that line from somewhere.

Then I had it. What the hell? Bugs Bunny?

31

This time, when I raced up the stairs to hammer on his door, Jordan was fully clothed. The air in his flat as he opened the door was even thicker with cigarette smoke than it had been the last time. He stood back without a word and let me in, sighing out a belt of a long, stale day. Evidently, he hadn't been relaxing all weekend, but had been losing sleep as much as I had – the deep pits around his eyes were even more sunken than usual.

Jordan looked how I felt, and I was comfortable the moment I stepped into his home. Sometimes, I considered myself too dishevelled and smudgy and clueless to blend in among Fabian's polished ornaments, but at Jordan's place, my presence was absorbed. The thought felt disloyal as I sensed the pull from Fabian, sitting outside waiting in the car.

I hovered next to the lumpy brown sleeper couch in front of a low melamine coffee table that had once been a crisp white democratic flatpack, and was now stained in eggshell wafts by the tobacco fug and pocked with butt-burns and stained with brown rings. Pictures of dead children were scattered across its surface between a coffee mug, a third full with a cold-slicked and forgotten brew, a saucer piled with cigarette butts and a bowl with orange chip crumbs pasted to its inside. Jordan came around, collected the dishes and took them to the kitchenette counter, then returned and gathered the dossiers up, squaring the photos and documents into neat stacks, flipping the manila covers shut and laying his notebook and pen on top of the pile.

I was afraid that whatever I said next might burst the bubble of motivation that had led him to fish out the old files and stay here all day looking into those dead children's eyes. If he sensed any pressure from me, he might snap closed, so I didn't say anything for a while, waiting for him to ask, waiting for him to offer. But as the seconds passed, I anxiously imagined Egus breaking through Vidal's security, somehow sending commands through the ether into Kira's fitful sleep. It bubbled over then; I couldn't keep it in.

'I was wrong,' I blurted, as if continuing a discussion we'd been having rather than avoiding each other's gaze in silence for the last twenty seconds. 'We can't let them go back.'

'I know,' he said.

I hurried to his front door and he followed, grabbing his coat, gun and holster from the stand in the hallway.

I glanced at Fabian as he drove. These past few days, so much had happened. He'd discovered I had a living niece, he'd been attacked in his home because of me, he'd been worried to death about me, yet here he was, willingly driving me to where Kira and the other Green Valley kids were being kept in an electronic shelter whose very existence must fundamentally disgust him.

Squalls of icy rain slapped against the window in the gloomy dusk, shattering and blurring the lights prickling from windows over the grubby sidewalk. We passed the Eet Mor's gap-toothed neon shining between the scuffed concrete columns on the sidewalk, and a blanket of warm yellow glowed from the back alley of Cubbington's bakery. We'd passed the bodega and the pharmacy by the time Jordan told Fabian to pull over.

'It's still a half-mile further,' I said.

'Yeah, but from what you've told me, we'll need to make

proper plans.' He took his junction set out of the back of the car and carried it to the junction-box in the alley.

What I remember most clearly about that night was Jordan's face when he saw Kira. He stood quite still, his back to me. She was slumped, plugged in and zoned out on her mattress, against the peeling wall of that dingy room.

So still, for so long.

Fabian stood next to me, his silence sending claws into my spine. I had to shatter it.

'Jordan?' I said, reaching out to touch his shoulder.

My touch seemed to start him up again, and he took in a long sigh, filling his smoke-lined body from toes to tip, then he finally turned to face me, letting out the air. His eyes were red and his cheeks were blotched with rage, picking up the yellow glances of the low lights along the corridor. It was then, I think, seeing Kira through Jordan's objective eyes, that the abomination finally sank into me as deeply as it could go.

'She looks like you,' he said.

'No,' I started deflecting. 'She's just like Odille...' But I ran out of excuses as I looked in on her through Jordan's eyes. He was right: that was *my* flesh and blood lying there, in critical need, and her father was not defending her. The duty was on me.

'We're going to make this right,' he said. 'Enough is enough.' Then he trailed his way along the third-level corridor, back the way he had come, walking in careful, deliberate steps as if he didn't trust the floor. Vidal saw him out, locking the landing gate behind him before going down and opening the turquoise door on the ground floor, checking on his hand-held signal meter as he went. I peered through the narrow gap in the boards in a vacant room on the street

259

side of the building, and waited until I saw Jordan stumbling out into the mist-blown night like a man disenchanted from a trance. Across the road, the dark and vacant window of Verla's coffee shop observed with no apparent judgement.

Vidal came back upstairs, pocketing his keys. 'All locked up. Even if he is wandering about in Stanton, David's not going to get in, so don't worry.'

'Do you need me to do anything?' I asked. 'Can we help in any way?' Cautiously including Fabian.

'We've got it all in hand. Sofe and Rainbow are a crack team. They've been doing this every night for weeks,' he said with a defensive frown. He wished we weren't there, but knew he had no option. 'Make yourselves comfortable,' he said, nodding towards Kira's room down the mildewed and peeling hallway.

'Are you sure Zeroth can't hack your signals?' I asked him. 'Do something to the kids from a distance? Get into their minds?'

'One hundred per cent.' He lifted his signal meter and tapped its screen. 'As long as the interference shield stays intact, we're a sealed system. No signal on this range can get in from outside.' Vidal's electronic shields offered me far less comfort than the two barriers of solid metal between us and the street.

'Keep an eye on that thing, will you?' Fabian said.

'Yup.' Vidal turned and went down to the kitchen, and soon we heard him talking softly to Rainbow and Sofie.

I brought two hard-seated schoolroom stools from a vacant room, dusted them off with my hand, and placed them beside Kira's mattress. 'Come, Fabe.'

He sat next to me. 'This feels like a vigil.'

'I know,' I said. The low brown light and the stagnant air reminded me of the house with the altar room in Green Valley. I shuddered the thought away before it took me too far down that broken house's hallway. 'She's better off here.'

'You're going to tell me some day, aren't you?' he said.

'What?'

'Exactly what you saw in there.'

I took a deep breath in, sighed it out. I said nothing.

'Was she like this last time?' he asked. 'Has she been in a coma ever since she came out?'

'It's not a coma. She's on The I, or a safe version of it. Watch her eyes.'

We both watched her eyelids jittering as her piped life played through her. For the first time since this had started, I felt a pause, as if I had time. Jordan's outrage convinced me that at last someone else was on my side, that something official would be done, and that I could relax minutely, let down my guard for a moment. Fabian and I sat and watched Kira as if we were a contented couple watching their child sleep.

It was absurd.

'I can't do it, Fabe,' I said.

He glanced at my face, waiting for me to carry on, shifting his knee an inch so that it touched me.

A tight burn clenched in my chest, a wet heat in my eyes. 'I'm not enough for her. She needs a mother – she always has, all this time. Odille died and I let her down.' Fuck it, I was going to allow myself to cry in front of him. 'This sweet little girl. All she needs is someone to care for her, someone to love her, and I can't do it.' Fabian touched two fingertips to my leg, while my face crumbled and the dam broke, and all that ancient loss came flooding out. 'Look at her. Isn't she lovely? She doesn't deserve what's been done to her.' I drew myself together and sat up straight. 'Nobody does, none of these children do.'

'No.'

'Goddamn David. I trusted him. He was so good with

her. He was spontaneous and patient and kind – I watched him with her. He laughed with her, tickled her toes, put his face to her skin and tried to breathe her in. When the three of them were together, they were an unbreakable unit. I was even jealous sometimes, I guess – Odille's perfect new love excluded me.'

'I'm sure it wasn't perfect. You know how things are different from the outside. It was probably difficult.'

I shrugged. 'When he wanted to take her to Green Valley, I trusted him. I trusted Zeroth, that it would be a good place for my sister.'

'Everybody believed in them – it's what they do. They sell dreams – not just to naive people, but to everyone. Everyone fell for them.'

'Now look at her little girl. How could I have let this happen?'

'Jesus, it's not your fault. Nobody knew that this was happening.'

'Didn't we? Didn't we, Fabe? You did. *He* did!' I said, poking a finger towards the door, towards wherever Vidal was scheming. 'The rest of us just looked the other way because it was easier.'

'But it looks like he's trying to do something about it, right?'

'But why now, why when it's so late? You don't know what it's like in there, Fabe. And he's known all this time. And it's only now he's started trying. He's got some fucking angle; I know he has.'

Fabian sighed. 'Perhaps. But at the moment, this is all that's important.' He gestured towards Kira splayed out before us, fighting her invisible demons. 'She's all that's important tonight. Vidal said they're weaning them from the technology, right? That they'll turn them off for a while tonight?'

'Yes.'

'So let's be here for her then.'

I took Fabian's hand and knitted my fingers through his,

squeezing a little too hard. It was seductive, the idea of ceding, of giving over, of giving up. How restful that would be.

Fabian seemed to read my mind, because he said, 'We can't change the world by ourselves, Luce. None of us.'

'I didn't think I'd ever hear you say that. You're always so… on the case. With your Omega friends.'

His lips twitched into a smile. 'Big changes take millions of small actions. It's inaction that allows entropy to set in.'

'And sitting here, doing nothing, is our action, right?'

Fabian nodded. 'We're not doing nothing. Right now, things are happening.'

'I don't think so. I don't think anyone in power's that concerned.'

'They're getting concerned. I've drawn people's attention to it.'

'Whose attention? I don't think even you have that power.' But I'd never really considered just how far his connections with Omega took him.

'I have influence. I don't abuse it, but I can use it when necessary. David made a mistake, breaking into our home,' Fabian said softly, with an angry steel I'd never noticed in his voice. 'There's physical evidence of a crime committed in Stanton by someone from Green Valley. Egus has been skirting the edge of every one of the ill-advised agreements we made with Zeroth, and this time he's overstepped. These children are proof of that. He's culpable.'

I shouldn't have been surprised. 'So now you have what you wanted all along: an excuse to go into Green Valley and shut Zeroth down once and for all.'

Fabian read my face. 'You feel sorry for Egus, don't you? Despite all this?' He waved his hand towards the doorways along the corridor that sheltered the addicted little shells lying on their small beds. 'Despite what he's done to your own niece?' He shook his head and puffed out a sigh of dismay.

And it was true. Despite everything I'd seen, I pictured Jamie Egus as a mad, sad, defeated king holding on to the last vestiges of his glory, and he was finally going to be brought low. With the combined power of Omega's corporate and social tsars and the government forces arrayed against him, he stood no chance of holding them off from his haunted, crumbling tower.

Fabian's cheeks flushed when I didn't contradict him. 'You feel sorry for a man who invaded and collected and commodified the private lives of half the world's population, sold them to the highest bidders, supralegal and untouchable. He wouldn't have stopped until he owned everybody in the world.'

I scoffed. 'Come on, Fabian. You're smarter than that. It wasn't just Egus.'

'Egus was one of them, probably one of the most important.'

'It was a system, incorporating us. The system changed. Is the new system any better?'

'Yes,' Fabian said, with a flash of the evangelical fervour he saved for his speeches, the same zealous fervour David pumped out in his product launches. 'Yes, it is far, far better.' What was it with the Sterling sisters and zealots?

I just shook my head. 'I don't know why I'm defending him. Of course I'm glad that someone's taking this all seriously, protecting these children. But not everything's as simple as you people make it out to be.'

'Which people?' Fabian said.

'All of you.'

Vidal looked over at us from where he was arranging bowls on a narrow table in the corridor outside, and noticing his attention drawing my way, Fabian edged closer to me. I was too drained to push him away.

Fabian and I had run out of words to bat at each other, so I watched my addicted niece in her opiate dreams and allowed the silence and the stillness in the building to lull me.

My eyes grew heavy, but every time they dragged shut, I saw the ram, felt smothered by the bristly ropes of its gory hair. I drowsed and started, drowsed and started, and Fabian, wired and fully awake, cupped the side of my head and drew me towards him. I leaned my head on his shoulder and must have slept for only a bottomless minute, but I snapped awake when the air changed. I could feel it, the soundless, vibrating thrum of the wireless signals dropping out of the air as Rainbow turned the mirror I off.

On her bed, Kira stirred and pushed herself up from her slump, her eyes trying to find meaning in the peeling murk of the room and her middle-distance gaze. As reality oozed in from the edges – the starch stew Rainbow was slopping into the bowls in the hallway, the prod of the mattress and the scratch of the army surplus blanket, the cough and moan of the other children, soft crying from next door – she turned her head to Fabian and me, robotically, neutrally trying to parse us. I could see her trying to summon an I readout on us, and frowning deeply when she failed. And now she smiled, having learned somewhere that ingratiating sweetness might save her from harm. Every one of her facial expressions was stagey and overblown and it struck me that this was how she had learned to interface with The I, using her face to control her avatar. Her smile was like a pantomime grin developed and amplified for thousands, and it was mortifying in the low light of this small room with its intimate audience.

'Hello, Kira. It's okay,' I said, softly and soothingly, as if to a scared animal. I reached my hand out slowly, watching her reaction.

She started to say something, only managing a weak hiss. She swallowed and tried again. 'Where am I?' she said, her dry, atrophied voice crackling around the words.

I glanced at Fabian, as if he might be able to help, as if

he might be able to tell us where we'd all ended up, but he was staring at her with his mouth open, his forehead creased with undisguised revulsion.

Sofie came through the doorway, saving me. 'Hi, sweetie,' she said. 'Here's some food. Do you need help?' Without waiting for a response, she knelt down on the mattress and started feeding Kira, and Kira ate passively, still looking with wide eyes around the room, as if it were a new level in a game, trying to figure out what it wanted.

'She's doing really well,' Sofie said to us. 'Waking up like this. She's not resisting. You can hear the other kids, how they normally react.' And from the other rooms along the corridor, I could hear gagging, crying, moaning, Rainbow and Vidal hurrying from room to room to soothe the worst hit.

Kira was docile as she finished her bowl of porridge, Sofie wiping her mouth with a flannel, their routine a grotesque, unfunny parody of a mother feeding a baby. All the while, Fabian was squeezing my knee and staring. His hand went tighter and tighter as he ground his jaw. I peeled my eyes away from Kira and looked at Fabian, the profound distaste he'd felt for Zeroth overspilling now into visceral disgust. He pushed up and away from me. 'We're taking her home,' he said, and when neither Sofie nor I responded, he stepped over to Kira and took her hand. 'We're taking you home.'

Now, seeing Fabian touching her, something I had barely managed myself, I was forced to respond. 'What? Fabian, wait.' I spoke softly, afraid Kira would shatter, being grabbed like that, and that Fabian's raised voice would rattle her fragile mind. But she didn't shatter; she stood and glanced between us with living eyes, almost like a real girl.

'We're taking you out of here, Kira,' Fabian repeated, with a gentleness that shamed me. 'We're taking you to a proper home. You don't belong in a place like this.' He turned to me. 'We can't allow them to do this to her, Lucie.

We can't allow them to violate her like this.'

'But we can't move her,' I said. 'The children need The I. She'll get sick if we take her away. She needs to stay here.' Vidal stepped into the doorway, glancing between us and Sofie, who hadn't moved. Both of them watched Kira like fascinated observers, as if she were a subject in an experiment. Had they observed the dead children suffering their withdrawal, watching to see how much they could take, waiting just to see what would happen? I thought of the little girl's jutting hips on Maya's shelf, of the strawberry-mint gum in her flour-coated pockets. 'She has to stay here,' I said again. *Otherwise she could die.* I couldn't bring myself to voice it.

'She's disconnected now, isn't she? She's doing fine. She said so.' Fabian pointed at Sofie.

'Vidal,' I pleaded. 'Tell him what you told me.'

Vidal looked between us all, his unwanted guests and his daughter holding an empty bowl and a dirty spoon on a grubby mattress. There was a scream and a wracking sob from next door. 'I don't know what will happen, but I can't stop you. I really haven't got the resources. Sofe, we need to help the others.'

'What do *you* want, Kira?' Fabian said, still clutching her hand.

'Stop it, please,' I said. I could see that Kira was becoming afraid, her eyes widening and welling. She couldn't understand what was happening to her; she'd been kidnapped from the only family she'd known and severed from her reality into the middle of this dark domestic battle.

'Do you like it here?' Fabian pressed.

Kira gathered her answer. 'No.' As she shook her head, a tear flicked off her eye and smeared down her cheek.

'That settles it.' He stood up and dragged Kira off the bed and down the corridor. 'Let us out of here, Barrett.'

Vidal didn't turn, just said over his shoulder, as Rainbow hurried into the screaming child's room, 'Let them out, Sofie. Make sure to lock up again, right?' Then his conscience may have provoked him, because he turned and squatted down to look at Kira at her level. 'I'm just glad for you that you've found someone to look after you.' He reached out and smoothed her hair down. 'You'll be fine.'

We trailed Sofie down the darkened stairwell, Fabian still clutching Kira's hand. She was looking around her groggily, still stuck in this murky dream. Sofie unlocked the gate to the landing, and we filed downstairs. We were going home, the three of us, and for a second that fake image of a neat little family was a feasible delusion.

As we approached the turquoise steel door, I softly put my hand to Kira's back, hoping it was an encouraging gesture. She stiffened. At first, I thought it was a flinch, my own flesh and blood repelled by my touch, but then she began to jerk and spasm, pulled around like a marionette.

'Something's happening,' I said. 'There's something wrong.' Kira was still gripping Fabian's hand, now painfully tight, and her eyes rolled back, small whimpers punching out of her as if shockwaves were shooting through her body.

I touched Kira and for the duration of a chemical flash, I knew what she was seeing. Less seeing than sensing the black hole it made in space. Semi-materialised, leaving a smudgy, half-drawn trail of soot as it went, reaching out for us, and beyond us, through the slats of the gate, its tendrils spreading around and past Fabian and me, through us, splitting up into a many-headed hair serpent as it trailed past us and towards the children's rooms.

Then it disappeared, leaving only a negative burn in my imagination. Kira slumped down on the stairs and rubbed at her eyes, trying to erase the image. A phone started ringing upstairs.

Vidal answered, and after a moment called down, 'Fabian, it's for you.' Fabian tore himself away from us and went back upstairs to the phone.

I put my arm around Kira's narrow shoulders and drew her to me. She didn't pull away. Her thin body quivered with fear, with life.

Then Fabian's voice. 'Hello? Yeah. Good.'

Fabian came back down, and stood behind us on the stairs. 'We've got them,' he said.

VIII

32

We got to the gantry early so that we could get a view right up against the railing. The past few days, the crowds had swelled so much that, by nine or ten in the morning, you'd need to queue up for the stairs and shove your way between bodies to see anything. By now, nine months after Egus and David were arrested, the dismantling of Green Valley was no longer our private moment, no longer even Stanton's personal victory. Tourists had begun to throng here from all over the world. Stanton city council was instituting a ticketing system, hastily erecting two more paid gantries before the wall was gone, Green Valley razed, and there was nothing left to see.

The destruction of the wall hadn't been planned as a public spectacle – in fact, those first few days after the arrests, even admitting the existence of the wall still seemed shameful, and the city had erected vast plywood barriers to screen the demolition. But people had kept prying and poking, peeping through the cracks on the off-chance of seeing something of the fallen invisible kingdom exposed behind the piles of grey rubble, of catching a glimpse of the dishevelled group of survivors being treated in the military tented camp planted on the office park's lawns; and the barriers had kept slumping over and toppling.

But this morning, it was just Kira and me as the late-spring sun, red in the warm dust, strobed between the clearing clouds over the horizon. I pulled the brim of Kira's hat further down over her brow, and made sure that her sunglasses were flush against her eyes.

'It's fine, Lucie,' she moaned, wriggling away from me and aiming her face like a sunflower towards the light. I stopped fussing and watched her soak in the rays, still and contented and painless for a moment, and my chest swelled.

Tentatively, Kira tugged at the fingers of her gloves, glancing up at me to see if I'd try to stop her. I let it go, helping her pull them off and bundling them in my pocket. 'Let's get some lotion on, okay?' Kira smiled and held her hands up, turning them, radiating them like toast in the red light. 'Just a few minutes.' Restricting, policing, monitoring: this, I'd soon discovered, was so much of what looking after a child entailed.

The machines started up with a roar and a clank, raising their hydraulic fists and hammering at the next section of concrete, beating at it until it shattered, slabs shearing down, rebar twisting and shrieking as it lost its purpose with a fight. Over the weeks we'd watched the hole in the roof grow wider, the wall decaying away, until Green Valley was more open to the sky and to the world than closed. This morning it was no longer an enclave, just a crumbled fortress.

People started to come onto the gantry, jostling and pressing, but still I was reluctant to move. Finally, the wind swirled, changing direction and funnelling a blast of peat from the site into our faces, and I took Kira's hand and led her down towards Green Valley for the last time. At the perimeter fence today there were just two city patrol officers on the gate, unlike that first night, when an industrial collection of police and unmarked cars, a military detachment and the mobile operations centre had been clustered outside the Zeroth liaison office. The lights and the rush had reverberated off the concrete shell and died in the fog, falling muffled into the nothingness that had enveloped the enclave. This morning, the wind had found new channels between the demolished teeth of the shell.

I showed the patrol officer Kira's special clearance letter and my guardianship certificate, and she let us in, scowling as her colleague pushed back a group of overeager young ruin-tourists who'd tried hopelessly to sneak past the public barricade and follow us in. A few weeks before, the *Observer* had published a photo of a hanged man outside the processing tents. The front-page suicide had ignited a flurry of theories about what was happening inside the tents. As survivors began to be processed out and reintegrated into Stanton life, the weight of testimony grew: about just how many people had died in Green Valley, how many had taken their own lives or been broken by withdrawal after it collapsed, ravaged by ancient diseases we thought were extinct, gone irretrievably mad. It was little surprise the remaining survivors were reticent as they stumbled out of their confinement into the sun, but gradually the truth had started to emerge with them.

'Through there?' I asked, indicating the liaison office door.

The patrol officer nodded, distracted by the shifting groups at the barricades.

The glass door, once the only public portal to Green Valley, slumped where the raiding team had smashed it in nine months ago, and now dust and leaves and litter lay in a clot on the threshold.

Kira's grip on my hand tightened as we stepped into the poorly lit office. 'Are you all right?' I asked. She pulled me further in.

A delta of rubbish and dust had swept through the doorway in a fan over the carpet, and rain had blown in, caking small pats of mud over the dust-coated floor. But deeper in, the room was much as I'd first seen it: the faded blue-and-green sofa, the patterned cloths and chintzy decorations, the catalogue reception desk and Gina's old-fashioned computer screen all left where they had been. But the signs of police and forensics investigations were also clear; apart from the ravaged front door and a broken chair, the coloured dots stuck on every item of evidence, numbered, photographed and classified, had been left to bond on the files and books and tea mugs, the paintings and wall hangings, on the spatters over the floor.

It had seemed a good idea to come back when we'd first been offered the chance. The police and forensics were finished with Green Valley and the enclave was about to be shut down finally, auctioned off, demolished, redeveloped, erased – whatever the intentions of the successful bidder. I'd discussed it with Fabian and Kira's counsellor, and we'd agreed that maybe it would be good for her to visit one last time, help her create an ending for this chapter of her life.

Was it safe for a child, I'd wanted to know. There's nothing unsafe, they assured me. Since the roof had been opened, the levels of airborne pathogens had dropped to acceptable; fungicides and pesticides had been pumped into the enclave before the second phase of the forensic work had begun; all human and animal remains had been appropriately disposed of. But what's it like, I pressed. Would you bring your child there? The person on the phone skewered me with a long, judgemental silence. Then she said, 'Other surviving residents would be grateful for the opportunity.'

But right now, I wasn't so sure. Shouldn't we all try to forget Green Valley like a bad dream, and move on? The rational part of me knew the area had been scoured and graded and that Kira would see none of the mortal decay that I'd seen, but still I couldn't bring myself to move. Looking down, I saw that my indecisive feet were rooted on a brown stain in the carpet.

'Lucie?' Kira tugged at my sleeve. 'There's a big man here.'

My heart punched at my ribs and almost escaped before

I had a moment to look up. But it was the man we'd come to meet.

'Hi, Jordan,' I said. 'Thanks for this.'

He'd emerged from the locker room behind the office and was beckoning us to follow him there. 'They collected all of the personal effects in the warehouse, and I've gathered some of the kids' things here. The stuff in… better condition. I don't know if she'll find anything that was hers, or anything she likes, or whether she'll…' He stopped talking when he noticed Kira looking up at him frankly, following the conversation he was trying to have over her head. He spoke to her: 'Do you wanna have a look through the toys?'

'Yeah,' she said with an excited trill, such a convincing facsimile of an undamaged, unafraid little girl. But when Jordan pointed the way into the locker room towards the plastic tubs of swabbed and sterilised toys, she hesitated and squeezed my hand. The room was sunken in the gloom of night lighting, and the switch at the door didn't work.

'Can we make it lighter in here?' I asked Jordan.

'Hang on.' Jordan went into the reception area and squatted behind the desk. He found the main board and the strip lights came on, spearing clean, bright light into all the corners.

'Better?' I asked Kira, walking with her to the containers, the paltry physical remnants of so many children's half-lives, her warm little hand in mine helping banish my fears too. She smiled and sat on the bench – the same bench where I'd allowed Gina Orban to invade my body – and leaned over the toys and started picking through them cautiously, as if something inside might still bite her. I ran my hand over her hair. 'I'll be just there by the door, okay? Talking to Jordan. Right here if you need me.' She was already more engaged with a plush leopard than with me. I went back to join Jordan, leaning against the door frame opposite him, where we could talk and I could still keep Kira in my peripheral vision.

'How's she doing?' Jordan asked.

'Fine,' I said. It was the short answer.

The last nine months had felt both like nine years and nine seconds. That night Fabian and I had gathered Kira up and driven her straight home.

Two blocks away from Vidal's office, we knew we'd made a mistake. Kira started bucking and writhing with pain, gagging but too cramped up even to vomit, a thin trickle of foamy bile pushing out between her gritted teeth. It was as if The I was clawing her back to its embrace by her entrails. And then, as we passed the invisible limit of Green Valley's radio signal, she slumped and relaxed, released finally, and we thought she'd be all right. We guided her into the lift – she managed to walk on her own legs, not needing to be carried, and we thought she'd be all right. We sat her in the tub, and she let us wipe some of the years of waste off her; we towelled her down, and we put her in our bed, warm and fragrant and at peace, and we thought she'd be all right.

But the dreams attacked her in the night, her mind rebelling, and she screamed as if she was being tortured. We took her back to Vidal's building, to the grey-eyed children and their colourful bedspreads, so that Kira could survive.

It had taken her three more painful weeks to wean from The I. While Vidal and Sofie dropped in and out of the children's world, Rainbow had always been there, nurturing and coddling and coaxing them as the children suffered through the withdrawal. We followed Rainbow's timetable, disconnecting Kira from the mirror I for increasing periods, taking her out to the local streets for longer and longer walks to help her acclimatise to her new environment. We gradually transformed her diet, and her body fought every mouthful but eventually adjusted. During that period, three more children died. This time their bodies were not dumped, but sent through official channels to Maya, who gathered data at the pathology lab to try to help other Green Valley survivors, sharing it with the social workers, psychologists and doctors who had been assigned to the programme. Five of Vidal's rescue kids weaned off safely, plus Kira, the healing process still a work in progress. The last three were still hooked up to the mirror I, the last I heard. Social services had matched some of the survivors with parents from inside, and more with family members from Stanton and beyond – I knew what these shattered families would be going through. I hoped that Maya was learning from the dead, and what social services were learning from Kira and the dozens of other children who'd been ejected from Green Valley would smooth out this mess in time.

'Yes, she's fine.' I glanced at my niece, who was humming a very quiet tune as she made a rubber tomato dance a waltz with the leopard. 'She's really doing well.'

She felt my gaze at the back of her head and broke her game off to look at me. 'I like this tiger,' she said. 'She doesn't talk. But I can make her sing with my mind.'

'She's very pretty,' I said. I was still learning not to contradict every misapprehension she'd picked up in there. I wanted urgently to fix what they'd done to her, to erase the junk code and replace it with the regular knowledge and the normal upbringing she should have had all along. I got it right just at this moment, but still my teeth gritted as I stifled my correction. I knew it was going to be a long and delicate process; my obsessive will to facts and what I'd learned to call truth – my tyrannical desire for re-education – would have to take a back seat. Kira's happiness and confidence were all that mattered right now.

'There's still no trace of him,' Jordan said. 'The department's engaged on the search like nothing before.'

Once Kira had been weaned from The I, and made it through a week in our apartment, I went back to Vidal's office to check on the other kids and bring Rainbow and Sofie a gift to say thank you. I had no idea what they might like. The weight of their mortal responsibility had made them prematurely adult; they barely seemed to sleep, never mind take time out to relax and want childish things. I ended up choosing half a dozen books I thought they might enjoy – a wide range of topics so that something might appeal. It was a stupid gesture, and I was feeling self-conscious as I approached the office, as if I was the little child trying to gain attention from these busy grown-ups, trying to curry favour, trying to impress these brave and high-minded women. But before I even got to the door of Barrett & Sanders, I could feel the emptiness. No need for fake surveillance loops and subterfuge this time: they were gone.

The front door had been left unlocked, but that hadn't stopped someone from smashing his way through the plate window at the front. The shattered gash had been pasted over with brown paper, waxed against the fog, and it sucked and rattled as the wind blew. All the furniture had been taken, even the sticks in their decorative vase were gone. All that remained was the sign behind the desk, smeared where someone with greasy fingerprints and no tools had tried to pry it off: Vidal's yellow rooster, consigned to the trash heap of his past. Was he still feeling a pull from his history, I wondered, or had he successfully abandoned it? Imagine being able to run far enough away to leave your past behind.

'I bet you wish for some spooky tech now, don't you?' I teased Jordan.

To my surprise, Jordan sighed. 'Yeah. Yeah, I really do.' His resignation seemed like defeat, and it made me sad, but I said nothing about Misty Vale or Roger Basson. 'After all this time, I don't know if we're ever going to find the other—' He stopped talking as Kira shifted and dug for another toy.

Part of me assumed Sentinel knew about the farm. I'd been granted indefinite leave from the records department while I looked after Kira, and Sentinel had closed ranks behind their mysterious door again as quickly as they'd burst out, so I couldn't know what they knew and what they didn't. They'd find out about the farm before long, if they hadn't already; I didn't need to be the one to tell them. Because the bigger part of me wanted Vidal to escape. Those three children and Rainbow – given that they had no home to go back to, that none of their parents had survived, I could only imagine that all of them were better off with Vidal and Sofie than in the middle of a heavy-handed police operation mopped up by overstretched social workers and straitened state welfare. I thought back to Sofie playing with Basson's dog in that dusty lot, and knew what I'd want for Kira: that if she needed a safe, happy place one day, she wouldn't be betrayed by some officious stranger. What would I want for Kira? That was my only measure now.

Jordan fished in his inner jacket pockets for a crumpled packet of cigarettes and his lighter and fired up. As he vented the first, deep drag, even after all that had passed, it still felt subversive and wrong in this space – smoothie-swilling Gina Orban's health club for one person and one ghost. Jordan's smirk as his Adam's apple bobbed and he sent out another flume was sweetly, satisfyingly sacrilegious.

'We could do with your spook department's help in finding her too,' Jordan said, poking his cigarette towards the reception office. 'We could ask her a few more questions, seek some clarification.' Gina Orban had disappeared on the night of the raid, a remarkable feat given that the liaison office had been crawling with police and Sentinel agents. All she would have needed was a small pocket to have carried off all of Zeroth's files into the darkness with her. The precinct-level investigation had uncovered personal journals and reams of logs, but with gaping holes gouged out before they'd been able to access her computer and files.

I'd been at Jamie Egus's arraignment the day after his arrest, and that had offered no answers either. He'd been beaten in prison, and his hair and beard had been hacked off in some brutal act of mortification, leaving red weals and rough patches, but still he bore himself as if he were greater than us, no matter how the mob had tried to reduce him. The judge asked him questions like a terrified inquisitor facing a powerful witch. Towards the end of the session, the judge asked, 'And have you ever managed to project an electronic avatar in a physical form?'

Egus drew himself up and laughed, filling up with a puff of that superior, lordly scorn. 'Materialise? If I could materialise ideas, do you think I'd be here?' He looked at his shackled hands and closed his eyes. What chilled me most was that he'd taken the question seriously.

Later, asked the same thing at his hearing, David had remained silent, slanting his eyes up into some distant future, as if imagining how he'd pitch an army of electronic minions to bidders at an arms fair, and just how far above all the dirty ethical concerns he'd be.

'I could ask Barbra and Schindler when I go back to work,' I said, but of course they either knew where Gina was and weren't telling, or they'd never know. First case far more likely.

'Barbra who?' Jordan said. 'Schindler who? They don't exist. Never did.'

I smiled. 'Now you're learning. I can tell you've been working with them.'

He shook his head. 'It was all in a dream.'

Kira was bored of the toys and stood up, her fragile bones crackling as she stretched her arms over her head.

'Can we go see Mommy and Daddy now?'

'Oh, sweetie,' I said. 'Remember what we talked about? That we'll go to the house so you can see it one more time, but David and Eloise won't be there.'

Kira's eyes deadened as a thump of disappointment hit her, and then I watched the life swell back into them as she fought to control her reaction. It was as if The I were still directing her moods, but I knew that wasn't the case. She was certified one hundred per cent clear, and what was controlling her moods was that purely human mixture – hope, shame, resilience, fear, bravery and love, each of them spurting its tiny natural nanorobots into her receptors.

I squatted down and gave her a hug, hard and warm.

She nodded, nodded again, convincing herself. 'Yes. I remember. We'll see them soon, though.'

'Yes,' I said, standing and taking her hand in mine. We'd go see David in jail on visiting day, and we could look at Eloise staring back from her ward, her mind dislodged and elsewhere. Egus – or David – had fried her mind for her betrayal, just as she'd feared. Poor Kira – she had nobody else but me.

So I followed her; I followed my nine-year-old niece down the exit corridor and into Green Valley. And the light from the sky was making grass grow, and the withered trees were sending tentative shoots out into the fresh air. Sparrows and blackbirds and pigeons and magpies were making the most of the rich and uncontested feeding grounds. Now, in the daylight, I could pick out patches and paths where we could walk without smearing our shoes.

I followed Kira, and she tugged me along. 'Look, Lucie,' she was saying. 'This is where I played with the girls when they started the battle aliens game and it's just round here we buried the treasure box. And here, and here, just round this corner, that's where they sometimes sell cakes. Not every day, but there's cake day. Mommy and Daddy take me sometimes when there isn't any work.'

Along Main Street and through the town square, and listening to her voice, I could just about fool myself into seeing it all through Kira's eyes. I let her voice guide me, and for her, I'd blind myself to the truth.

ACKNOWLEDGEMENTS

Thank you:

to Oli Munson, Prema Raj, Vickie Dillon, Florence Rees, Hélène Ferey and Jennifer Custer at A.M. Heath, and Michelle Kroes at CAA, for working to get my books into the right hands;

to Sam Matthews, Joanna Harwood, Lydia Gittins, Katharine Carroll and the production and publicity teams at Titan for all their enthusiastic efforts on *Green Valley*;

to Tim Müller at Heyne Verlag for taking the first affirming bite;

and especially to Bronwyn Harris, Sam Greenberg, Adam Greenberg, Rosa and Houdini, who lent me time and warm companionship while I wrote, and rewrote, and rewrote, this story.

ABOUT THE AUTHOR

ouis Greenberg is a renowned writer in his own right, having been shortlisted for the Commonwealth Writers' Prize for his debut novel, *The Beggars' Signwriters* (Umuzi, 2006), but is perhaps better known for his work with Sarah Lotz as one half of internationally bestselling S.L. Grey. *Green Valley* is his first solo novel to be published outside his native South Africa. He is currently based in England.

For more fantastic fiction, author events,
exclusive excerpts, competitions, limited editions and more

VISIT OUR WEBSITE
titanbooks.com

LIKE US ON FACEBOOK
facebook.com/titanbooks

FOLLOW US ON TWITTER AND INSTAGRAM
@TitanBooks

EMAIL US
readerfeedback@titanemail.com